Deeper Realms

Volume 1

Chronological Edition

© 2018

Ian Roberts

Deeper Realms

Deeper Realms, Volume 1, Chronological Edition,

By Ian Roberts

ISBN 9781731325419

For Flash Fiction, thoughts and more on Ian RobertS' eclectic time travelling world visit: www.scipio6.wixsite.com/the-wardrobe-door or keep up with his latest tweets @IRobertS_author

#DeeperRealms

I'll take your brain to another dimension.

The Prodigy

Part 1

The Girl from the Book

(Dinosaur Girl)

The UEM

E ve Wells fought the urge to glance across the crowded student concourse.

It was *not* the girl from the photograph, it couldn't possibly be.

She took a deep breath, forcing herself to concentrate on the notes in front of her, but before she could stop herself, her eyes had darted to the figure by the window once more. It just couldn't be her – and yet there she was: the same confident features, the same Mediterranean complexion.

She blinked a couple of times as if hoping the figment of her imagination would disappear; but the girl was still there, gazing lazily at her phone - dark eyes focussed on the glowing screen. Eve looked briskly away trying to put the stranger out of her mind. But it was impossible.

With a troubled sigh she snatched another glance then looked down, trying not to make it obvious she was staring. There was just *no way* it could be her. She drummed her fingers against her coffee cup, trying to recall every detail of the photo in the book, then dropped her gaze as the girl glanced up from her phone. She swallowed, trying to pull herself together - a breakdown was the last thing she needed: the scramble to the end of term was always pressured, but this was something else.

She was *not* going mad.

Tearing her gaze from the dark haired girl she swiped determinedly through her tutorial schedule – just one more seminar and then the day's teaching was done, just another fifty minutes.

And then there were the hallucinations.

She cursed her own mind, longing for it to cut her some slack, but the memories kept coming. The worries. She felt her thoughts beginning to run down the road of weird sensations and events she had experienced since beginning her first degree at the University of the East Midlands, and the horrible knowledge that the terrible anxiety she had suffered during childhood was returning full force.

She took out her pen and began to doodle, swirls and spirals, dark cross-hatched vortexes and strange reptilian shapes. She smiled ironically. Drawing, after all, was what had come to define her – the skill which had led to her unique specialism as a palaeontologist.

She sighed, finding herself able to push away her concerns about the girl just long enough to return to the session ahead. A fifty minute class on palaeontological reconstruction techniques: the science of putting flesh and skin on long dead bones - the magic of resurrecting the past. She forced herself to be positive. At least she was doing what she loved, teaching and working on vertebrate reconstruction – until her contract ended at least, and then ... *more worries.* What if Professor Stokes' new replacement didn't arrive before the end of the semester – what if her funding was pulled?

Her phone chimed and dropping her gaze to the screen she cursed with annoyance.

Hey ginger. About tonight, I'm really not going to be able to make it. So sorry. Catch you Tuesday?

Rich.

What was it, dump on Eve day? She almost screamed with frustration - now the only guy in ages

11

who'd shown her any serious interest was getting cold feet - and what was with the whole *ginger* thing? She was closer to strawberry blonde! She stuffed her phone into her pocket. Maybe if she could lighten up a bit, try not to take life so seriously.

You need to broaden your horizons Eve – talk about dead things less.

She cringed as she remembered her flat-mate's droll advice. She'd laughed along with her joke, but deep down she knew it was true: she was passionate about her work and sometimes it just seemed to take over. She took off her glasses to massage tired eyes. Again, that horrible sense she needed to change herself to fit in with everyone and everything around her.

She glanced across the concourse once more as if expecting to see the dark haired girl watching her, but she was now staring absent-mindedly out of the window. Eve sighed. Just to make it through to Christmas - just a couple more weeks! She pushed her glasses up her nose and sipped at her drink – it was all just her stressed mind playing tricks – hardly worth thinking about, hardly worth ... Across the concourse the dark haired girl finished her coffee and ditched the take-out cup in the nearest bin.

Eve tried to ignore her, flipping briskly through her notes, but still she couldn't stop herself from watching as the young woman walked across the room.

She was maybe twenty-five, petite and athletic, dressed in fashionable clothes: just another post-doc killing time between lectures. She hesitated, desperate to follow, the photograph flashing once more before her mind's eye – the picture in that old book. It was clearly the same girl, the similarity uncanny. But it just *couldn't* be her. That would be impossible.

She was nearly at the door now, ponytail bobbing as she wove between the tables.

Eve forced herself to look away – forced herself to put the book out of her mind as she scanned her lesson plan; but the urge to follow was near overwhelming, an almost visceral tug in her gut. She had to do it – had to find out what on earth was going on - if she didn't follow now she would lose her chance - and she needed answers. She glanced up to see the young woman vanish through the door, and with an impulsiveness which surprised her, grabbed her bag and made to follow.

Pursuit

'**S**orry,' Eve breathed apologetically as she muscled her way between two guys chatting by the second set of automatic doors, trying to keep her gaze on the athletic figure as she entered the Kincaid Library.

As the doors slid aside she was enveloped by the gentle lull of the huge purpose-built structure, plush and unashamedly modern. She felt her guts twist with concern. It was midday and the ground floor was choked with students, some hurrying to cram in last minute prep before tutorials, others gossiping the lunch break away by the entrance to the coffee bar.

She had to find the girl. She had to get answers! Her thoughts began to race as her pulse quickened, her memories rushing forward to overtake her - she was in the tram carriage again, the old book in her hand, caught between nostalgia and regret – how she'd loved it as a kid - and then she was glancing up from the pages to see a face she felt sure she had seen many times before, a face she had known for years but couldn't quite place. She was frowning as she glanced down at the natural history book her dad had sent her that morning, turning the page as she struggled to remember – and then the image was leaping up off the page – glancing up as if seeing a ghost: for across the aisle sat the young woman from the image, a dark haired girl hunched over a dig site somewhere in the US. And it wasn't possible.

A thought hit her with an almost visceral nudge. A memory. She had looked at the young female palaeontologist in that book as a child thinking: *one day I want to be like her...*

The young woman had seemed oblivious to her, swiping through photos on her phone, but the resemblance was so uncanny it was scary. She tore her gaze from the photograph and flipped quickly to the publication date. 1977. But that was impossible, the girl in the photo had to be in her mid-twenties and that would make her ...

Eve tried to focus, hurrying onwards as the dark clothed figure was swallowed momentarily by the crowd, and with a curse she wove between the milling bodies in pursuit. Above her rose a three storey glass wall behind which lay reading tables and shelving stacks, work rooms and IT stations. Directly ahead were twin staircases behind a central island help-desk and more stairs to her left and right. Where the hell was she? Then her heart leapt as she caught a glimpse of her ascending the right hand flight of steps.

She crossed to the stairs, weaving against the flow as she ascended two at a time, trying to close the gap between them. The dark haired young woman never turned, never faltered, but it was clear she was trying to lose her, making random shifts and turns as she bypassed the private study rooms near the social sciences bay and disappeared around the glass balconied walkway of the internal mezzanine.

'Damn.' Eve cursed as the girl's reflection disappeared from view, lost behind a gaggle of chatting undergrads, and hurrying past them came face to face with a conundrum. The Earth Sciences reading room or the Lee-Harvey periodical stacks? Two large doorways to choose from, one adjacent to where she stood - the other straight ahead. She hesitated, glancing over the balcony as if expecting to see the girl from the photo magically walking away across the foyer below. 'Excuse me,' she said turning to the girls on the balcony, 'you didn't happen to see which way …' They hadn't got a clue and she cursed inwardly, knowing that whichever option she chose would give adequate time for the girl to slip away through the other.

There was movement from the periodical stacks and she took a gamble, turning to her right through the smaller door to find herself in a long low room with row after row of moveable shelving. She hesitated, wondering if she should call out some kind of challenge, then thought the better of it. The room was dimly lit and eerily quiet, the only way out through the door she had just come through – at least if the girl was in here she had no way of getting past her.

She strode forwards, her boots oddly loud despite the carpeted floor, glancing down each stack in turn and finding with an odd sense of relief that each was empty. 'Hello?' she called after a moment. The low buzz of the library beyond seemed to fade with every step, 'Hi, is anyone in here?' A faint sound came from up ahead. She quickened her pace, brushing her palm against one of the hand wheels which crowned the end of each row - the somewhat retro mechanism which manoeuvred the space-saving periodical stacks on their runners. 'Hi, I only want to talk to you!'

She was sure she heard a cough to her right and with a flash of triumph burst around the corner of the next row. *Nothing.*

'What?' she frowned, carrying on for a few paces, running her gaze along the titles of the spines: obscure journals on theology and metaphysics, ancient volumes on miracles and the abstract philosophies of ancient thinkers. 'Hello?'

For a split second she felt sure she glimpsed dark eyes peering at her through the shelving, from the other side, then movement and muffled footsteps. 'Hey!'

Before she realised what was happening, the shelving unit to her left was moving, sliding gently towards her so the carpeted area on which she stood grew less and less by the second. 'Hey – what the hell!' She twisted back towards the end of the row, her heart thumping with panic, hardly able to believe what was happening. 'Hey!' The stack had stopped moving and she put out a hand to pull herself towards the end of the row, her thoughts racing as movement sounded in the walkway beyond. She swore, breaking into a run, knowing that the girl was getting away, and swung briskly onto the walkway.

'Eve?'

A tall figure stood right in front of her and she jerked back, apologising profusely to the woman she had walked straight into. 'Eve? Is everything alright?'

She blushed, her mouth opening uselessly as she took in the tall brunette who now stood with her hand on her shoulder. Dr Laura Highcroft was one of the department's greatest assets - a leading light of popular palaeontology and the university's chair of science engagement.

'Sorry,' she said hastily, 'I ...' She wished the ground would open and suck her down. Highcroft was one of her most imposing seniors, eminently experienced, coolly confident and classically beautifully. Could she have made herself look more stupid in front of the member of the department she most admired? She looked away then felt her gaze drawn past her to the mezzanine beyond, a part of her desperate not to lose the girl.

'Is something wrong?' Dr Highcroft enquired with a concerned frown, 'you look like you've seen a ghost ...'

'I ...' her voice seemed to fail her and a shudder ran down her spine, followed by a horrible creeping sensation of dread. *A ghost*. The book was from the late 70s and the girl in the photo ...

'I …' she swallowed, and realizing with sudden horror that she was about to cry raised a hand to feign scratching her cheek.

'Hey,' said Dr Highcroft, a frown of concern wrinkling her brow, 'is there something you need to talk about?'

'I'm just …' she began, but didn't know how to continue, longing with an almost visceral tug to tell the weird secret she had been holding in. 'I – I keep …' Emotion began to surge with almost tidal power.

'Come on,' said the senior tutor, directing her towards the mezzanine and before she realised what was happening she felt the woman's arm around her shoulder. 'I've got office hours till five – no teaching – let's find somewhere quiet. If there's something you need to talk about it will be better to get it off your chest.' Eve nodded, feeling horribly embarrassed as she held back the tears and with a nod stepped out onto the stair-well, forcing herself not to scan for the girl.

Highcroft

'**S**o you don't think I'm going mad?'

She was sat opposite Laura Highcroft in one of the bustling coffee shops which had sprung up across campus since she had begun her first degree. Dr Highcroft stirred her Americano thoughtfully but said nothing. Eve found herself scanning her attractive features for any trace of what she really thought. She had always thought of her as a busy professional, blunt-speaking, even a little aloof – a jaded hard-ass, resenting the managerial role her position now required – but in her calm presence, she found a comfort she desperately needed. Highcroft chose to ignore her question.

'It was all a bit different in my day,' she said glancing out across the plush leather sofas, filled with undergrads typing on their Macs, sipping lattes, with their noise-cancelling headphones and designer bags.

21

'Student life was supermarket pasta sauce and scribbling essays in the library...'

Eve forced a smile, still unsure of where the conversation was about to go. It had taken everything to admit the hallucinations – not just the girl from the 70s book, but the sense that even in wakefulness she kept glimpsing other places: smelt forest loam and heard the calls of strange creatures. Highcroft sipped her coffee.

'You're not the first highly creative person to think they're going mad, Eve,' she continued, picking up her comment, '– and I don't like to use that term.'

'Sorry,' she fumbled apologetically. She felt vulnerable, tired and confused, yet somehow relieved to have got it off her chest. 'Nor is *seeing things* particularly unusual.'

Dr Highcroft sat back in her chair. 'People have been reporting unexplained events since the dawn of recorded history.' Eve frowned. She had not been expecting that. 'Stories of strange beings and people slipping into other realms have been with us since the very beginning – pervading every single human culture.' Eve almost did a double-take. It was the last thing she had ever expected the pragmatic professional to say.

'Yes, that's true but ...'

Laura Highcroft looked at her almost challengingly. There was a look in her eye, a knowing look. The buzz of conversation seemed momentarily to die away. 'We are in no place either to prove or disprove such stories, Eve. They are just there: stories, experiences – and *seeing things* is perhaps, well, normal.'

Eve took a sip of her drink to cover her surprise. 'Normal?' *If you're a nut-case!* She thought, but said nothing more. Her superior gazed at her thoughtfully as if assessing her, then shrugged.

'There are more things in heaven and earth than are dreamt of in your philosophy.'

It struck her suddenly that Dr Laura Highcroft had likewise seen things - that she too had witnessed strange beings and seen other worlds, yet even to think it let alone voice it seemed utterly ludicrous. 'Hamlet,' Highcroft added to fill the pause, 'have you ever studied Shakespeare?'

Eve shook her head.

'So you're saying?'

23

Highcroft dropped her gaze to the table and began to toy with the corner of a ring bound report she had been carrying.

'If you were to ask me any question Eve - about how I could help you - what would it be?'

Eve wrung her hands feeling utterly awkward. What was this, some kind of test? Would her senior colleague recommend she be placed on sick leave if she admitted the full extent of what she had experienced – her obsession with the girl in the book she had loved as a child? Yet she couldn't take back what she had already told her. Crockery clattered noisily behind the counter and the hiss of the milk steamer momentarily prevented her from speaking. She took a shaky breath.

'Dr Highcroft, like I say, when I'm alone, strange things seem to ...'

'Eve,' her superior interrupted with a friendly smile, 'that isn't a question. Perhaps I didn't express myself properly – so try again, what question would you ask?'

Eve looked into her dark eyes then swallowed.

'How do I make these hallucinations stop?'

'Good,' Highcroft replied and let out a long breath, 'that's a good question,' then pushing her cup aside rested her weight on the table, smiling at her through arched fingers, 'expand on that.'

Eve tried not to frown. What was this?

'Why do I see things – why do I visit strange places in my dreams … keep seeing ..?'

Highcroft looked at her thoughtfully, a half-smile playing across her intelligent features.

'Eve, it's not physically inconceivable that someone could catch a glimpse into another space or time – see someone from the past. Highly improbable yes - as far as current scientific knowledge goes – but not theoretically impossible.' Eve felt suddenly as if the world had stopped spinning. 'Electricity would have seemed like magic to someone from a hundred years before Edison patented the light bulb,' Highcroft continued then broke off as if to give her time to consider the comment.

'In the fifties a young heating engineer was working in a York basement when all of a sudden an entire column of Roman infantry came marching out of one wall and off through another. He could hear them, but they could clearly not see him. He could describe them in extreme technical detail – a man who had no archaeological or historical background.' Eve swallowed. 'Was he mad – no ... was he hallucinating?' she shrugged. 'I could tell you many other stories Eve, but I get the feeling that they wouldn't help convince you that what you have experienced is totally normal.'

Eve frowned as she sipped her coffee. 'So you're saying visions are normal, fair enough, but what should ...'

'Go easy on yourself Eve,' Highcroft replied calmly, '– don't let them play on your mind ... and get some rest.'

'Yeah, but -,' she broke off and glanced away. 'Sorry.'

'Don't worry,' the older woman smiled back confidently before finishing her coffee. 'Just get some rest – I'm pretty sure everything will make sense in the fullness of time.'

Rest - *seriously?*

'I'll try,' she smiled weakly as she rose to grab her bag, then paused. A sudden impulse crept upon her.

'Dr Highcroft, have you …'

'I have a free afternoon,' the academic cut in casually, 'I can take your 3 o'clock class – go home, rest – or at least just draw if you have to work!'

Eve hesitated, then smiled and abandoned the question.

'You sure? Thanks - *really*.'

'Don't mention it,' Highcroft shrugged. 'And if I don't see you before, I'll catch up with you at Prof. Stokes' do.'

A dark cloud seemed to overshadow her thinking at the thought of her mentor's farewell party but she pushed it away.

'Yeah, thanks – see you then,' and with an odd feeling of confusion she left the room.

Evening

Eve sighed, unable to sleep.

TV was rubbish, she'd tired of sketching, and hadn't the focus to read. She picked up her phone absent-mindedly, forcing herself not to glance at the books and folders piled on her chest of drawers - nor the documents and notebooks on her desk. An unfinished PhD in artistic vertebrate reconstruction, forty undergraduate essays and an unfinished post for the pop-science blog she manned. A literal ton of work to do – but she needed to rest. To take a break and *relax* as both Aisha her flat-mate and Dr Highcroft kept telling her.

She scrolled through her messages then played a music video which usually improved her mood, but this night it seemed to make no impact on her at all. Facebook was no better. She sat, listening, trying not to think, bathed in the unearthly glow of her phone's screen, the room seeming suddenly to swirl with discordant shadows. She clicked off her phone, bored of scrolling through social media and turned on her bedside lamp, bathing the room in a more homely glow. She felt like a square peg in a round hole: parties, dinners, selfies, fashion, holidays, hot guys … she was becoming depressed, yet at least it was still an abstract, an observation she could control.

'Get a grip!' she whispered involuntarily. She needed to distract herself, to wind her racing mind down. She glanced at her piled desk, almost giving in to the temptation to work on her PhD then let her gaze drift to the book shelf. She would read. Something homely and familiar, maybe Pride and Prejudice or one of the Narnia stories which took her mind to a happier time – but before she could stop herself she had realised her mistake, and before she could push the thought of the woman from the photograph away she had thought of *the* book.

It seemed suddenly to goad her, calling out to her from its forlorn resting place, crammed horizontally above the volumes on her over-loaded bookcase. For a heart-beat cold dread seemed to tug at her and she shivered as if caught in a raging blizzard, then it passed.

She set her jaw. *Exposure*. She would read the damned book, tackle it head-on and before she lost the will to do so she rose from her bed and grabbed it briskly as if taking charge, then returned to sit cross-legged with the large volume resting on her lap, the smooth-skinned lizard-like model of an Allosaurus staring back at her menacingly from the cover.

'Okay,' she said belligerently, 'do your worst!' As if in answer the lights flickered but she pretended not to notice, and with a sigh opened the book, flipping briskly to the page in question. That page. That photograph. She forced herself to look at the photo of the girl. The picture sat midway down the right hand page in the chapter entitled *Digging up the Past*, sandwiched between text and illustrations demonstrating how fossilisation took place. She read the subtitle below: *Palaeontologists at Work, Montana N. America*.

Despite the obvious fact that there was no way it could possibly be her, she could not escape the fact that the young woman she had been seeing – time and time again since the book had arrived – looked exactly like the woman in the photograph. She ran her fingers across the image. So that was that. No rushing wind. No plunge into sudden darkness, no Hollywood special effects. It was a photograph in a book about dinosaurs from the seventies; and some over-agitated part of her subconscious had been seeing one of the intake of new students and making a subconscious association. The palaeontologist in the photo would be at least sixty by now! She let out a long sigh, then putting the book down pulled the covers over her. She'd flick through the book, read the words she'd had read to her –and later read herself – so many times as a kid, and finally put this stupidity to bed.

A strange creaking noise came from the door of her en-suite bathroom. She ignored it – just the heating. She rolled onto her side and took off her glasses. She so needed a good night's rest, to let her mind switch off. The creak came again, then the sharp slap of the door slamming closed. She sat up, her heart thumping.

What the ..? She felt her pulse begin to race out of control.

Her bathroom door was clearly moving, a sliver of darkness opening up discernibly as she watched. She crammed on her glasses and edged into a sitting position. There was something in her bathroom! The door continued to open a few centimetres further then slammed close abruptly. She swallowed, her mind racing and fumbled for her phone. What on earth? It began to open once more and this time she could sense the sigh of a warm wind pushing the door open a few inches before abating as the door was sucked closed again. *A draught?* But where the hell was that coming from? Her bathroom abutted the next flat and the only ventilation came from an extractor fan above the shower.

Forcing herself up, she slipped her feet into her boots and crossed the room, pushing away the childish urge to call out to her flat-mate. Just a draught. She watched the door begin to open slowly once again, and this time she could hear the gusting wind and the distant cry of what sounded unsettlingly like a bird of prey.

Oh God!

She paused just inches from the door, her heart thumping, somehow knowing what lay beyond yet unwilling to believe it. She felt the hairs on the back of her neck stand on end. She was going mad ... A fine dark mist seemed to be spilling from the narrow gap, the atmosphere intensifying, rich and warm. A part of her wanted to turn and run from the room, but she had to end this, to put the madness to bed once and for all. She took a breath and gritting her teeth pushed it open - stepping forward briskly - then gasped, realizing her mistake too late.

The Pliocene

Eve's thoughts seemed to accelerate to the speed of light as the ground rushed up to meet her: she was stumbling over the edge of a rocky escarpment, some rationalising part of her brain knowing her face was about to impact the ground, while another simultaneously found itself unable to believe it. Her vision blurred, then the air was crushed from her lungs as she was yanked sideways, the counter force crushing her rib-cage as a grip like iron grabbed her left arm. She was alive. Dangling.

Twisting awkwardly she saw a woman's face above her, then yelped as her saviour let her go, dropping her unceremoniously to slide six or seven feet to land on her hands and knees. She took a breath, then felt her heart thud out of control as the face above her registered: it was the girl from the photograph.

She took a few slow breaths, trying to get a handle on what had just happened, then gawped as the young woman swung her legs over the edge and scrabbled down to land at her side. They were at the bottom of a low rocky outcrop, an uneven surface of rocks and grassy tufts spread out in front of them. The girl seemed to be ignoring her completely and began to scan the area cautiously. She was dark haired and very attractive Eve noted subconsciously as she unslung something from across her back. It took her a moment for her confused brain to process what it was.

'Is that a pump action shotgun?' she asked in a daze.

The young woman turned to her distractedly. She was wearing a fur-hooded bomber jacket and Ugg boots like she'd just stepped off the high street; the weapon seemed unbelievably incongruous in her hand. Eve gawped, her terrified mind struggling to keep up, watching in a daze as the girl pulled something from her belt.

'Yes - and this is a 1940s British Army issue Webley,' she replied in strangely accented English, 'can you fire a pistol?'

'I ...' she began, feeling utterly overwhelmed. Thirty seconds ago she was stepping into her bathroom and now she was being handed a gun in a desolate wilderness. The revolver felt like a lead weight in her hand.

'Don't worry,' the girl from the photograph continued dismissively, 'I hope you will not have to use it – just make sure you do not point this bit at *me*.' She gestured to the barrel, 'or any part of your own body ...'

Her accent was unusual, Eve noted with a strange detachedness. Eastern European? Mediterranean? Yet somehow well-spoken like a foreign dignitary who'd learned English at a prestigious finishing school. Before she could muse further, the girl had turned away to scan the desolate hillside once more. 'We cannot go back the same way,' she said pensively glancing up the precipitous slope, 'that would be too obvious...'

Obvious? Obvious to whom?

She set off without a word. Eve hesitated for a moment then followed. She felt light-headed – overwhelmed – but what else could she do?

'Where are we?' she dared to venture after a while, struggling to process the rugged terrain they were passing through; the scrub which tugged at her clothes and the wind which stung her cheeks. It was a dream – it had to be – but if felt so painfully real.

'No talking,' replied the woman with the shotgun, barely turning to glance at her, 'we must keep our senses sharp, yes?' Her mind couldn't take it in. They stood in a land of vast prairies, scrub and craggy outcrops. It was utterly impossible – but it was clearly happening. She slowed to a halt, staring in disbelief, then shivered. The shock of the fall was wearing off and with a jolt of realisation she noted the fact that she was still wearing her pyjamas. The girl with the gun turned.

'Take this,' she said, stripping off her jacket to put it round her shoulders. Though the dark haired girl was shorter and more athletically built it was a surprisingly good fit for her slender frame. 'Come,' she continued gently, 'follow me quietly,' and levelling the gun once more set off into the swaying prairie grass ahead. Eve shivered again as she zipped the jacket up, but not with the cold: it *felt* so real – so horribly real.

They skirted the ridge, passing stunted trees she couldn't identify, and as they wove between dusty boulders she plucked up her courage to speak. 'You're

36

the girl from the book,' she said as they neared a rocky depression bordered by fractured crags. She felt as if she was in a daze, the world around her ethereal and dreamlike. The girl glanced back at her for a moment, her dark eyes brooding and for a moment she thought she would refuse to answer.

'Yes,' she replied curtly, 'a photograph of me during a dig in 1976 was used in the book of which you speak.' Eve swallowed. She felt suddenly warm, a sickly light-headedness beginning to creep over her. 'I look good for my age, yes!'

She didn't know how to respond. 'You … we've travelled through time,' she said unsteadily as the vastness of where she stood hit home, the never-ending desolate wildness. The world seemed to be throbbing with some barely-perceivable energy, the rough ground beneath her feet more tangible than she had ever experienced, the wind keener on her cheek, every strand of hair it rustled almost painfully obvious. The girl from the photo nodded.

'Obviously.'

Eve shuddered, her mind overwhelmed by the sounds and sights of the virgin landscape, the sweet musk of the rippling grass-lands and the pine-fresh smell of the gnarled shrub-like trees almost overwhelmingly heady. She felt small, tiny amid a primeval vastness, a place so huge and wild her human impact was of almost no significance. .

'Are you ... from the future?' she asked, turning from the view across the plain as the idea struck her suddenly.

'No Eve Wells, I am not – *from the future*,' the girl replied making quotation marks with her fingers in the air, 'far from it.'

Eve frowned as a thought struck her. 'How do you know my ...'

The screech of a huge carrion bird wheeling high overhead caught their attention and she broke off abruptly. The girl paused, her face etched with a knowing smile, then dropped her gaze to the scrub ahead.

'Ah, here!' she said in a low tone, then gestured for her to squat down. She obeyed willingly, then following her gaze saw something which made her heart leap. The girl grinned, her eyes locked on a strange, stretched-looking animal reminiscent of an otter or a weasel – but the size of a leopard. It stood about ten metres away licking delicately at bloodied paws, before leaving the carcass it had found to sniff briskly at the air. It moved with a jogging swiftness, pausing to dip its head and sniff the foliage, then turned its large tapering head in their direction. Eve froze.

'My god…'

From its sagging mouth projected two thick fangs the length of her hand, protected by weird jowl-like protrusions on its lower jaw. The dark haired girl raised a hand to hush her. So far, they had not been noticed, but Eve hardly cared, her fears forgotten as she stared in rapt fascination, unable to believe what she was seeing. For a moment, crazy excitement vied with her sense of disbelief. It was a creature she had studied and drawn endlessly for her undergraduate thesis. A creature whose disarticulated bones she had carefully reassembled and catalogued in the stores of the UEM's zoological museum. A creature which hadn't walked the earth for over three million years.

'*Thylacosmilus.*'

Even as she said it the world seemed to lurch disconcertingly. She gasped, then stumbled, her head spinning with such violence it took her breath away. She felt her legs buckle, the strength seeming to flood out of her body as a migraine-like sting engulfed her and her stomach began to churn. The time travelling girl from the book made a disparaging sound.

'Sorry …' Eve gasped, then gagged and was violently ill, bracing herself on her hands and knees as the world seemed to turn upside down.

'This is only natural,' the girl with the gun said calmly, 'as your mind adjusts. It will pass Eve Wells … but let it pass quickly, that animal will soon have our scent – particularly as you are now vomiting.'

She crouched feeling shell shocked and dazed, her hands trembling uncontrollably as she braced herself against the cold rocky wall, but before she had time to recover herself, the girl from the photograph had cursed and was dragging her by the armpit towards a low rock shelter between fallen boulders. There was the sound of movement close behind, mammalian sniffing and a strange gurgling bark. Eve felt her pulse lurch wildly, scrabbling forwards into the darkness with an almost animal desperation. They flattened themselves against the back of the cramped cave, the shotgun ready in the stranger's hand.

'So, tell me about this creature Eve Wells,' said the girl in a reassuringly measured tone, as if trying to distract her, '– this *Thylaco-smilus*.' She thought of the pistol the girl had given her, but her hands were shaking too much to even consider using it. She paused for a moment, her mind reeling, watching with horrified fascination as the young woman took a handful of cartridges from her pocket and began to slide them steadily into her weapon one after another.

'I – It's a marsupial mammal,' she said shakily, 'one of the dominant carnivores of South America during the Pliocene...'

South America. Her head began to spin once more, forcing her to take a series of deep breaths. How the hell had she stepped from her bedroom into South America over four million years ago?

'Go on.'

She was trembling, the gun in her jacket pocket seeming suddenly to weigh her down.

'It's sometimes referred to as the marsupial sabre-toothed cat. But it's not a feline...'

'Uh-huh...' The dark haired woman nodded without looking at her, her eyes fixed on the foliage just visible through the bright entrance of the overhang.

'It's a member of the *borhyaenids* – a group of mammals with both bear and dog like features …'

'*Hush!*'

The dark haired girl had raised her hand, her eyes locked on the strip of light before them.

'What?' she whispered anxiously, 'what's happening?'

A huge head lurched into the musty space, temporarily blocking out the light as viscous fangs raked the length of the entrance. In the cramped space the sound of their shocked screams was deafening.

'Too shallow!' the girl with the gun yelled desperately, but Eve was too busy screaming to hear her, flattening herself instinctively into the furthest corner of the cave as the snarling mouth jerked towards her followed by a sharp-clawed foot. The dark haired girl snarled angrily, grunting as she struggled to cock the weapon and manoeuvre it past her own feet with the animal's muzzle so close. 'More facts Wells!' she yelled angrily, kicking out at the grasping paw as it sought to hook her ankle, 'give me more facts!'

Facts! What the hell was she on about! The fangs jerked out towards her, ripping a five inch tear in the arm of her jacket. She screamed incoherently, her senses overwhelmed by its stinking breath, dust and dirt cascading from the ceiling above.

'I need information Wells,' the girl yelled angrily, 'vulnerability, weaknesses …'

Then she understood, and though, for a moment, she felt sure her mind would be paralysed, her thoughts went suddenly into over-drive.

'Their mandibular fangs!'

'What?'

'The sabre fangs …'

'I am well aware of the sabre fangs Eve Wells!' the girl exclaimed desperately as the raking teeth scythed through the dirt by her leg.

'Brittle!' she gasped hoarsely, '- their teeth are surprisingly brittle!' she yelled desperately, 'built to slash throats and give suffocating bites - not strong enough to crunch laterally through bone!'

'Boom!' said the dark haired girl and abandoning her attempt to use the gun began to kick wildly at the beast's muzzle with her boots. Eve flinched as it began to growl menacingly, writhing and slashing as its whiskers tickled her calves, the time traveller yelling and kicking as she sought to smash the slashing teeth away; and then, with a grunt of pure desperation the dark haired girl's boot hit home, snapping the nearest incisor with a sickening crunch.

The Thylacosmilus let out a hideous whining snarl, its huge head jerking backwards, and as blood flecked the girl's legs she whipped up the gun and fired two rounds in quick succession.

Eve closed her eyes, clamping her hands firmly over her ears, and when she opened them the cave was empty.

'Has it gone?' Her terrified voice sounded like it belonged to someone else – she'd never been so scared. The girl nodded casually.

'The noise and the smell have driven it away – I try never to take life unnecessarily ...'

Eve glanced at the gash in the jacket the girl had given her and let out a horrified whimper. The time traveller seemed not to notice. 'Well done Eve Wells ... and that is why I have found you.'

She dusted off her hands and picking up the shotgun crawled out lazily as if nothing had happened.

Eve slumped against the dusty wall, watching as the dark haired girl ambled casually away, forcing herself not to sob.

'Who are you?' she called weakly after a moment.

'Your guardian angel,' the girl replied casually, 'you can call me Ravenna Friere.'

Debrief

'So, you have considered my proposition Eve Wells.'

It was nine-thirty in the morning and they were sitting over coffee outside the student concourse, bathed in winter sun.

Eve shuddered as she sipped her cappuccino. Yes. Yes, she had considered the crazy girl's insane proposition - mulled and mithered and lost hours of sleep over the unbelievable request she had made. She took a breath.

'Look, you've got to appreciate that this is all a bit much for me ...'

The Mediterranean girl looked at her levelly, her eyes hidden by mirrored aviator sunglasses. She raised her eyebrows, then turned her attention to the plate of chocolate fudge cake in front of her.

'With respect Eve Wells, I do not see the problem. You have something I need and I have the ability to protect you in return.'

Protect her – protect her from what – from going mad? Eve put down her cup and gazed at the girl's confident features. In her designer parka and tight black jeans Friere looked more like an Italian super-model at a ski resort than a postgraduate student. She had never felt so confused, nor so conspicuous. She glanced away as two passing guys tried to catch her eye.

'Cheer up Eve Wells,' smiled the time traveller before stuffing her mouth full of chocolate cake in a most un-super-model like way, 'you survived … you saw the past … you have me to protect you. Is this not wonderful?'

Eve said nothing. *No.* No it was not wonderful. Her understanding of reality and the universe in general had just completely disintegrated and this crazy stranger was asking her to take it all in her stride.

'I'm sorry,' she said, plucking up the courage to voice the decision she had made, 'about last night - whatever it is you want me to do …'

'You cannot pretend last night never happened Eve Wells,' the girl said softly, 'and I *need* your knowledge …'

Eve shook her head. Everything within her screamed that she should walk away – that it was madness, that she was literally going mad. 'Look, please, you've got to appreciate …'

'You must try to relax Eve Wells.'

'*Relax!*' she shot back, 'look – I barely know who you are and you're treating me like I should accept what happened as normal!'

Ravenna Friere removed her aviators.

'Eve Wells, as you are about to discover, there is no such thing as *normal* …'

Part 2

A Most Extraordinary Form of Animal

Eve

The two young women at the station greeted each other with pensive nods. Though they had never met, each knew the presence of the other meant they were both in pretty deep.

'Polly Nightingale?' began the taller girl, lean and sandy-haired, her jeans and down jacket discordant against the other's mid-century dress and overcoat.

'You must be Eve Wells?' replied the brunette, gaze wary above freckle dappled features. Eve returned a discombobulated smile as behind her the guard's whistle blew. Less than ten minutes ago she had been kissing her fiancé goodbye on the edge of campus, yet now she stood amid the steam and bustle of a crowded Scottish railway station at some point in time she couldn't quite fathom. A man in a fedora frowned at her over the top of his *Edinburgh Standard* and she glanced away nervously, yet Polly Nightingale seemed more concerned with the headline of his newspaper: *Monster Fever Grips Caledonia Once Again*. Her brows knotted. 'Things must have become pretty serious if she's brought you along as consultant ...'

Eve looked away. In her everyday life she taught palaeontology at a Midlands university and the very fact she'd been called upon could only have one logical conclusion. It took every ounce of effort to keep her mind from drifting to the memory of the last time she'd been contacted – the crazy events which had turned her understanding of reality upside down.

'She's not here yet?'

'You know what she's like!' Polly grinned and they shared a conspiratorial smile. Though strangers, they were linked by an unspoken secret, mutual acquaintances of the most truly remarkable person. 'Here, let me give you my number, it'd be good to catch up after ...'

'Yeah,' Eve agreed, '- is it right you both ..?'

From what she had learned from their mutual friend, Polly worked at a prestigious London museum, yet her curatorial role had become a doorway to something entirely more incredible.

The girl inclined her head, her expression watchful. 'Best not talk about that now.'

With a nod they stepped behind the nearest pillar, discreetly shielding the glow of their screens from two mothers with perambulators and a gang of workmen packing up for the day.

'Tut-tut ladies,' said a disapproving voice and Eve whisked around to see a diminutive dark- haired figure dressed in vintage hiking gear. 'I see you cannot separate yourselves from your devices - will I need to confiscate them?'

Eve felt a host of memories clamour within her. It had been almost a year since the enigmatic speaker had invaded her life, yet still she had the power to unsettle her. 'All good Dinosaur Girl?'

Eve nodded hesitantly.

Classically beautiful, Ravenna Friere looked like any other confident twenty-five year old, but, as Eve reflected with a sinking feeling, the dark haired woman was anything but. 'I'm sure you can imagine the consequences of this kind of technology being noticed? We are here to untangle chronological problems, not create them!'

Eve cleared her throat as she pocketed her phone, her gaze drawn out across the platform, now thronged with smartly dressed school children; a businessmen tapping out his briar pipe glanced up to meet her gaze. Would any of them ever suspect where they had come from – or how archaic the dark haired girl was? She glanced back to Ravenna. With her flawless Mediterranean complexion and unusual accent they would probably take her for a tourist dressed for a week in the mountains. She looked down at her own clothes and took a step back behind the pillar. 'Where are we?' she ventured, sure the businessman was still watching.

'Later,' the Mediterranean girl replied, 'and as you know well, the question is not where, but *when* ...' She broke off to look her up and down disapprovingly, 'we must get you into something less conspicuous Wells.' And handing her a satchel of clothes gestured towards the ladies conveniences.

Ten minutes later Eve emerged looking like something from a vintage railway poster advertising bracing outings in the country. 'We must do something with your hair,' commented Ravenna, and with Polly's help began to force it into some approximation of mid-twentieth century style. Eve admired herself in Polly's compact, then glanced down at her feet and grimaced.

'Where the hell did you get these hiking boots, the torture chamber at Warwick Castle?'

'No complaining,' the dark-haired girl frowned, 'we have important work to do.'

'So what's the gig?'

The Mediterranean girl hesitated before turning towards the exit.

'We are three school chums on a jolly girls' get-together near the Moray Firth,' Ravenna replied over her shoulder, 'off for a spot of Highland air.'

'But I thought we were taking the sleeper?' Polly frowned, with a glance at the waiting locomotive.

'Things are moving rapidly,' the dark haired girl replied as they descended the steps, 'faster than I could have envisaged - and we must make up for lost time.'

'*Lost time* – but ...' the words died on Eve's lips. A small motor car was awaiting them, parked with a couple of others across the street.

'Austin Seven,' the Mediterranean girl said curtly, 'we can travel direct and non-stop - no connections to make nor time-consuming hikes into the sticks once we get there.'

'Do you want me to drive?' ventured Polly, making for the driver's door as if this was standard procedure.

'Do you know how to double-declutch Nightingale girl?'

Polly seemed to hesitate, then shrugged and took the front passenger seat as Eve headed for the rear with her satchel of modern clothes. 'Do you want me to stick this bag in the boot?'

'No,' Ravenna said sharply, 'I would not open the trunk here – not unless you want to cause … something of a stir.'

'*O-kay,*' Eve replied slowly, and throwing the bag on the leather seats got in and began looking for a seatbelt.

'I would tell you to buckle up,' Ravenna said with a grin, 'but there are no lap belts - they will not be mandatory until 1983 …' Eve noticed Polly Nightingale smile wryly, and knowing they would get along well sat back as Ravenna moved jerkily into the traffic.

Hell it was unreal – yet somehow every time the enigmatic Mediterranean girl called her back into the past she managed to adjust. She sighed, knowing it ought not to be possible, but as she lost herself in the long-dead world beyond the window knew that it clearly was.

'Now Nightingale,' the Mediterranean girl continued, 'your phone – we need some banging tunes for the journey.'

Road Trip

Within fifty minutes they were bumping along country lanes, heading out of the city into bigger countryside to a soundtrack of upbeat dance music.

The scenery made Eve's head spin: beautiful, unspoilt, *archaic*. It was time for the hay harvest and men in cloth caps and neckerchiefs were rigging up strange looking machines to shire horses ready for the cut. In the front, Ravenna gunned the engine like a rally-driver, squeezing every ounce of grip out of the thin tyres as she raced along the winding roads.

'Seriously, you're not using up my battery playing house music!' Polly was complaining as the time traveller bobbed her head to the pounding beat, 'what if someone hears us?'

'Who will hear us with these puny speakers Nightingale girl?' Ravenna returned incredulously.

Eve cleared her throat, suddenly desperate to make sense of the crazy road-trip she had found herself on.

'So where *are* we going?'

Ravenna glanced at her in the rear view mirror.

'A body of water between Fort Augusta and Drumnadrochit.'

She nodded and they carried on in silence for a long time, the scenery becoming steeper and more mountainous as they passed into a wooded valley.

'And what are we going to do at this *body of water*?'

'Always questions!' replied Ravenna, while Polly smiled to herself. Eve sat back and turned her attention to the window. Perhaps it was better she didn't know – after all, her specialism could only mean one thing – yet after a while Ravenna relented. 'We are going fishing Eve Wells – or perhaps I should say hunting. This deep ocean inlet is twenty miles long, ample room for a large aquatic animal to hide in – hence the legends which have grown up around the place.'

'*Legends?*' she frowned. Then the penny dropped. 'Oh - you're kidding me!'

'Read this,' said Polly, passing her a sheet of A4.

The Loch Ness Monster - a fairly exhaustive history of the legend printed off from Wikipedia. She scanned it with growing incredulity. She'd heard of the story since childhood but had never really given it any serious thought. As she read the long list of accounts and sightings a feeling of concern began to tug at her gut.

'I have spoken before of places where the weave of time pulls tightly,' Ravenna continued, 'and even touches – *close places* – and it has been bought to my attention that *this* is such a place.'

An almost Nordic scene had opened up before them, steep mountains soaring high above an immense steel-grey stretch of water. Eve nodded pensively. She still couldn't get her head around the fact that time was not a line but a knotted tangle, yet their very presence in this place was living proof. 'I believe the fissure in the temporal weave has happened only a handful of times before in this place.'

Eve glanced down at the sheet. 'Like when St. Columba defeated the monster with the sign of the cross in AD565.'

'And when Donald Mackenzie of Balnain saw the monster in 1871,' Polly added, realisation clearly dawning, '... which would explain why there have been so few sightings.'

Ravenna nodded, her gaze fixed hawk-like on the road. 'Indeed - the rift here is clearly cyclical, and ever since George Spicer saw the monster in 1933 – this very year – it has happened roughly every decade: Peter MacNab's famous 1955 photograph and sonar readings, Tim Dinsdale's film of a wake across the Loch in the 60's, Anthony Shiel's '77 photo of a long-necked creature and so on.'

Polly nodded seriously. 'With six sightings between 1933 and '38 something is clearly going on at this particular point in time.'

Eve frowned. They were passing a wooded stretch near the water's edge. 'This section of road is the very one on which George Spicer and his wife allegedly saw "a most extraordinary form of animal" crossing the road in front of their car, they claimed it had a body around four feet high and twenty five in length, it's neck long and ...' She broke off as Polly yelped unexpectedly, and looking up saw the last thing she had ever expected to see. 'Oh, and here it is!' Ravenna added in a matter-of-fact tone as Eve's heart leapt out of her chest, her stomach lurching wildly as Ravenna threw the wheel hard right, sending the car skidding towards the grass verge.

She twisted her head as she grabbed the back of Polly's seat. A mound of grey flesh - elephant-like at first glance, but more whale-like on reflection - a cracked yet blubbery mass - was lumbering across the metalled road with the undulating motion of an elephant seal.

'Holy ..!

The car struck the verge with a disconcerting lurch, making them scream as they ricocheted past the creature's vanishing tail, before coming to an abrupt halt against the bank. Ravenna was out in a flash. 'Did you see it Wells, did you get a clear glimpse?'

Eve was nursing a bruised shoulder.

'I – *yes*, but I don't really ...'

Ravenna scowled at her darkly. 'Brilliant, *Dinosaur Girl,* that was maybe our only chance to identify it in daylight!' She threw open the door and Eve stumbled out to gaze desperately at the swaying foliage left in its wake. There was nothing but an eerie silence now as if the woods were holding their breath.

'Must be its regular run,' Polly mused, glancing at the deep gouges and flattened foliage.

Eve nodded. 'The latest research seems to suggest many aquatic dinosaurs came to nest on land at night …' she broke off, hardly able to believe what she was saying.

'Come,' said Ravenna grimly, 'we are in the right place – now, roll up your sleeves, we must move this car …' But Eve hardly heard, still staring at the place the creature had disappeared.

'Woah - I've just seen the Loch Ness Monster.'

The Guest House

'Not hungry ladies?'

Polly and Eve glanced at each other as Ravenna calmly shovelled poached egg into her mouth. Food was the last thing on Eve's mind, she felt homesick and mildly nauseous. 'Well, waste not, want not!' Ravenna continued, reaching for Eve's plate.

Eve turned her attention to the view beyond the net curtains. The guesthouse stood next to a vicarage a stone's throw from the Loch - the perfect base from which to explore its brooding waters. She shuddered. It seemed almost impossible that it had once sat beneath a primeval ocean – the ocean from which the monster had no doubt come.

'So Eve Wells, your professional verdict?'

She looked up briskly, shooting Ravenna an anxious glance. 'On what we saw?'

'Yes, Dinosaur Girl,' the dark haired girl replied impatiently, 'of the creature by the loch.'

Eve hesitated. 'A plesiosaur of some kind – *elasmosaurus ... cryptoclidus*? There are at least twenty species of long-necked *sauropterygians* which would fit the bill.' She broke off as both women looked at her blankly, but was saved the trouble of elaborating by the appearance of Mrs McLeod, the proprietor, who entered to clear away the plates.

'All finished there girls? Would you be wanting the wireless on in the sitting room?'

'No, thank you,' Ravenna replied primly in a neat Oxbridge accent, 'would it be possible to have some more tea?'

The woman nodded and left the room.

'But I thought the classic monster sightings had been dismissed as hoaxes?' Eve ventured once she had gone, 'the long-neck-out-of-the-water picture at least – a plesiosaur could never extend its neck directly upwards like that ...'

Ravenna shrugged. 'Something is in this Loch and I now firmly believe it is a chronological anomaly ...' She broke off as the door opened again. To Eve's surprise it was not Mrs McLeod: a tall young man stood in the doorway in a dark suit and dog-collar.

'Oh, sorry ladies,' he said apologetically, 'I had no idea there were guests still breakfasting.'

'No problem,' said Eve instinctively. Polly added:

'Don't mind us!'

'No, of course ...' he replied bashfully, 'I'm James Roberts – the curate of St Mary's- I was just calling on Mrs McLeod ...'

'Cool,' smiled Eve without thinking. The young man frowned.

'Right, well, I'll be getting along now - parishioners to visit and all that ...'

'Have a good day,' said Ravenna neatly. The young man nodded awkwardly then left the room.

'*Hashtag hot vicar,*' grinned Polly after a moment and they all laughed.

'*Cool*,' tutted Ravenna with a disapproving inclination of her eyebrows. 'That term will not be used widely for at least another sixty years! Now children – down to business.'

A thoughtful hush fell.

'So, we have some idea what we are up against,' Polly ventured, sipping her tea, 'but in the deepest stretch of inland waterway in the UK - which as you said is over twenty miles long - how on earth are we going to find a creature the size of an elephant?'

'A small whale,' Eve corrected but Polly ignored her.

'Simple,' Ravenna replied with a matter-of-fact inclination of her eyebrows, 'bait – we find its favourite food.'

'*Which is*?' Polly challenged.

Ravenna smiled and made a gesture towards Eve with her fork.

'Ammonites?'

'*Boom*,' the dark haired girl smiled, 'and this, Eve Wells, is why I have brought you!'

*

'This plan is sheer simplicity,' Ravenna was saying as they unloaded an assortment of duffle bags from the car.

Eve looked on nervously, dreading that the landlady or some guest would appear and start asking questions. 'We go out onto the Loch at night and take a dive. We use our abilities to open a rift to the Mesozoic seas, we allow through some smaller aquatic fauna of the sort a plesiosaur would love, use it to attract the *monster*, then usher it back and seal the rift.'

'So simple,' replied Polly glibly, 'no danger involved at all.' Ravenna shrugged.

'If you have any better ideas Nightingale ..?' But Eve interrupted before she could reply.

'What? You're going to *dive* in Loch Ness? But it's connected to the Moray Firth – it's practically deep ocean!'

'I have few other options,' Ravenna returned darkly, then broke off as footfalls crunched on the gravel behind her.

'Ladies,' said the young curate they had met earlier. They smiled back warmly at the passing man, Polly giving a friendly wave; but as she did so the canvas bag she was unloading fell open and a scuba hose slipped out onto the gravel. Eve felt the breath catch in her throat as the young man's eyes darted to it, Polly moving swiftly to push it back in, while Ravenna cursed under her breath. 'Well, I'll be on my way,' the young man continued briskly, and to their relief hurried off towards the village.

'So what now?' asked Eve a little shakily.

'We take a hike,' Ravenna replied tersely, 'and find a place to dive.'

The Loch

Eve massaged her aching feet dejectedly.

'Much as I like the outdoors, we've spent hours walking and haven't heard of a single monster sighting.'

They were perched on a timeworn landing stage, gazing out over the mirror-like surface of the water. Ravenna seemed not to hear, staring stoically across the Loch at the castle which shimmered in the late-morning air. The Mediterranean girl frowned then glanced back to the guest house behind them, its ivy clad walls just visible barely twenty yards up the lane.

'This place is as good as any,' she mused quietly, 'now all we need ...'

She broke off, and Eve glanced up sharply as a dark shape appeared on the water, moving steadily towards them from the east about twenty yards out. Eve felt her scalp prickle, but as she stared on in silence the shape became more distinct: a rowing boat with a single occupant.

'*Magna Mater*,' Ravenna muttered then stood to watch the approaching vessel.

As the boat came alongside the jetty, a grizzled man in his sixties glanced up at them with interest, nodding curtly as he threw up the rope.

'So you're the three lassies hunting monsters are ye?'

'Oh – yes, we – erm …' Eve replied awkwardly, but Ravenna interrupted with a confident smile.

'We're just up for a weekend's hiking,' she interjected calmly in a prim tone, 'fresh air and wide open spaces.'

The old man looked up at her sceptically then began to unload a rod and tackle. 'You's been asking a lot of questions about monsters for three young ladies who aren't particularly interested in monsters.'

Eve shot Polly a concerned look.

'Fresh mountain air and fair prospects are all we're here for,' Ravenna continued, 'and if we happen to bump into a monster, then all the better.'

The old man inclined his head and made a sound in his throat which may have been a chuckle. It certainly seemed unlikely: three young women alone in the wilds hunting mythical creatures. Eve felt her heart sinking. 'You're reporters aren't ye?' he added as he climbed up onto the jetty, 'newspaper types from London up for a story ...'

'I couldn't possibly comment,' Ravenna replied with an evasive smile. The old man shook his head wryly.

'Well, I've been fishing this Loch for nigh-on forty years and have nare seen hide n' hair of any beast, metaphysical or otherwise.'

Ravenna returned a pert smile then glanced at his tethered boat. 'Well perhaps we'll get lucky ... we'll give you ten bob if you leave your boat here tonight and turn a blind eye, twice as much if we get a photograph.'

The fisherman shouldered his rod and looked at her levelly. Ravenna dug in her back pocket. A smile cracked the old man's lips and he nodded, extending his hand.

'But don't go making a song-and-dance about it will ye now, for the bailiffs are devilish keen on feeling a poacher's collar – if you get my meaning.'

'We certainly won't,' the Mediterranean girl replied demurely. The man raised a hand in farewell then went on his way.

Eve glanced at her sceptically. 'So let me get this straight: this is really happening - we're about to try and catch the Loch Ness Monster?'

Ravenna turned towards the guest house gesturing to Polly and with a sigh Eve followed.

Encounter

I t was pitch dark after the brightness of their room and Eve's eyes struggled to adjust. It was overcast – a moonless night – and the mountains seemed to glower down upon the valley draining all colour from the land.

'Come on,' said Polly squeezing her arm, 'let's get this over with before Mrs McLeod wakes up and finds us sneaking out.'

Ravenna appeared at her side. 'You two finish getting the kit ready and I'll make sure the old man has been good to his word.' She dumped a bag on the gravel with an overly loud crunch then disappeared, leaving them to sort the dive gear. Eve shook her head in disbelief. It was madness.

'Right, I'd better get set,' sighed Polly, and taking her wetsuit headed for the shelter of the garden wall.

Eve shivered as she contemplated what lay ahead, her eyes lingering on the ink black loch, but then, unexpectedly, Polly hissed a warning. She jerked her gaze towards the drive and to her horror saw light flare.

'*Hey!* You there ..!'

She turned briskly to find herself staring into the worried face of James Roberts. 'This must stop now,' the torch wielding curate said shakily, 'I don't know what you're up to, but I'm calling the police – I knew there was something rum about you from the first – your strange turn of phrase and the fantastical gear in your car – I'm putting a stop to this nonsense right away!'

'Please!' she whispered back but he took no heed.

'I've heard what's happening in Germany ... voices saying there may be another war ...' he took a shaky breath, 'you're spies aren't you, foreigners gathering information!'

'No!' said Eve desperately, 'you've got it wrong!'

'You're coming with me,' he continued firmly, taking her arm, '– and your friend who's hiding behind the wall!'

Eve felt panic grip her, watching helplessly as Polly stood slowly, but as she did so, a shadow rushed out of the darkness and the clergyman crumpled unexpectedly.

'Forgive me Father for I have sinned,' Ravenna Friere whispered in a tone which left Eve unsure if it were ironic or sincere, and promptly began dragging the unconscious clergyman behind the wall. 'Well, what are you waiting for? Let's go!'

Eve just stared, but the Mediterranean girl seemed not to notice.

'Put this on,' said Ravenna, handing her the down jacket she'd taken off at the station, 'just keep calm and try to relax.'

'*Relax!* she shot back incredulously, 'You've just knocked out a vicar! And I can't wear this! What if someone sees us – you heard what he said! Hell, if anyone finds us here with all this stuff - there's kit here which could change the outcome of the Second World War, the entire shape of the future!'

'Put the damned jacket on,' said Ravenna firmly, 'you are panicking Wells – it will be cold on the Loch.'

She hesitated, then consented, struggling to keep her gaze from where the young man lay.

The Loch Again

Ten minutes later they sat enveloped in darkness, bobbing on the brooding surface of the Loch about fifteen metres from the shore. Eve shuddered. Their tiny boat seemed dwarfed by the vastness of the landscape. Ravenna looked resolute but there was something unsettled in her dark expression.

'Anything we should know Wells?'

Eve glanced anxiously at the waves which lapped against the boat. 'The early Cretaceous oceans were vast and tropical – sea levels were at least three hundred feet higher and there were tons of reefs; less land mass than today - you'll be pretty deep.' Polly nodded pensively. 'And the Mesozoic Marine Revolution meant the arrival of modern fish – and predators to feed on them, loads of big creatures like plesiosaurs and pliosaurs ...' She broke off seeing Polly's expression darken.

'Our thanks for your heartening words,' Ravenna said grimly, before ducking down to busy herself with her dive kit.

'Sorry,' Eve whispered apologetically. Polly's face was ghostly white against her wetsuit, her eyes unnaturally large. She returned a weak smile as she perched her diving mask on the top of her head. 'You okay?'

'Not really – I'm terrified of deep water – and this is my second ever dive.'

'Oh,' Eve replied awkwardly.

'Hay-ho,' the museum curator shrugged, 'I've got to do this, it's only me and Ravenna who can ...' Eve nodded appreciatively, still hardly able to believe what was about to happen, then squeezed her shoulder reassuringly.

'All ready?' Ravenna whispered loudly. Polly gave Eve a reassuring look and with a nod they put in their regulators and dropped backwards over the side.

Polly

Polly forced herself to breathe evenly as the frigid waters engulfed her, an abyss of gloom and muffled noise containing god-only-knew-what horrors. It took every ounce of self-control to keep her head, following as Ravenna kicked downwards, out and away from the boat, the pressure building slowly as they descended through silt and streaming bubbles. She scanned the gloom anxiously, wary of every shape and movement, expecting at any moment for some primeval thing to manifest itself before her mask. The horror of it seemed to crawl around her, the sheer stupidity and the danger, the water like a living presence pressing down from every side.

She tried to focus her mind on Ravenna's kicking fins. The dark-haired girl seemed to be quickening her pace, pushing deeper as they spiralled into the darkness. She tried not to gulp her air as she struggled to keep up, but Ravenna - by far the stronger swimmer - was pulling ahead; and with a stab of concern she began to kick harder, concentrating on her stroke, forcing herself not to check her depth gauge. When would she deem it deep enough?

Her thighs were aching now, muscles burning as she began to gain, yet just as she drew level with Ravenna, something surged out of the darkness to her right. She gasped, jerking back instinctively, twisting in a panicked stream of bubbles – only to see a large fish flash away into the blackness. Dizzy with relief she skulled for a moment then looked down with concern. Ravenna was already far below her, seemingly oblivious. She followed with a desperate kick of her fins, descending into the emptiness, further and further from the apparent safety of the boat; but at last the time traveller slowed and turned, gesturing that it was time. Polly took a breath, hardly able to believe the ancient secret she had been drawn into, then replied with a nod.

Drawing strength from the confidence in the other girl's eyes she focussed her mind as Ravenna raised her hands. Almost instantly, living shadows seemed to writhe and deepen, swirling and arcing outwards to twist and fuse. A pool of inky solidity shimmered before them and with a nod Ravenna bid her swim into it. She held her breath as darkness surrounded her, then gasped as it gave way to light.

The temperature was changing, growing discernibly warmer. A hazy tropical light filtered down from the surface high above: the Mesozoic ocean. A searing headache lanced unexpectedly across her forehead and Polly had to fight to stay upright. For a moment she panicked, but with a rush of relief felt Ravenna grip her shoulder. She tried to breathe evenly through her regulator - just her brain adjusting to the titanic shift in time it had experienced - she made the *okay* gesture and the dark-haired girl continued with a nod.

They swam for fifteen minutes or so, seeing nothing but silvery fish and jellies, then headed up towards the light. Breaking the surface Polly began to scan desperately for any sight of land.

'*My god!*'

They were in an ocean, miles from shore, the white sand of tropical islands just visible below swaying palms. 'This is incredible!'

Polly took a breath to clear her head. They were bobbing amid powerful waves, salt stinging her lips as strange sounds swirled on the warm breeze - the call of long dead things - but Ravenna seemed unmoved.

'What are those?' she said impatiently, then putting in her regulator ducked beneath the waves. Polly frowned. It took a moment for her to realise what the strange shapes bobbing a few yards ahead were, and with a gasp of excitement pulled down her mask and followed.

Ammonites - the iconic spiral-shelled marine creature - some bobbing serenely while others jetted swiftly with explosive squid-like expulsions of bubbles. She floated for a moment, mesmerised, aware that she was seeing something generations of scientists had longed to see. There was a tap on her shoulder and Ravenna made a stabbing gesture with her finger: *go grab one*. She replied with a nod. They rounded on the creature slowly, trying not to disturb the water with their fins, but as Polly got within a couple of feet it sensed the other woman and jetted away making her jerk back violently.

Ravenna scowled behind her mask. *Try again.*

Another ammonite – about the size of a car tyre - bobbed a couple of metres above them. She skulled forward gently, extending her hand towards the seemingly docile creature. It did not move. A thought struck her and she began to wriggle her fingers gently, imitating some passing sea creature. With a surge of triumph she saw its squid like tentacles begin to emerge, dipping gently from the aperture at the base of the spiral. Ravenna gave her an approving nod, her hands almost closed around the shell. She was grinning as she wriggled her fingers closer, knowing the hardest part was now over, but then – to her horror – the gently waving tentacles shot forward to latch themselves around her hand with a horrifying grip. She cried out instinctively, wrenching her hand away with an impulsive jerk, realising her mistake too late as her respirator blew free in a blinding explosion of bubbles.

She spiralled, flailing wildly, trying to shake the powerful creature from her hand, clamping her mouth closed as her lungs began to burn. She kicked and punched as panic overwhelmed her, the vice-like grip crushing the bones in her fingers as she fought the instinct to take a breath. Her vision blurred - the world a chaos of turquoise and silver bubbles - and then the regulator was being pushed into her mouth, the grip on her hand vanishing almost instantly as a familiar pair of eyes looked firmly into hers.

Swim up, gestured Ravenna. She had the ammonite tucked under her arm like a parcel and a knife in her right hand.

Polly fought not to sob as she pushed up her mask to examine her fingers: they were badly bruised and cut in several places, the wounds stinging fiercely. She had almost drowned and the shock was beginning to make her tremble.

'Come on,' the Mediterranean girl said gently, 'well done Nightingale girl.'

She nodded weakly, wiping saltwater from her face as she struggled with the pain in her hand. Above them large shapes where wheeling, the air filled with the unearthly cries of circling pterosaurs - but there was little time to contemplate them. 'We have what we came for - now for the hard part.'

Great.

She nodded, and dropping her gaze to the living fossil in the other girl's hand pulled down her mask.

Monster

There were lights moving on the shore, the sound of shouting and the barking of dogs carrying clearly across the stillness of the loch.

Eve swore and flattened herself against the bottom of the boat as torch beams lanced overhead. She gritted her teeth, heart pounding, wrinkling her nose at the smell of stagnant water. What the hell was she going to do? A voice was calling out, bellowing loudly, but she couldn't make out the words. Where were they? She fought panic. Their chances of bringing back an ammonite as bait seemed suddenly more than ludicrous. She paused for a moment longer, her heart thudding, then, daring to glance up, saw the last thing she had ever expected.

Her heart missed a beat, the lights completely forgotten. A dark shape was moving with surprising swiftness across the black surface of the loch ahead of her, its white V-like wake clearly visible in the gloom.

'*Oh god!*'

Eve swore as she realised what she was seeing, some primeval instinct screaming at her to escape – but there was nowhere to go. The head broke the surface ten yards from the boat, huge liquid eyes and finger-length spines of teeth like an angler-fish. A strangled noise gurgled inside her throat but she was frozen, paralysed with terror as the creature closed on her. The calls from the shore became a distant blur.

She felt suddenly detached, her mind seeming to baulk at the impossibility of what she was seeing, longing for it to be some crazy dream. Yet there it was, the smooth ridge of its spine now visible, its broad muzzle opening and closing as it eyed her. An odd part of her felt she ought to be fascinated, to note some scientific observation, but she felt only primal terror, the utter horror of a creature which could end her life.

Eight yards away … seven yards. It was heading straight for the boat, eyes glistening.

Cold sweat broke and trickled down her back, her fingers aching from where they gripped the seat so

tightly. Hell, these things were supposed to be fish eaters
– perhaps it thought the boat was a rival male?

It moved almost silently – with a dreadful yet
serene predictability – six yards … five. It was going to
ram the boat and pitch her into the icy blackness. She
ducked and screamed, then driven by some instinct she
didn't quite understand made the sign of the cross as she
screwed her eyes firmly shut.

*

Polly broke the surface with a gasp, scanning
desperately, disoriented by the shift from tropical day to
Caledonian night.

For a second she couldn't place the boat and
panic flared, but then she saw it, a dark shape about
seven yards away, stark against the hills. She sensed
Ravenna at her side and with a nod they swam briskly

towards it – but as she did so became aware of an anxious voice calling from the vessel.

'It's here!' hissed Eve as she put her arm over the side, 'it's in the water … I … I made the sign of the cross and …'

'Like St Columba,' Ravenna said thoughtfully as she hauled the ammonite up into the boat. '*Deo Gracias!*'

'My god!' Eve replied as she saw the huge mollusc, 'is that ..!'

'Yes, but it is dead,' Ravenna said curtly, 'Nightingale forced me to dispatch it.' Polly felt too weak to reply. Her hand was aching fiercely, her head swimming with the pain. Then realisation struck her: *it's in the water!*

She gasped, the urge to climb into the boat near overwhelming, but even as she thought it, a beam of light washed over them. She froze instinctively. Lights were blazing in the cottage, whistles blaring. She heard Eve swear under her breath.

'What if they put a boat out - we've got to get out of here!'

But Ravenna seemed unmoved by the commotion. 'Nightingale – find out where the monster is!'

'*What?*'

'Just do it Nightingale girl!'

She knew there was no other option. Pulling down her mask with trembling hands she ducked beneath the surface and was met almost instantly by the sight of a swift moving flipper about the size of a car door. She panicked, sculling away in a flurry of bubbles and breaking the surface grabbed desperately for the side of the boat.

'Well, is it there?' Ravenna asked angrily. She nodded dumbly, feeling hysteria begin to tug at her as she desperately clutched the bulwark. She needed to get out of the water, needed to get away … a dark shape broke the surface a few yards to their rear and she yelped in synchrony with Eve.

From the shore more torch beams were scanning the surface of the loch and they ducked instinctively as painful light fell across the boat once more. 'What the hell are we going to do?'

Ravenna took a shaky breath, then gritting her teeth said: 'Pass me the ammonite Wells - I'll lure it down and close the gap!'

Polly stared at her incredulously, disbelief momentarily overriding her fear. 'But how the hell …' She would have to do it from the inside – from the Mesozoic.

'You must stay with Eve – get her out of here – back to her home!'

'You can't …' she stammered, 'I'll come with you …'

But Ravenna had already slipped in her regulator and was disappearing in a flurry of fins.

'Go after her!' Eve gasped wide-eyed, but Polly found herself unable to release the side of the boat, horribly aware of the thing which still eyed her from the stern.

'I –,' she began, but then the monster vanished abruptly and with a jolt of realisation she knew she had to follow. Shoving in her regulator she twisted forwards and with a pounding heart propelled herself into the gloom.

At first there were bubbles, the clear sign of movement, but after a moment they began to fade. She dived deeper, the pressure pushing at her chest, but there was now no sign of either Ravenna or the creature. She swam and swam, the blackness pressing down on her for what seemed like hours, and then, remembering her air tank, checked her gauge and with a sting of concern kicked sadly upwards.

'Ravenna?' asked Eve as she grasped the side of the boat.

Polly pushed back her mask and clawed at the tears which stung her eyes. Eve took a breath and began to haul her in.

'She must have done something,' the fair-haired girl said quietly as Polly struggled into the boat, 'I got this headache - about ten minutes after you went after her – and when I looked up the shore was deserted.'

Following her gaze Polly saw that the lights along the shore had indeed gone. She took a breath to calm herself and pulled back the hood of her wetsuit.

'She must have done it – she must have changed time - lured it to the Mesozoic and closed the rift.'

Eve nodded hopefully. 'No monster, so no monster-craze, so no reporters – just three crazy school friends on holiday in the Highlands.' Polly swallowed away a lump in her throat.

'Two friends.'

Eve looked at her, then cuffed at her eyes.

'Do you think she'll be okay?'

Polly forced herself to be resolute. 'She *has* been dead before,' she said with a melancholy smile, '- hell, this is insane!'

Eve gave her a hug then began to help her out of her buoyancy jacket.

She must be out there – *surely*. If she had died in the past they would never even know that she existed - they never would have met. The thought was almost too much to process. She took a shaky breath. Even after all this time she still had no idea who Ravenna really was or how she did what she did. A girl who had long ago slipped through a door in time? A phantom, or perhaps - as she had once thought– an angel? She glanced down at her aching hand. She still had no clue whether what she could do was science, magic or a miracle.

'So what now?'

Eve seemed trapped between horror and relief. They were just two girls alone in a boat. It could have been any time.

Polly shrugged. 'Now The Loch Ness Monster really *is* just a myth … I get you home. We keep in touch - we wait …'

Eve nodded. 'We wait until she contacts us again – wait until she calls on us.'

Polly smiled sadly. 'Until the next time.' She focussed her mind, watching fascinated as dark tendrils of mist began to writhe across her palm.

Eve Wells closed her eyes. "Til next time …'

Part 3

Unconfirmed Sighting

Stuck

The young woman stumbled as she negotiated the uneven path. Yet again the mist was closing in, rolling down from the glowering outcrops which flanked the fields, drifting wraith-like to obscure the world beyond the hedges and drystone walls. She grunted in frustration, then collecting herself pressed on with only the briefest glance behind.

The farmhouse, with its plastic wrapped bales and decaying tractor, was already partly veiled, consumed by the drifting mist. Crazy stories flitted through her head, the sensational headlines of newspaper reports and the warning words of old locals. She pushed them away, straightening her pack as she focussed on the directions he had given her. She had a job to do and no amount of scaremongering was going to deter her.

And then she saw it.

The stunted copse loomed up unexpectedly, tangled branches appearing out of the mist barely a handful of paces away. She hesitated, listening, sensing suddenly that there was something different about this place. She paused to check her phone – no signal – then took a couple of photographs before stowing it with a sigh. Nearly a week of wandering the area, following up every possible lead and she had seen absolutely nothing – and yet ... Her mind returned to the prints he had shown her and with a surge of determination she pushed in between the twisting branches.

Brambles plucked at her walking trousers and she cursed as her pack snagged on a branch. She was sure he had been hiding something, and with a sudden sting of excitement knew with utter certainty that this was it. There was a path here, but not a path forged by people.

A blackbird shot away in a noisy explosion of sound; small things scuttled through the loam. She was in a primeval place – a place of moss covered rocks and ancient trees - a dark and skeletal mass of gnarled branches, barely navigable even in autumn. She fought through a thicket of hazel and mountain ash. There was movement ahead.

'Hello?'

Something large was moving through the undergrowth about three yards to her right.

'*Hey* … hello?'

She pressed in deeper, ducking under an overhanging branch as she followed, twigs clawing at her face and hair. She was about to call out a third time when something made her hesitate. Perhaps this was it! Her heart began to pound. She strained her eyes, now certain it wasn't another person, the silhouette far too low. It was clearly a mammal – yet bigger than a fox or a badger - and moving with the fluidity which suggested it wasn't a loose sheep or stray dog. She stood, pulse thudding – this was it, her first sighting!

She quickened her pace, excitement mingling with fear: *hard evidence* – what no-one else had ever been able to find!

The animal was ahead of her, moving stealthily, forcing her to cut through tangling brambles as it veered to the left. Ignoring scratched fingers she stepped awkwardly over a fallen log then paused, her breathing loud in her ears. The birdsong had died away: dead silence. Some instinct told her not to make another sound and fighting the urge to retreat to the safety of the field she hesitated, listening. She took a breath, gathering her courage as she gazed into the thicket ahead, but saw only blackness and shifting shadows.

She pressed on, but cautiously now, moving branches delicately aside, treading as gently as she could - knowing it was near. And then, before she had even realised it was happening, the world around her was changing – the air growing moist and warm. Sweat began to bead her forehead so that she found herself longing to unzip her waterproof jacket, though she didn't dare, fearful of the noise it would make.

Perspiration broke and trickled from her hairline. It was hot now, unusually so – tropical almost - and the thing was still moving, twigs crackling as it wove briskly across the leaf litter ahead of her. She had to follow – had to find …

'Oh god …'

She stopped dead, unable to believe what she was seeing.

There was a clearer view ahead where the branches thinned, and it was misty – but the warm mangrove-like mist of a forest - damp condensing on the foliage around her.

A searing pain ran through the back of her head. What was this – what the hell was going on? And then she heard the snarl and her heart missed a beat.

It had been leading her in, drawing her to this place – and it was not alone.

Something large and mammalian flitted past to her left, visible momentarily through the shafts of light lancing through the canopy. She twisted, terrified, then stumbled with a yelp, her feet sinking deep into sucking ground.

She gasped, hands scrabbling desperately, sensing more movement behind her, a horrified scream gurgling up inside her throat: and then she froze. Huge dark eyes were ahead of her gazing straight into hers.

Eve

'*S*eriously! Did you *really* have to rent the

creepiest holiday let in the whole of Cornwall?'

Dr Eve Wells shuddered as she gazed at the ivy covered cottage in front of her, nestled gloomily between spreading beech trees. The dark haired young woman who was placing the key in the lock said nothing, swinging her rucksack off her shoulder as she pushed the door aside. 'Does it even have electricity?'

The girl turned sharply, her brow creased with annoyance. 'What *is* your problem Eve Wells?

Eve found herself momentarily lost for words in the face of what she had just experienced. '*My problem?*' *Seriously!*

She stared, unable to frame a reply - because until about forty-five minutes ago she had felt sure the Mediterranean girl who was addressing her was dead.

Her mind flew back to the crazy events of an hour before which now felt like some dream-like fantasy. The knock on her flat door – her heart leaping as she had stuffed the last of her things into her over-night bag - the anticipation of the romantic getaway about to be realised – and then …

'Come on Wells – we haven't got long.'

'We never have,' Eve muttered glibly as she followed the athletic young woman into the gloom of the stone-flagged kitchen.

She felt her shoulders sag, visualising the five star cottage she would not be staying in, remembering the excitement with which she had struggled into her down jacket while grabbing her keys and bag – how she had opened the door so expectantly. And then the shock: for instead of Adam, Ravenna Friere was standing in the doorway as if she'd never been away.

The keys had fallen from her hand. *'Oh god!'*

'Not quite,' the Mediterranean woman had replied thoughtfully, *'but I am only a little lower than the*

angels.' And then the attractive twenty-five year old was pushed past her – and she had found herself trapped between the sensation that she had just seen a ghost and the realisation that her weekend plans had just evaporated.

'Ravenna! I thought you were dead!'

'You have such little faith,' the enigmatic young woman had replied, *'nothing that has been made can ever truly be unmade Eve Wells.'*

Ravenna flicked on a light bringing her thoughts back to the present. She sighed and unzipped her jacket, then paused, resolving suddenly to make her point.

'Look, Ravenna – I know that what you do is important ...' *what you do*: it seemed mad even to contemplate the secret which Ravenna Friere had called her into.

The Mediterranean girl snorted as she began to unpack her kit with pointed brusqueness, '- but Adam and I haven't been away for an age and I'd had this weekend in Galloway booked for months ...' Ravenna just kept emptying her bag. 'Look, I can appreciate that whatever it is you're doing here is necessary ...'

'We are doing,' the dark haired girl corrected.

'Okay, what *we* are doing - but you don't know how much I needed this!'

'Need?' the Mediterranean girl said tersely.

'We were going on holiday!' she found herself replying more heatedly than she had expected, 'like now!'

'Lives are at stake,' the Mediterranean girl said softly.

Eve looked at her for a moment then closed her eyes. They always were.

'So what's the problem?'

She set down her bag with a resigned sigh. As a doctor of palaeontology there was every chance that Ravenna would be calling on her specialism, and the thought of what that might entail filled her with a horrible sense of unease.

Ravenna gazed at her for a moment then smiled. 'Eve Wells, we are about to search for something which is "right-up-your-street" as your unusual phrase has it – I would not have come for you if it was otherwise.'

Eve perched on the arm of the living room sofa, choosing not to remove her coat. 'So what's the deal … and can we put some heating on - its freezing?'

Ravenna began searching for a thermostat giving her time to glance at her phone – there was no reception and none of her apps were working, a message warning that no stored data could be found.

'So when are we?' she asked, placing her phone on the coffee table. Ravenna turned her attention to the wood burning stove.

'Today – *almost* … we are currently three days in the past as you understand it.'

Eve blew out her cheeks. She did not understand it – she never did and most likely never would, however many times the enigmatic Mediterranean girl dragged her back into the past. 'Look, no offence, but couldn't you have just called on Polly, she's more experienced at this stuff after all ..?'

Ravenna looked up at the mention of their mutual friend, the museum curator who'd accompanied her on their last insane journey together.

'Polly Nightingale has … other pressing matters to attend to,' the dark haired girl said evasively, '– and you must know I would not call upon you if it were not strictly necessary Eve Wells.'

Eve let out a despairing sigh.

'But Ravenna, I mean, I'm so glad you're okay, but you've got to appreciate I'm a little annoyed.'

'Then let us distract ourselves,' the Mediterranean girl said expressively and turning to her bag threw a bundle of papers onto the table in front of her.

'What's this?'

'Research – a little light reading to take your mind off the relaxing romantic weekend you are not having.'

'Thanks.'

She opened the folder cautiously. The material was an untidy bundle of grainy photos, computer print-outs and dog-eared newspaper reports all connected to the North Cornwall moors.

As Ravenna knelt down to the wood burning stove once more Eve turned over the first document and felt her heart sink.

'No – please no!'

'Like I say Wells, this is right up your proverbial *via* yes?'

Eve felt her temper begin to flare, pushing her glasses up her nose to cover her annoyance.

'This is nonsense,' she said tersely, discarding the tabloid clipping, with its poor quality photo and sensationalist headline, 'a total load of old …'

'You are not even a little intrigued Dinosaur Girl?'

Eve stood angrily. 'It's a blatant hoax Ravenna! Take me back, I've got a sleeper to catch to Scotland, Adam's waiting for me and …'

To her surprise Ravenna shrugged. 'As you wish Dinosaur Girl, I will soldier on and face this danger alone.'

'Thanks,' she said grudgingly, stooping to grab her bag.

'I mean, it is probably – as you say – just a hoax … the trail of devastation and missing person notwithstanding.'

Eve paused.

'What?'

'Slaughtered cattle and sheep, fresh reports of some unidentifiable animal at a place renowned for sightings – I mean, it's probably just coincidence. Apart from the woman who went missing.'

Eve leaned her rucksack against the table leg once more.

'Go on.'

'Jess Flynn, an expert from Cambridge writing an article for *Current Palaeontology* - missing up near the river Fowey for the past ten days - local gossip has it that ...' She flicked her gaze to the newspaper cuttings on the coffee table. Eve looked down and took a breath. 'Cup of tea?'

She nodded dejectedly.

'So where do we start?'

'Research,' the Mediterranean woman called from the kitchen, 'this is what you do best, yes?'

Eve turned her attention to the pile of cuttings, all trashy tabloid reports – and yet ... She shuddered, even with the wood stove crackling and a steaming cup of tea, there was something utterly unsettling about such a persistent story.

'So you will help Wells?'

Shadows danced across the old plastered walls.

'Yeah,' she conceded, 'lives are at stake.'

The time traveller smiled. 'Good – but do not get too comfortable Eve Wells, for we have someone to meet.'

*

'So – how long is it before I'm attacked by some horrifying primeval creature – a couple of hours? Ten minutes?'

They were sat in a quaint tea room with the pile of cuttings strewn between them. 'That's what all this is about isn't it,' Eve continued glibly, 'It's the only logical reason you've bought me here?' Ravenna seemed not to hear. Eve shook her head and pushed back the net curtains a little. A seemingly endless expanse of mist-shrouded moorland stretched out behind the cottage garden, a rolling land broken up by ancient copses and monolithic rocky tors. 'So when does the Hound of the Baskervilles make an appearance?'

'I think I freaked out the lady at the counter asking for your decaf skinny latte,' Ravenna said absent-mindedly, '– they seem to make most of their trade in tea and scones.' She smiled her thanks as a waitress put a huge cream tea in front of her, accompanied by an almost industrial-looking pot of tea. 'I presumed you'd be off your food in the face of such terrifying circumstances.'

'Thanks,' Eve replied with little attempt to veil her annoyance

'Come Eve Wells, what does your laptop tell us?'

She turned her attention back to the screen, which by some miracle was able to connect to Wi-Fi despite the lag in time. A quick search had given several useful hits, mostly newspaper articles debunking the myth of a large unidentified mammal on the moors. 'A keeper at Plymouth Zoo allegedly released three pumas on transit to their new home at a wildlife park in 1978,' she began, 'only two pumas in the consignment arrived and there were five tags in the cage – couldn't stand to see them go back into captivity …'

'And this is when the *legend* started?'

Eve nodded. 'The evidence was strong enough for the government to launch an official investigation in 1995. Numerous sightings – livestock mutilations – but nothing conclusive was found.' She shuddered as she clicked onto another window: photos of a dismembered sheep carcass and grainy stills from an amateur video showing a large dark creature running across an open field.

'So maybe this creature is just a descendent of that breeding pair released in the 70's - or perhaps …'

Eve shuddered, longing – just for once – for there to be a rational explanation. 'It says here that a lynx escaped its enclosure in 2016 … maybe it's what people have been seeing …'

Ravenna bit into her scone, and began to talk between mouthfuls.

'*Maybe*. But here is another story: in the mid 90's a farmer called Mrs. Jarrod reported numerous sightings of a large mottled predator on her land. She claimed her sheep were attacked regularly and heard the animal up in the copse by her farm on a daily basis – even captured a sound recording of it …'

Eve looked up at her pointedly.

'She claims it was as big as a lion.'

Eve shook her head, telling herself it was just an exaggerated fantasy.

'I don't buy it,' she said frankly. 'I remember that one - the Natural History Museum were asked to research a skull found by the river Fowey. For a while everyone got all excited but it was found to be from a leopard – an egg case from a tropical cockroach confirmed it most likely came from an imported leopard skin rug.'

Ravenna frowned at her. 'We covered it as a case-study during my first degree – *mysteries of vertebrate palaeontology* – we even got to look at the original sample.' Eve sipped her drink. 'Basically, it's a load of … anyway, despite numerous sightings and lot of half-eaten sheep, no one's ever really proved anything and there hasn't been a sighting for years …'

'Until two months ago.' Ravenna said pointedly. Eve looked at her sharply. 'A local farmer reported two of his sheep mauled and a neighbouring smallholder says she saw the beast itself.' There was an odd look in her eye.

'And?' Eve asked with a frown.

'The farmer is called Steve Jarrod - he is the son of the late Sarah Jarrod, who claimed she saw the *beast* regularly during the 90s.'

'Ah,' Eve said, 'so what you're saying is ..?' But at that moment the door opened as a sturdy woman in her late fifties entered the café, heading straight to their cutting-strewn table.

'Here about the beast are you?' she began without introduction, 'like that other girl? Well, I hope you keep your wits about you – she didn't last five minutes, and neither will you if you're not careful – because, as ever, no one will take this seriously and send some proper wildlife control ...'

'Mrs Whitchurch,' Ravenna interrupted warmly, 'why don't you take a seat – *tea*?'

'To be honest it's a ruddy disgrace,' the woman continued without ceremony, 'the government's known there's a wild cat population here for years and they've done next to nothing about it – they've been dragging their feet since the nineties and only ever send token …'

She broke off apologetically and Eve dropped her gaze.

'So, what can you tell us Mrs Whitchurch?'

'Well, I've seen it,' the farmer said belligerently, 'seen it plenty of times – right outside my kitchen window.' Eve struggled not to gawp at the comment. 'Makes a fearful sound – strange high whine – and it's big, big and speckled …'

'Like a leopard?' Eve ventured, reaching for her sketch pad. The woman shook her head.

'No, nothing like that – more like … a jackal or some kind of wild African dog, but bigger – much bigger.'

'*O-kay.*'

'Listen,' the woman replied, catching the note of disbelief in her voice, 'I've been farming up near Tor Wood for over thirty years – lived there all my life - and we've been hearing – and seeing – these animals for as long as anyone can remember.'

'And you knew Sarah Jarrod?'

The farmer nodded. 'Sarah reported that cat over a dozen times – but they wouldn't believe her …' she broke off and sighed. 'Her son still lives up there – and he's seen it too – maybe you should be asking him more questions?'

'Maybe we should,' said Ravenna with a nod.

Eve glanced at her briskly then took a sip of coffee, the legend now feeling unsettlingly real.

The Moor

'You believe her?' asked Ravenna as they trudged up the rocky footpath behind the village.

Eve took a breath, focussing her attention on the rugged landscape around them. It was a wild and lonely place – a landscape in which one could easily imagine some unseen creature lurking. In truth, though she longed to disbelieve her, there was something unsettling about the woman's story which nagged at her.

'Look, Ravenna, there are thirty-seven species of modern wild cat and none of them fit the bill of what Mrs Whitchurch described – pumas and jaguars would be far too small, and they're fast, you wouldn't see them hanging around stalking, not in these climes anyway.'

'So it is a chronological anomaly, yes? Our work here is valid?

Eve sighed, consoling herself that there was every chance they were dealing with a perfectly natural explanation for the *beast*: 'Alien big cats – ABC's - are nothing unusual, there are hundreds of sightings yearly across Europe, tales of leopards and panthers in the wilds, from Denmark to New Zealand, creatures well outside of their natural range.'

Ravenna nodded thoughtfully.

'Yet have I not told you that the many and varied phenomena which humanity has struggled to explain over the ages can most often be put down to this breaching and slippage in time within which I walk?'

'Yes, but …'

'Sasquatch, the Yeti, the Australian Drop-Bear … there are still many such anomalies Wells.'

Eve made a face. 'But this is rural Cornwall!'

Ravenna shrugged. 'It is a point on God's earth like any other …'

A darker thought struck her which made her frown. 'And the expert from Cambridge who went missing?'

'There was a police search but no body was found.'

Eve shuddered. 'Then you think?'

'I try not to second-guess,' the time traveller said thoughtfully, 'I grew out of it after the first two or three times ...' Eve frowned. '*Lifetimes* Wells – anyway, I have long since learned to *listen* rather than to guess.' They walked in silence for a few moments, Eve longing to press further, the hollow noise of their boots the only sound. *To listen.* 'And then there is this Steve Jarrod whose mother saw the creature regularly almost two decades ago ...'

'So you're saying this is no coincidence?' Eve ventured, 'you think it's some kind of a cyclical event?'

The mocking chuckle of a curlew echoed overhead making them both gaze skyward instinctively.

'I am saying we must speak to this Steve Jarrod who has seen the beast,' Ravenna replied coolly.

Eve sighed under her breath. 'But seriously - *The Beast of Bodmin Moor* - if it were possible I'd be dialling a taxi right now … you're mad!'

'Quite probably,' the Mediterranean girl replied, but before she had a chance to respond, something flashed across the rocky skyline dead ahead, there for a second, stark in silhouette before vanishing amongst the boulders.

Eve felt her heart skip. 'Did you see that!'

'What?' Ravenna frowned.

'There - up there on that outcrop!' Her scalp was prickling. Something large had descended between tumbled boulders – she was sure of it. 'An animal …' she blinked, wondering suddenly if it was her mind playing tricks - it had been little more than a silhouette, but fast and large. Her heart was pounding.

'Come!' said Ravenna with sudden determination, and then, despite her misgivings they were running.

The Beast

'You're loving this, aren't you!'

Eve paused, her heart pounding. They had just slithered down their second rocky tor and despite her anxious mood Eve was beginning to feel thoroughly frustrated. At first she had been stung by an odd mixture of fear and exhilaration, yet after the best part of an hour following the slight trace of indistinct tracks her mood was hitting an all-time nadir.

Ravenna paused to examine the ground at her feet once more and Eve sighed, bracing her hands against her knees. 'This is just my perfect Sunday morning.'

'*Hmm?*' Ravenna muttered absent-mindedly, still poking at the ground.

'Freezing my proverbials off in one of the most barren places I've ever visited - with a monster on the loose somewhere just out of view ...' She turned an anxious eye to the tumbling landscape ahead.

'Nonsense Wells – you love this place, the primeval beauty - I challenge you to deny it!'

Eve sighed grudgingly. They were stood between tumbled outcrops, gazing out over a heather clad hillside which sloped gently towards distant fields. The wildness was in truth captivating, despite the mist and stinging drizzle, but the thought of some unseen presence was seriously taking the edge off her appreciation. She turned a nervous gaze to her friend.

'What have you found – anything?'

'More tracks,' Ravenna mused, 'I think ...'

'You think?'

She saw unease in her friend's expression. 'There are two sets of prints where there was only one here Wells.'

Eve shook her head and swore silently, a thrill of fear running down her spine.

'Maybe it's just a pair of dogs?'

'Be my guest,' Ravenna gestured and she stooped with a grunt of annoyance, but the smeared prints were too indistinct to decipher as either canine or feline. She straightened and ran her fingers through her hair. The wind was getting up and rain was spotting her glasses. It was pointless – stupid and pointless. She began to clean her lenses.

'Look, Ravenna, maybe it was just my imagination ...'

'Silence!'

'*What?*' Eve whispered loudly. There was nothing – just the howling of the wind.

'Do you hear that?'

'No – I can't hear anything?'

'Exactly!' the time traveller hissed, 'the corridor of silence ...'

'What do you mean ...' then the penny dropped.

Eve felt the hairs on the back of her neck stand on end in a way they hadn't since the first time Ravenna Friere had dragged her into the past. *The corridor of silence*, the path a hunting carnivore created as the lesser wildlife fell silent at its approach. She swallowed, straining, hardly daring to breathe.

'It is here, Wells, watching us ... somewhere amongst these boulders ...'

She froze, heart thudding, hardly daring to breathe as she allowed her eyes to scan the crumbling outcrops. Then, to her horror, sensed movement immediately behind.

'*Hi* – you alright there?'

They both turned with a start.

'Sorry,' said a guy in his late twenties, 'You were looking lost - hope I didn't scare you.'

'Not at all,' Eve smiled back instinctively feeling almost weak with relief. A handsome young man with a close-cropped beard and work stained clothes was grinning at them from the tree lined path he had just ascended. 'No problem.'

'Let me,' whispered Ravenna, pushing past to extend her hand.

'Hello,' she began in a slightly horsey Oxbridge accent, 'I'm Dr Wilding from the Cranfield Museum in London and this is my colleague Dr Eve Wells, we're here looking into the phantom big cats which have been reported recently.' Eve fought not to roll her eyes at the Mediterranean girl's well-worn academic alias. The young man looked at her quizzically.

'*The beast?*' His handsome face broke into an almost amused smile, 'then you've come to the right place! I've seen the beast alright, more than once – I can take you up to where I saw it if you like?'

'Really?' said Ravenna enthusiastically as if astounded by her good fortune, 'that'd be great - thank you, Mr ..?'

'I'm Steve Jarrod – I farm down the way there …' He gestured with his hand towards tiled eaves nestled close by a tangled copse. Eve caught Ravenna's eye. *Steve Jarrod, the son of Sarah Jarrod who had seen the beast two decades before.* 'My Land Rover's just over the rise …'

They followed as he led them up and over the tree lined trackway, Ravenna leaning close to her as they stepped into the shelter of the trees.

'Helpful … and quite cute yes?' she grinned, before falling in step with the farmer.

'So you have seen the animal once Mr Jarrod?'

125

'More than once – it's come up after my ewes at least three times - seen it in the bottom field over there,' he gestured to an almost square patch of land nestled between a mid-sized farmhouse and a tangling copse. 'Look, if it's an interview you want, I can tell you everything I've seen – I'm heading back to the farm right now if you fancy a cuppa?'

Jarrod smiled as they made eye contact and Eve found herself doing the same, feeling her cheeks begin to flush unbidden.

'I …' she began, but Ravenna spoke over her.

'That would be wonderful Mr Jarrod … is it right your mother reported seeing the beast?'

He hesitated then replied in a more guarded tone: 'Yep, mum saw it too – but I expect you know all about that.'

Ravenna smiled. 'I guess we do.'

The young man shook his head wryly. 'Come on then, this way.'

He led them through a gate to where a Land Rover stood parked by a tumbledown wall. 'Hop in – you look frozen Dr Wells - I'll turn the heater up.'

She floundered bashfully.

'Come Wells,' Ravenna whispered once he was out of earshot, 'he is your type, yes? Hardworking and honest – you must go to his farm and use your girl-next-door charm, see what you can find out about his family's involvement with this creature ...'

'*Ravenna!*' She gasped, but Jarrod was rounding the side of the vehicle, opening the door for her to get in.

'Ladies ...'

Ravenna smiled and gestured for her to enter first. 'And remember you're spoken for,' she whispered pulling the door closed behind her with a grin.

*

Steve Jarrod frowned as they paused by the gate to his yard.

'You sure you won't come in for a coffee Dr Wilding, the weather's definitely closing in.'

'Oh no, but thank you,' Ravenna said sweetly, pulling up the hood of her waterproof jacket, 'we're really pushed for time and I need to get some photos for the report – but Eve here will stay and jot some things down, won't you - I'm sure you'd *love* to chat.'

Eve smiled hesitantly at the young man, then shot Ravenna a *what the hell are you up to?* kind of look.

Ravenna just returned a twee smile, and then she was turning away with a wave and Jarrod was ushering her into his kitchen.

'Tea or coffee?'

She unzipped her down jacket and hung it on the back of the chair 'Tea will be great thanks.'

She seated herself and was about to put her bag on the table when something caught her eye. Amid the clutter was an open folder containing cuttings about the beast – and on the top was a report about the missing expert, Jess Flynn.

'Interested in the beast, then?' she said with a frown.

Jarrod laughed softly as he filled the mugs. 'Mum was pretty big on exposing the beast – letting the world know the truth and getting the government to do something about it … it was pretty much all she ever talked about when we were growing up …' there was a distant look in his eye, 'and I've kind of carried it on - I heard it too, you know' he added, 'as a kid, weird sound – long high note.' Eve looked at him pensively. 'Mum did some research and reckoned it was similar to the cry of a black panther calling for its mate.'

She broke eye contact and pulled out her laptop and sketch book, the latter falling open at a detailed drawing of a hyena skull she'd been working on.

'These yours?' he ventured as she booted up her computer, gesturing to the sketches of running hyenas doodled in her pad. 'They're really good – incredible.'

She smiled bashfully.

'I'm a palaeo-artist – I reconstruct extinct species.'

He seemed to hesitate then smile, 'you're really talented.'

She fought not to flush. *Damn, he was good looking*. 'So when did you last see it?'

He sipped his tea. 'Bout a week ago – Saturday – no Sunday – night.' She nodded.

'And can you describe it?'

He made a face as he considered. 'Powerful limbs - clearly a big cat of some kind.'

'Uh-huh. And did you see it close up?'

'Kind of … well, not exactly.'

'Not exactly?'

He shrugged. 'When I got close it took off round the corner of the barn down the way there.'

Eve hesitated. 'And how large would you estimate it was?'

'It was big, certainly, seven – no, eight – maybe nine feet long … perhaps nearer to ten.'

Eve lifted her gaze from the word document she'd created, 'somewhere between seven and ten feet long?'

'It was dark,' the farmer said casually before sipping from his mug.

A ghostly feline between seven and ten feet long. She frowned.

'You're making this up aren't you.'

Steve Jarrod's momentary hesitation was enough to let her know that at least a large proportion of what he was saying was total fiction.

'Look, it was dusk, and to be honest …'

She closed her eyes, realisation dawning. 'This whole thing's just an excuse to hit on me isn't it …' She shut her laptop with a decisive snap.

'Look, Miss Wells …'

'Dr Wells – and it's okay, I'll let myself out.'

'Listen, I'm sorry …' She could hear his stool scraping behind her.

'Lonely up here is it?' she needled, grabbing her bag and coat, 'Haven't seen a woman round these parts for fifteen years?'

She crossed the kitchen briskly, stuffing her sketch pad into her bag, barely pausing at the door to put her coat on.

'Please, I didn't mean any …'

'And I'm engaged,' she called over her shoulder, 'getting married in five months …'

A damp chill enveloped her - she could hear him a couple of paces behind.

'I saw it,' he said firmly, 'and that's no lie. Down in the bottom field two nights ago.'

She turned to face him, trying not to shiver as her body adjusted to the cold. '– and in the morning three of my ewes were gone.'

She gazed at him coolly as she zipped up her jacket to the throat, but could only see sincerity in his eyes.

'Look, Dr Wells – *Eve* – I'm sorry …'

'Thanks for your help,' she said testily, and turning away headed off to find Ravenna.

Tracks

E ve shuddered as she navigated the rutted farm track, picking her way gingerly between mud and exposed rock. Ravenna was stood in a small field up ahead, paused behind a pile of plastic covered bales.

'He's talking rubbish,' she began as soon as she had joined her, 'reckons he's seen something but he's clearly making it up – probably trying to cash in on the legend to bring in a bit of publicity.' She recounted all he had said disdainfully, '– he's got a whole heap of photos and reports about the beast on his kitchen table, bet he wants to bring in some tourist money …'

Ravenna held up a hand to silence her.

'You have a fair point Wells, but what about the sheep he has lost?'

Eve hesitated. 'So? Maybe it's just an escaped lynx or a descendent of those pumas released in 1978 – all that rubbish about it being ten feet long …'

'And this?'

Ravenna had dropped her gaze to the soggy ground behind the tattered plastic encasing the bales. 'What do you make of these Dinosaur Girl?'

Eve stooped, frowning as she gazed at what her friend was indicating.

'No – *oh no!*'

Clearly visible in the soft dark mud was a large four toed paw print.

'And here,' Ravenna indicated, pointing to another, 'and here – and also here …'

'*Oh god.*'

She slipped off her bag and pulled out a tape measure before handing the rucksack to Ravenna.

'You carry this with you always?' the time traveller said in mild amusement. Eve ignored her as she knelt to lay the tape across the nearest print, then checked it against the next. Each deep impression had a large almost triangular pad and the toe marks terminated in prominent claws.

'And?' Ravenna asked, 'your professional opinion?'

Eve hardly heard her as she extended the tape, holding the end out for Ravenna to take. 'Give me a hand, we need to take some measurements.' The time traveller nodded as they began to measure the distance between the prints. A light rain began to fall but Eve was too engrossed to notice.

'Wells?'

Eve hesitated. '*Erm* ...'

'Come Wells, tell me what you have found.'

She swore under her breath, chill fear prickling her scalp. The footprints were unmistakably feline but too big for a puma – way too big.

'This is evidence of a big cat, yes?'

Eve let out a slow breath and closed her eyes momentarily, almost unwilling to reveal the fact, as if to say it would somehow make it real. She nodded. 'Whatever made these prints is massive – far bigger than a puma or lynx.'

'A lion? Ravenna mused quizzically, 'a Bengal tiger?'

Eve shuddered, trying not to dwell on the horrible conclusion her mind kept leaping to: *far bigger than any living feline*. 'The jury's out for now,' she said dismissively, busying herself by squatting to make more measurements and key them into her phone, 'here, can you help me with the tape again.'

When she finally stood back, she found Ravenna gazing steadily into the stunted copse which lay barely three hundred yards behind. 'Ravenna?' she said questioningly.

'That is where the prints begin and end Wells,' the time traveller said slowly without moving her gaze from the rain slick branches, 'I explored it thoroughly and found nothing – and yet ...'

Eve swallowed, feeling a sudden sense of foreboding. 'So you think ...'

'Come,' the time traveller said briskly, 'we must get back to collate your data.'

Encounter

E ve looked up from her laptop to massage tired eyes. It had grown dark outside and the room was now shadow-cast, the table bathed in the screen's eerie glow. She shuddered and replaced her glasses. Getting freaked out by the dark was the last thing she needed.

Hunkering down into her scarf she turned to her sketch pad and began to doodle idly, dragging the soft pencil across the neat pad of cartridge paper to create a thicket of shaded lines. She shaded and cross-hatched, her thoughts tangling and converging as she mulled over the images in her mind: the twisting strands of comments and observations, the video footage, the photographs and footprints. She turned her mind to the pile of cuttings Ravenna had given her. Half the reports were clearly hoaxes, the others most likely genuine – images of escaped jaguars and pumas, probably now long dead - yet none of the descriptions fitted the prints they had found.

She let her hand do the thinking; drew mottled pelts and sinuous limbs, sketched soft padded feet and long graceful tails – and fangs, always long tapering mandibular fangs. Sabres: scimitars – her mind echoing with the images and the names – *homotherium, meganterion, smilodon fatalis* – a roll-call of long dead feline species, animals so massive and powerful as to put all modern big cats to shame.

She tapped her pencil against her lip. Hell, she'd even helped articulate a *smilodon* skeleton for an exhibition at the University of the East Midlands' small museum, handled its bones first hand – marvelled at the power of the muscles which must have attached to it. The sabre toothed tiger – yet tiger in name only - more lion like perhaps if a modern counterpart were to be found. She pulled up an image of a male African lion and used it to draw the creature at rest: *smilodon* yawning lazily as it basked in the late Pleistocene sun. Noble, graceful – not some dangerous monster.

She put down her pencil. *Hell, who was she trying to kid.*

She looked at the images she had created and shuddered – since Ravenna Friere had invaded her world her palaeontological reconstructions had taken on a new life – a near-unbelievable realism which had won her endless praise. She sighed softly: how often she'd longed to share the secrets of where she had gained her insights.

She forced her mind back to the databases she was working with and pulled up yet another window. Analysis of the paw prints was proving more time consuming than she had expected - matching the pattern and size against a multiplicity of fossil specimens was no mean feat - and though engaging, the process of calculating the distance between each impression to give an estimate of its gait and likely height at the shoulder, was a seriously laborious task. She lingered over opening the next window, taking a breath to calm the sting of panic which flared every time she contemplated the implications. An image of a large articulated skeleton, mounted in a North American museum.

Whatever had made the prints was massive – substantially bigger than *Panthera leo*, the African lion, the largest feline on the planet – and unless by some horrific chance a freakishly large big cat had escaped from a local circus, then something seriously unusual was happening. She bundled her scarf up over her chin and clicked off the picture: whatever had made those prints had not walked the earth for millennia.

Something tapped against the kitchen window and she looked up sharply.

'Just the wind,' she reassured herself, watching the old rosemary bush which had grown up against the glass dancing wildly, 'get a grip.'

Where the hell was Ravenna? She'd headed out after dinner to search for the animal once more but had still not returned.

She sighed and closing the laptop stole a glance at the wood burning stove. She had been so absorbed it had almost died right down and she rose dejectedly to stoke it. She knelt as she opened the glass-fronted door, her gaze melancholy as the orange flames danced. It was quite beautiful in its own rustic way – the whole cottage was – and under other circumstances would have seemed quite cosy. Her thoughts flew to Adam and the break in Galloway she was *not* having. Her spirits plunged, longing suddenly to be curled up in front of the fire with a bottle of wine, longing to talk over all she had found with him, to get how crazy and terrifying it was right off her chest.

She rose and glanced at her watch. It was nearly 7 PM and there was still no sign of Ravenna. With a sigh she glanced towards her sketch pad once more, but had had enough for one day and taking an anxious glance towards the darkening window headed to the kitchen to make a cup of tea.

The kettle boiled noisily as she stood watching the darkening world, the faint purple haze of a distant cloudbank stark against the skyline beyond the garden wall. She thought again of Ravenna, out there alone and was torn between anxiety and frustration.

'She's more than capable of taking care of herself,' she said out loud, but somehow her words didn't reassure her.

With a shiver she flicked on the kitchen light, the fluorescent tube fizzing and clunking as she turned to the window once more. Her reflected features looked pale against the pitch darkness, her eyes wide and anxious.

Relax, she thought, forcing herself to stare at the blackness. There was still every chance that whatever they had found was an elaborate hoax. Beyond her reflection she could just make out the slabs below the wall, lit by the kitchen's pale glow. Whatever *was* out there, the chances of it making a beeline for human habitation were almost …

A dark shape moved above the gloom of the garden wall, a pitch-dark shadow which appeared with near unbelievable swiftness. She swallowed, eyes scanning desperately, trying to make out what on earth she was seeing.

'Ravenna?'

Something huge hit the window with such force the panes of glass rattled, making her scream involuntarily. She stumbled back, heart pounding, as for a split-second bright shapes flashed in front of her face. Then blackness and her horrified expression – there were grease stains on the glass, mud and saliva – and a long crack snaking up the corner of one pane.

'Oh god!' she heard herself exclaim shrilly, unable to drag her eyes from the window. What the hell? She recoiled, her mind racing – had she really just seen the flash of sharp mammalian teeth. *'Oh hell!'*

She stood, frozen, the blood hissing in her ears, barely able to drag her gaze from the grease smeared window – then, to her horror, she heard a noise to her left – something outside the kitchen, knocking over the bins – her gaze shot to the kitchen door. She swore – the door wasn't locked. Something was outside, something large and powerful, and with a pounding heart she realised the danger. *It can't get in* she told herself, *the door's closed, it won't even* … another noise echoed in the kitchen yard and she flinched involuntarily. Her gaze flew to the twin wrought iron bolts - she *had* to push them home.

With a tremendous effort she forced her limbs into action, her legs feeling leaden as she crept across the old stone flags of the floor. It had seen her – did it have her scent? Fear stung the pit of her stomach as she made herself reach for the uppermost bolt. If she moved slowly, then perhaps it wouldn't hear her, perhaps it would just pass by.

She made a face as the bolt creaked angrily, so stiff it would barely move. She winced, applying more pressure - it sounded loud enough to wake the dead in the confines of the silent cottage – then broke off to listen, heart thudding. Something was nearby - she could hear it clearly - soft feet getting closer. She resumed her efforts with renewed vigour. It was just outside the door and the damned bar wouldn't budge!

There was movement barely inches away.

Panic took her and she began to fight desperately, jiggling the bolt wildly to free it a few millimetres. 'Come on!' she gasped as the old latch groaned – just another centimetre or so - but then, before she knew what was happening, a force pushed against her and the door burst open, filling the cottage with cold night air.

'Did you see it Wells?' Ravenna Friere exclaimed almost excitedly, 'Did you see the beast?'

Eve stood panting, fighting a withering wave of faintness as she looked into the other girl's eyes.

'Yes,' she said shakily, the apparition flashing in front of her mind's eye, 'yes – I saw it … and I think I'm going to sit down now.'

Night Hike

Eve stood shakily, trying to stop herself from glancing towards the blackness beyond the open door. It was drizzling lightly, windblown drops flitting like fireflies across the pitch darkness beyond.

She turned her attention to the large case which Ravenna had laid out on the kitchen table. 'What's that?' she said hesitantly.

Ravenna glanced up at her with annoyance.

'What does it look like Wells, it is a tranquiliser gun.'

'And why do we ... oh god - you're not seriously ...'

'Do I ever joke Wells?'

Only at my expense she mused grimly, then took a deep breath. 'You seriously want to follow it? Have you ever tranquilised a wild animal before?'

'I must admit it is not in my sizeable *skill-set*,' the time traveller replied glibly, 'have you?'

'Do you have any ideas how much it will weigh – what the correct dose will be? We'll never be able to move it, let alone ...'

'Estimate its weight for me Wells.'

She sighed then obeyed. It was madness, but it was clear they had no other option.

'Time is of the essence now Wells,' the dark haired girl replied briskly, 'it could already be miles away but we must try.'

'So how do we ..?'

'With skills I picked up long ago – and by following the tracks I found earlier – it is an obvious run and it is doubtless headed for Jarrod's farm where I believe the rift it came from lies.'

Eve donned her jacket in a daze while Ravenna loaded the weapon and shouldered her bag.

'Ready Wells?'

She nodded dumbly. They were going to hunt a monster.

*

The trek across the moonless moor was a nightmare. Eve shivered, yet the encumbrance of wearing nearly every item of clothing she'd brought with her only seemed to add to her discomfort. Her boots were soggy, her extremities frozen and the damp seemed to be chilling her to the core.

'So why the hell did it come to our cottage?'

Ravenna shrugged. 'Your alluring scent ... my magnetic personality?' Her features were eerie in the torchlight – her near-crazy grin less than reassuring. Eve looked away, trying to focus on the skipping patch of light cast by her torch, forcing herself not to scan the shifting shadows. She felt panic begin to overwhelm her, almost visceral revulsion of the cloying darkness: there was a big cat out there beyond the beam, and to all intents and purposes she and Ravenna were its prey.

'So brief me, Eve Wells,' the time traveller said softly in a clear effort to distract her, 'What am I up against here?

Eve swallowed. 'Well, at first I was thinking *Homotherium Latidens* – the European sabre tooth – a scimitar tooth actually – which once roamed the landmass we're now standing on ...'

'But?' Ravenna said seriously.

Eve swallowed. 'To be honest it wasn't much larger than a modern jaguar.'

'So?'

'*Smilodon fatalis* – maybe even *populator*,' she replied, trying to keep her thoughts objective - trying not to surrender to the horror of what her words implied.

'Sabre-toothed yes?' Eve nodded. 'And bigger than a modern lion?'

Eve forced herself to nod. Much bigger. 'The fossil evidence suggests they were ambush predators that worked in a pack – they were powerful, but not sprinters like cheetahs or leopards ...'

'And those teeth? The sabre fangs?'

Again, she forced herself to remain calm, dragging her gaze from the shifting shadows to the barrel of Ravenna's readied gun.

'The fossil record suggests most extinct big cats were sabre toothed. Unlike modern felines which can pounce on prey and bite into the back of its neck while moving, these animals were bigger and more powerful - they would hold a struggling herbivore down and deliver a massive suffocating bite to the throat … those teeth would never survive going through bone …' She broke off, realising what she'd just said, beginning to feel suddenly very sick. And they were out there – somewhere in the darkness …

'Wells!' Said Ravenna sharply, 'you say they worked in packs – how do you know this?'

Eve took a breath to clear her head. 'Some of the fossil bones we have show signs of healing after injury – it suggests that old and sick animals were cared for by the pride …' Ravenna nodded thoughtfully. 'The evidence suggests they primarily hunted herbivores of their own body weight or less – antelope and young bison, primitive camels and early …' she faltered, realised what she was saying, 'early humans.'

The clouds had drawn back to bathe the woods ahead of them in a pale and silvery light and at her side she saw Ravenna nod thoughtfully. 'I thank you Eve Wells – this knowledge is most useful to me …'

She could see Steve Jarrod's farm now, the sloping roof picked out by the moon as if in silver filigree. They fell into silence as they descended into the shadow of a hedgerow fringed with trees and there Ravenna raised her hand.

'What …'

'Silence Wells,' the time traveller hissed, 'turn off your torch.' She stood staring into the dark tangle as her eyes adjusted to the gloom. Even a vole would sound like an elephant amid this silence she reminded herself as a faint rustling met her ears. Ravenna took a tentative step forward. There was something moving beyond the hedgerow to their right, something swift and large. Eve felt the hairs on her scalp prickle with utter terror, her stomach stinging with fear as some instinct she had never experienced primed her for desperate flight. There was a large animal in the foliage – far bigger than a vole.

Ravenna stooped closer, peering steadily, her gaze unwavering as she unslung the tranquiliser gun -

then laughed under her breath as her search was rewarded with a pitiful bleat.

Eve swore with relief. 'It's just a sheep!'

And then the creature struck. It happened so quickly that she was barely able to process what was happening. One moment the lost ewe was bleating at them from behind the hawthorn and then it was gone, whisked backwards by a swift-moving shadow, lost in a blur of snarls and movement, before the spectral form shot ghost-like into the gloom. Eve's scream was drowned by the thud of Ravenna's weapon.

'Damn – missed it!'

Eve stumbled, gasping desperately, eyes wide with horror; there was just enough moonlight to see the pile of flesh and fleece which had been the unfortunate ewe.

'Oh my …' she heard her own voice say shakily, 'oh hell … oh …'

'Come on Wells!' Ravenna said grabbing her arm, forcing her trembling legs into action. 'It is heading for the sheep pens!'

*

'Go left,' Ravenna ordered, 'I'll circle the buildings – we'll corral it into the corner of the yard.'

'I …' Eve protested, but knew that it was useless to argue. She swallowed, trying not to contemplate what was about to happen as she watched Ravenna disappear behind the building to her right. She stepped forward in a daze. Somewhere within the farmhouse a dog was barking madly – surely Steve Jarrod would come out at any moment? She paused by the large galvanised gate of the pens, forcing herself to breathe evenly.

'You can do this.'

A large open-fronted structure made up one side of the farm's yard and nearing it she was met by the sound of bleating and the sickly stench of animals packed close together. The sheep were spooked. Terrified. She forced herself forwards, trying to focus on the fact that Ravenna was armed.

The drizzle had turned to rain now and for a moment her view of the yard was obscured. Ahead, the raindrops flitted like sparks in the glow of the farm's security light; to her left was utter darkness, the shadows of disused outbuildings. Where was it?

The thumping of her heart seemed to reverberate through her chest.

She took a breath. It was here somewhere, waiting in the darkness - the bleating of the sheep increasing as she forced herself past the gloom.

Her heart began to beat out of control. It was *here* – somewhere – *and it had torn the sheep in two* … it took everything to take another step - and then she heard it: just the faintest movement to her left and a little behind her. But how could it possibly? Her own words leapt to the forefront of her mind: *the fossil evidence suggests they were ambush predators that worked in a pack.* She swore. There were at least two of them – and she was utterly defenceless.

*

Eve cursed at her mistake – while they had been pursuing the creature another had been stalking her.

Something moved in the darkness and Eve broke into a run, snagging her jacket on the gatepost as she charged towards the light of the yard. Part of her was desperate to pound on the farmer's door - yet the creature in the darkness was barely seconds behind. Her feet moved almost beyond her control, carrying her into the nearest outbuilding, smashing her shoulder painfully against the dry stone wall as she stumbled inside. She twisted, gasping breath, feet slipping on dry straw - then realised with a sting of horror that the building had no door.

She hesitated, fighting panic, scanning for anything with which to block the entrance. Metal fencing from a sheering run lay stacked against the wall. She lunged for it, tugging desperately, but the legs of the panels were overlapped and the whole stack collapsed towards her in a useless tangle.

She yelled in desperation, heard the creature growl as it stalked forwards, then driven by some instinct to survive scrabbled into the shadows behind the tangled heap. She flattened herself against the sheep-pen wall, breath coming in sharp ragged gasps. It was out there in the darkness, eyes glinting in the light of her fallen torch, breath misting on the cool night air.

She longed to close her eyes but didn't dare. She saw sinuous movement, heard soft feet padding on the cobbles, the flicker of whiskers through the bars of the fencing and the glint of huge sabre fangs. A shriek of pure terror began to rise up inside her, acid fear stinging her chest as her body tensed for god-knew-what action. Her mind seemed suddenly to drink in every detail - the cobwebs around the wire caged electric lamp, flecks of dry manure in the old straw. There was blood on her knuckles where she'd fallen against the wall, scratches on her cheek. Oh god it would smell her – it would have her scent!

Its huge eyes were searching, scanning, its mouth opening gently as it sniffed the air.

She closed her eyes momentarily, willing it to turn away. It was coming for her, snarling as it padded softly. Gritting her teeth she fought not to tremble, unable to tear her eyes away.

Ravenna

She paused, listening, closing her eyes to perceive beyond the residual sights and sounds which overwhelmed her mind. *Use all your senses girl*, her old *lanista* had told her. She could see his careworn face as if it was yesterday, the scar which bisected his left temple prominent like a badge of honour. Her mind flashed back to that exercise – to the day he had made her close her eyes, the soft swish and rush of air as he had lashed the *rudis* at the side of her head. *Now block me*, he had said dispassionately as she reeled from the pain. *Sense the stick, girl – feel it – use more than your eyes and ears.*

Rain lashed the cobbles of the yard, branches creaking softly as heavy drops dripped steadily from loose guttering.

Again! Feel it.

There was a presence out in the darkness, a sinuously moving force, breathing so gently as to be barely audible. *Close – and getting closer*. In her mind she caught the wooden *gladius* inches from her face, grasping the training stick before yanking it from the old man's hand. She could sense the gentle rise and fall of its flanks, hear the soft scrape of foliage against its soft-moving hide.

She took a breath, steadying her pulse, then opening her eyes stood utterly motionless, scanning the patch of woodland which bordered the old stone wall of the yard, forcing her mind to untangle every detail beyond the security light's residual glow. Mottled patterns seemed to move between the branches, diffused spots and speckles brushing past the twigs and leaves. Softly, she let out all her breath, allowing adrenaline to fuel her ready muscles.

'*Parakletos*,' she whispered softly, gazing steadily, her eyes unblinking, and almost in response the mottled patterns moved and vanished as something turned away. She filled her lungs again, ignoring the rain which dripped from her chin and nose, unhitching the weapon slung over her shoulder as she strained to pierce the darkness.

Slowly, steadily, she flicked off the safety and took a breath, steadying herself as she nestled the stock of the weapon into her shoulder. The shapes in the thicket kept moving steadily – the flash of a mottled pelt, or just her mind, playing tricks? She steadied the barrel, aiming low to compensate for its recoil and emptied her lungs.

A sound rang out to her left, frantic movement in the yard – feet clattering on cobbles: *Wells!* She broke contact, aware of stealthy padding – aware that something was prowling behind her - and swore silently. There were two of them – maybe more.

She began to turn, ignoring the movement in the hedgerow before her, blanking it out as she focussed on the barely discernible shape in the shadows six feet behind. She lowered the barrel and the creature twisted a little, bright irises glinting suddenly in the light of the yard. She swallowed - momentarily mesmerised by its huge yellow irises - banishing her fear to that place she had long since learned to stow it: she had seen men face creatures like this before and live, take them on amid the blinding heat of the arena sand. She said a silent prayer, saw its huge fangs loom out of the shadows as its body tensed to spring, saw the rain dripping from its graceful whiskers.

It dropped its weight to pounce and she threw out her elbow as she steadied her weapon. And then the world went mad.

Prey

The noise was deafening in the confines of the disused pen, the shotgun's report leaving Eve's ears ringing.

She stared open mouthed as the smoke cleared.

'Out,' said a firm voice, familiar yet oddly stern. She obeyed dumbly, limbs shaking – it felt like her body belonged to someone else. She emerged blinking in the light from the yard, dimly aware that the rain had eased.

'It's gone,' Steve Jarrod said more coldly than she would have expected. She nodded briskly, unable to drag her gaze from his shotgun's barrel as she backed shakily out of the space.

'Did you …'

'Kill it?' He shook his head, 'why would I do that love, it's far too valuable alive …' There was something less than reassuring in his expression.

'Valuable?'

'I said the same when the other girl came asking questions.'

'The other girl?' she said without thinking.

'Come on,' he said firmly, ignoring her question, 'I guess you know all about it anyway ...'

Jess Flynn, she thought suddenly, *the expert who had disappeared*. 'I ...' Eve swallowed, but he was already gesturing across the yard, the gun held low at his side, a veiled threat – he wasn't inviting her in for a cup of tea.

She nodded and began to walk, feeling suddenly light-headed. It was as if she were watching herself walking out into the night – as if someone else had found themselves in the middle of the madness and she were watching her, screaming at her to get away.

She plucked up her courage. 'Where are you taking me?' her voice sounded odd in her own ears. There was blackness ahead – blackness and god-knew-what.

The farmer tapped the small of her back with the barrel of his weapon and she swallowed, suppressing a whimper as she stumbled across the field.

'What I've found is unbelievable Eve – maybe the most important thing anyone has ever found *anywhere* ...'

Valuable enough to kill for she thought desperately? Her mind shot back to Jess Flynn.

But before she had a chance to contemplate further, he was nudging the barrel of the gun into the small of her back again, silent as he herded her down towards the copse. She suppressed a whimper, trying to focus as her feet slithered on the muddy ground. He was going to kill her, going to take her where the cats had come from.

It was horribly dark and she strained her eyes, just able to make out skeletal swaying branches. This was where the palaeontologist had ended up – this was where she had disappeared.

'*Please!*' she pleaded, but the gun was still at her back, his hand pressing down on the crown of her head.

'In!'

She felt hollow as she ducked into the tangle of low branches, nauseous and hollow. They walked for a few moments, her breathing seemingly crazily loud in the silence, struggling through the dripping twigs as they

162

stumbled into the blackness. And then the air was changing – the atmosphere growing warmer – the light getting greyer with every step.

'You can't,' she said shakily, '*please*, we've got to stop this!' But Jarrod only nudged her forwards.

'In!' he ordered, but as she readied her limbs, a voice split the silence.

'Drop the gun.'

Ravenna Friere stood behind them, haloed in the faint light of the farmhouse, the tranquiliser gun aimed squarely at Steve Jarrod's chest.

La Brea

To her horror Eve felt the farmer raise the weapon to her neck.

'You drop yours,' the young man replied bluntly. She could feel the cold metal jerking against her skin, sense his agitation. 'I'm guessing you've already fired that thing and you haven't had time to reload it.'

Eve stood rigid, almost lightheaded with terror, hardly able to believe it was happening. Jarrod jerked the barrel violently against her throat. She whimpered and in a moment of despair saw Ravenna close her eyes then cast her weapon aside.

'In!' ordered the young man, and then they were both walking side-by-side, Eve stumbling forward in an utter daze.

'Courage Wells!' Ravenna muttered, but the farmer growled at her to be quiet.

They ducked and crawled, feeling their way through the tangle of dense foliage, struggling amid the cloying heat.

'Steve,' Eve pleaded, 'please, we don't belong here … we won't last five minutes!'

'Shut it,' he replied gruffly. She felt her breaths coming in tremulous gasps.

Around them the world was changing; night becoming dawn, heat replacing autumnal cool – they were emerging into woodland flanking the edge of sunlit savannah, light streaming around them in gleaming shards. And that was not all. Ravenna coughed pointedly, making a subtle gesture with her hand. They were being pursued, flanked by cautious movement to their left. *The beast*. Eve shot her a horrified look, but Ravenna's expression was firm.

'Keep moving!' their captor urged.

*

'You're going to leave us here, aren't you?' said Ravenna, feigning despair, 'strand us like you stranded that other girl.'

The farmer grunted.

'She asked too many questions – took the lead I'd given her too far. All I wanted was a bit of exposure, but then she went and stumbled into this …'

Eve swallowed. What the hell was he planning to do? Her thoughts began to race. Jess Flynn … the beast … this rift into the past. They were walking in a sun drenched world, feet squelching through rich smelling loam - and all around them the forest was alive. Birds called noisily in the branches above and small creatures scuttled all around: but there were other noises too – commotion and grunting calls; the distant sound of bellowing. She walked open mouthed. It was a resurrected fossil wonderland but doubtless it would become their grave.

'Keep it going,' the young man urged as her pace began instinctively to slow. She swallowed away her fear. The sounds of commotion were growing steadily louder - the cacophony of many animals. There was a huge creature up ahead, frantic movement visible through the tangling branches.

'What the hell?' Jarrod breathed, the barrel of his gun drooping as they all paused to stare at the scene before them. An animal was struggling on the edge of a water hole like a scene from an African wildlife documentary, a huge elephant-like creature, hind legs half-submerged in cloying tar, struggling and slipping as it fought to ascend the bank.

Eve let out a breath, the momentary euphoria that she was seeing the death-throws of a North American Mastodon almost instantly drowned by the sheer terror of the danger they were in. The sounds around them didn't just come from the struggling beast, nor the bellowing herd of its fellows across the lake – but from a myriad of eager predators all biding their time as the mastodon trumpeted and thrashed. She heard Steve Jarrod swear, and glancing up glimpsed bright eyes watching them before disappearing ghost-like through the tall grass: a long extinct dire-wolf massive and shaggy.

'What is this?' the young man said disbelievingly.

'I – I know where we are,' she began shakily, 'the Rancho la Brea tar pits!'

'What?' Jarrod frowned.

'This is like LA, but 40,000 years ago!'

'Quiet!' Jarred growled, 'keep walking,' but she could sense his attention drawn to the unbelievable world around them, his concentration waning as they skirted the animals in the clearing.

'He intends to strand us and run,' Ravenna whispered, 'but there are two of us, yes?'

Eve nodded, but felt horribly weak, finding little consolation in her words. 'Just watch your step!' she observed with a glance towards the loamy ground, 'there are tar deposits seeping up everywhere … sometimes there's just a thin layer of sand or leaves across the top.' Ravenna nodded almost imperceptibly.

'Keep walking!' the farmer ordered.

Ravenna shot her a side-long glance and whispered: 'distract him!'

She walked for a couple of paces, her mind racing, then took a breath.

'This is one of the best known palaeontological sites on the planet,' she began slowly, 'I'd know it anywhere! It's yielded up millions of fossils since people first started digging in the 1870's …' There was a crashing of vegetation to their immediate right and they veered away instinctively.

'Herbivores came down to drink the water pooled on this tar and ...'

Movement flickered close at hand. 'My god!' whispered the farmer as they all slunk back into the foliage. A massive animal with bulky limbs and huge clawed paws was stripping leaves from a pine-like tree just a few paces ahead of them.

'Giant ground sloth,' Eve whispered disbelievingly, some childlike thrill of excitement beginning to stir despite the horror of what was happening. Her mind rocketed to the site she had always longed to see - photos of bones being dug from huge slabs of fossilised tar, modernist museum displays of hundreds of carnivore skulls. 'Oh god this is insane!' Facts shot through her mind as she watched the heavy snouted mammal stripping leaves with its flexible tongue ... *over 600 species identified from the pits, spiders, fish, camels, horses ... big game ...*

'What is it – what the hell's going on?' Jarrod demanded sharply ... *over seventy percent of the fossils from la Brea were of predatory carnivores.*

'The tar pits,' she whispered hoarsely, 'the big herbivores became trapped in naturally occurring asphalt, stuck like insects on fly-paper ...' In her mind's eye she saw an image she had seen of a wall display made entirely of sabre toothed cat skulls, *smilodon* after *smilodon* – a host of carnivores who had perished hunting the rich pickings of the pits, 'this is like a Pleistocene fast-food restaurant for big cats ... we can't stay here!'

The sloth seemed to pause as if sensing something, letting the branch it was stripping swing free as it dropped down to gaze around on all fours. Eve felt her body tense instinctively. It was massive, far bigger than any animal she'd ever encountered, at least six feet at the shoulder. Jarrod readied his gun at his side. The sloth took a tentative step in their direction, sniffing the air as it walked on its knuckles - its claws were horrifyingly large. She felt Ravenna touch her arm.

She was struggling to keep her breathing under control, her palms sweaty while her body itched to flee. It turned slowly, head dipping as it eyed them cautiously – she saw Jarrod shoot a desperate glance towards the clearing they had left behind.

'*Now!*' Ravenna yelled, but at that moment something exploded through the foliage ahead of them.

*

Eve threw herself behind a fallen log in time to see a massive big cat latch itself onto the creature's shaggy flank. Yet even as she processed the unexpected movement another lunged in from the left, attempting to topple the sloth under their combined weight. She gasped, flattening herself to the ground, spitting loam as the bellowing ground sloth shook the first cat free, swiping with its fore-claws as a third appeared to goad it.

She tensed, dragging her gaze from the flashing sabre teeth to the barrel of Jarrod's shotgun which wavered barely two feet from her face. The farmer looked appalled, clearly too stunned to fire. Ravenna crouched beyond him, likewise recovering herself, but as she gestured for them to break and run something massive snarled close at hand.

Fear flooded her body like electricity, the hairs on her neck standing upright as large eyes flashed beyond the foliage – the *smilodon* which had been stalking *them*.

171

'Go!' Ravenna yelled, and then they were sprinting, spewing dust and dried leaves, feet flying as the cats snarled and squalled. She gasped air, running blindly, praying the big cats would concentrate on the sloth; but pawed feet were following, the blood hissing in her ears as she heard Jarrod yell. She stumbled, twisting to see the farmer and Ravenna sprinting wildly with the big cat bounding close behind. She heard her own voice yelling, saw Jarrod twist the barrel to fire, then gasped as Ravenna barged him aside, the first shot missing the big cat by millimetres as they tumbled to the ground.

Then Jarrod was cursing, pulling himself free as the creature wheeled into cover at the sound; and Ravenna was shouting too, grabbing for the gun, growling at him to stop. She watched, horrified, dragging herself into a crouch as she sensed the big cats close at hand. 'Stop!' her friend was yelling, '– we must collaborate ..!'

She saw Jarrod hesitate but then, to her horror, jerk the stock of his shotgun up into the side of Ravenna's head. She hardly had time to take it in – and then he was running, firing wildly to his side as he twisted away, pursued by a flash of mottled fur. Eve yelled as Ravenna crumpled, throwing herself towards the Mediterranean girl as Jarrod and the swift moving feline were swallowed by tangled foliage.

'You okay?' she gasped desperately, helping her to sit. There was blood on her temple, the wound caked with dust.

'… had worse,' the time traveller mumbled groggily, wincing as she reached for the side of her head, then gestured in the direction they had come: 'help me Wells!'

She obeyed, hefting her weight with some difficulty, 'we must find the rift and close it …'

Eve's mind was racing. 'You saved the *smilodon!*' she breathed without thinking. Ravenna was breathing hard as she took a shaky step. 'It meant us no malice Wells – unlike Jarrod - and besides, it would not be good for the shape of the future.'

Eve scanned the undergrowth desperately as her mind worked on the comment - but what of Jess Flynn's disappearance in the past – and now Jarrod's? They stumbled. The scrub around them was alive with life, but she pushed the thought away, struggling to comprehend how some crazy hernia in time could link two places so geographically different over such a long chronological

173

sweep; but such questions were completely irrelevant - they were soft targets now – injured game.

They skirted the place the sloth had been, aware of it crashing away to the right pursued by the snarling felines, then paused to get their breath.

'They are gathering again,' Ravenna mused, wiping her forehead with her hand as movement registered in the trees. Around them the tangled scrub had fallen deathly silent, 'how big were the packs they hunted in?'

In truth she did not know.

'Come on,' she gasped, reaching for Ravenna's arm, but the time traveller shook her off.

'I am fine Wells – it will be faster for you this way.'

'Faster?' she frowned, 'look – Ravenna …'

'Just keep moving Wells – I will be right behind.'

Eve pressed on cautiously, horribly aware of Ravenna's limping and the movement in the foliage to their side, sure that some unseen creature would burst upon them at any moment. Fear threatened to overwhelm her as she scanned anxiously between every branch and frond; neither spoke as they retraced their steps, gesturing to familiar branches and their own marred tracks - Eve feeling as if she would explode with tension - sure she sensed stealthy movement at every turn. She paused to wipe her forehead, slowing as she became aware that Ravenna had fallen behind.

'Just keep going,' her friend called firmly, but as she glanced away Ravenna let out an uncharacteristic yelp. Eve turned, heart thudding, to see her friend knee deep in tar, her hands black and sticky where she had fallen and now scrabbled for the bank.

'Well?' the time traveller exclaimed desperately, struggling as she grasped at a rotten log, 'don't just stand there!'

Eve hesitated, casting around for a stick to extend to her - Ravenna was already up to her thighs in the sucking mixture of oil and sand - she felt her heart beat out of control. Around them the brush was quaking with movement. A few feet away something growled.

'Hurry Wells!'

Grabbing the nearest stick she stumbled forward, crouching as she reached for her, bracing herself to take Ravenna's weight; but as she did so she overbalanced, adrenaline stinging her gut as she stumbled, her boots slithering in the tar.

'I can't reach!' she exclaimed desperately, retreating a pace or so, 'you're too far away!' Panic began to overwhelm her, 'I'm sorry, I can't ...' There was a rustle in the chest high grass. '*Oh god!*'

'It is good to call to him, yes!' Ravenna exclaimed desperately, lunging forward once more to slither for the bank, but Eve's attention was elsewhere, her gaze fixed on large eyes peering out at her from across the pool.

Smilodon fatalis.

It stared at her fixedly, yellow eyes locked firmly onto hers, its huge fangs dipping slightly as its mouth began to open. Something disturbed the scrub behind her and she cried out involuntarily. They were here, gathering for the kill, cutting off their escape; she saw Ravenna's eyes widen, braced herself for the worst, but as her mind struggled to take in what was happening she felt a rush of air pass her shoulder, then another – spear shafts whistling - and then the predators were twisting away, disappearing spirit-like into the bush.

A knotted chord of plaited grasses fell across the mire in front of her and she turned with a disbelieving gasp.

'Grab on,' said a girl's voice and to her surprise she found herself looking into the sun-burned face of a woman only a little younger than herself. 'We'll pull you out.'

Eve just stared. Though the young woman was wearing travel soiled modern clothes, the people who stood around her were something else entirely.

'My god,' she breathed as Ravenna took the makeshift rope without hesitation, finding herself staring into the eyes of her long-dead ancestors. She gawped, reality seeming suddenly to become fluid, struggling to make sense of the clothing and tools – and the faces - so familiar and yet so unlike any modern person - faces much closer to their African origin than any modern race; and her own world seemed suddenly to vanish, viscerally caught in this moment, tens of thousands of years before her birth.

The young woman spoke on their behalf. 'My name's Jess,' she said with a hesitance that suggested she hadn't spoken English for quite a time, 'Jess Flynn – I ...'

'You went missing two weeks ago,' Eve said shakily, 'looking for phantom big cats...'

The young woman hesitated, her expression becoming pensive. 'Two weeks - but I've lived here two winters at least ...'

Behind her one of the men shifted his weight and began to speak in a soft tongue-clicking language. The girl listened for a moment then nodded as he produced a hide blanket which she took and offered to Ravenna. Eve found herself lost for words. Ravenna continually talked of time and reality as a fluid concept but nothing had prepared her for this.

Jess Flynn's eyes were swift and vigilant, darting continually to the bush around them. 'The elders speak of a way to another place,' she said guardedly, '– a door – many doors ...' She gazed past them to the tangle of foliage they had come from as if remembering, 'but it's not always open.'

'I can make it open,' Ravenna said gently, 'and close it forever.'

Jess Flynn hesitated then returned a thoughtful nod. 'But first we must help you.' At her side a woman produced a wodge of moss from a woven bag and after explaining in gestures pressed it to Ravenna's wound. 'Come - come and eat with us, tell us your story – and then …'

'Then we can take you home,' Eve smiled warmly, but to her surprise Jess returned a perplexed frown.

'Home?'

Her gaze darted to the man at her side before drifting to Ravenna's tar spattered clothes. She spoke a few words in the same clicking tongue the man had used then said: 'let us share with you what we have.'

'Our thanks,' said Ravenna before Eve had a chance to reply – and then they were moving, weaving off into the bush as the hunters began to chant and sing; and Eve was left staring, watching almost dumbly as the Mediterranean girl allowed a woman in clothes of hide to help her - and then she too was walking, following her ancient ancestors from the clearing in a daze.

Questions

'So she seriously wanted to stay?'

The sunrise was dazzling, a blaze of scarlet and gold from where they sat feet dangling on the edge of a rocky tor, gazing out across the shadow-stretched wilderness. Ravenna shrugged, her expression hidden by mirrored aviators.

'What she has gained is - for her - far greater than what she has left behind.'

Eve frowned. Somehow that didn't work for her. 'But what about her family ... her modern life and her career? And what about modern comforts – hell, what about the constant danger?'

Ravenna Friere cocked her head on one side.

'Sometimes that which is easy is not always that which is most fulfilling, Eve Wells.' Eve shot her a look.

'She has found friendship and community Dinosaur Girl, found a simplicity her soul longed for ... real adventure – perhaps the rawest and realist life that anyone could ever live.'

Eve sighed. 'But won't it mess reality up – her disappearing into the past, I mean?' Ravenna shrugged. 'That is not my call to consider,' she said lightly, 'but I felt it was acceptable.'

'You felt?'

Ravenna yawned and stretched theatrically, clearly unwilling to discuss what motivated her interventions.

'She is a part of the legend of the beast now - all's well that ends well, yes?'

Eve said nothing. It did not seem like a happy ending: a missing specialist whose family would never have answers and now a farmer obsessed with the legend gone without trace. She shuddered. That was fitting at least – and now he too would become part of local folklore.

Ravenna pulled a granola bar from her pack and began to munch.

'Well, that was different.'

Eve wrinkled her face in disbelief.

'Different! I've just been through one of the most terrifying physical experiences of my life and all you can say is *that was different*!'

Ravenna shrugged. 'You cannot deny that it was *different* Eve Wells?'

Eve just gazed at her in disbelief then sighed. 'And Steve Jarrod – do you think he's ... I mean, after he ran ..?'

Ravenna shrugged. 'Do not contemplate it Eve Wells, he chose his path and he must walk where it leads.'

'Even if it changes time?'

Ravenna kept her gaze on the glowing horizon.

'Like I say ...'

'But you saved the *smilodon* ...'

'That was different.'

Eve frowned, but Ravenna spoke before she could interject. 'Turn your mind to pleasant thoughts Eve

Wells – it is over, the rift is closed and the beast is a legend once more. Cheer up! You get to go home and spend a couple of days with your beautiful man, while I …'

She broke off to scan the silver flecked clouds which scudded briskly on the stiffening breeze.

'Where are you going?' Eve asked thoughtfully.

'I will press on to my next engagement.'

She frowned. 'But how do you - listen, Ravenna …'

'Come, Eve Wells,' said the time traveller, dusting down her jeans as she rose, 'it is time to go – and if you are quick you will just make the sleeper.'

Eve hesitated for a moment, her mouth opening to object, then checked herself. Her questions could wait – they always could – and shouldering her bag she stood to watch the sunrise paint the world anew. And though a host of unanswered questions flitted through her mind she allowed herself – just this once – to choose blind faith over reason, letting go of the impossibility of it all. Her questions could wait - until next time.

Part 4

Last Known Outbreak

Eve

The young woman on the tube kept her gaze fixed firmly on the strip of floor in front of her, blanking the interested stares of the commuters who had just entered the carriage.

'Sorry,' she said apologetically, lifting her unusual luggage onto her lap as a man squeezed into the seat next to her.

'Cheers,' the commuter grinned, then added, 'I think it's going to be a pretty heavy vet's bill!'

Eve Wells smiled weakly, pushing up her glasses as she fought to stop her cheeks from flushing. 'Fine looking animal,' the man continued. She found herself lost for words, wrapping her arms almost protectively around the large glass case.

'It's from a museum,' she replied awkwardly, glancing down at the unusual contents.

'You don't say,' her fellow commuter replied.

When she had agreed to drop off *a parcel* at her friend Polly Nightingale's workplace she had never imagined she would have to cross London carrying a dead cat.

Eve cleared her throat. Thus far the weekend break in the capital had been run-of-the-mill – just a chance to catch up with one of the few people who could truly understand the strange experiences she had been through - but some sixth sense told her that things were about to change. She suppressed a shudder as her gaze dropped to the beady eyes of the snarling Victorian wild cat in her arms, glaring up at her from its fake tussock, back arched in anger.

Just drop it off in my department, Polly Nightingale had said over cocktails the night before, *I've got a couple of errands to run before work, just make yourself at home – explore the museum.*

Eve coughed nervously, struggling to avoid both the wild cat's glare and the commuter's grinning gaze, trying not to speculate about what lay ahead. *I'm a palaeontologist going to a natural history museum,* she reminded herself reassuringly, *just returning a specimen - what could possibly go wrong?*

Darkness engulfed the windows, the rhythmic hum of the carriage momentarily overwhelming her senses. She felt her mind drawn back through deeper darkness - through the rush and pull of a different blackness to the sights and sounds of places so incredible she could barely believe she had seen them; she heard again the growl and skitter of long dead beasts, felt the chill breeze of an icy Scottish Loch decades before. Then the train began to slow, the sigh and clatter of the carriage changing pitch as light and movement filled the windows once more - the white tiling and curved billboards replacing her near-unbelievable memories.

Her phone chimed – no doubt Polly checking on how things were going – but as she struggled to retrieve it from her pocket her face fell. The message was from Ravenna Friere.

'This is my stop,' she said as the platform came into view, apologising as she struggled with the bulk of the attention-drawing taxidermy.

'I could have sworn it just blinked!' exclaimed the man at her side, but she was already pushing towards the door, forcing herself to ignore his comment, somehow knowing that however weirdly her day had begun it was about to get a whole lot weirder.

Nineties

'But she's going to be okay?'

Eve's head was spinning as she fought to focus, barely taking in the words of the woman she had just been introduced to. Yet the hesitation before the other speaker replied strongly suggested the person in question was *not* going to be okay, the woman's face drawn with worry.

Eve forced a sympathetic smile, feeling totally out of her depth. Barely thirty minutes ago she'd been walking through the contemplative depths of a London museum, yet now she found herself enveloped by the disorienting light and sound of what reminded her of every bad wedding disco she had ever hated.

She fought to ignore the nausea which nagged at her, trying to shrug off the disorienting shift in time as the track changed from *Return of the Mack* to Gina G's

Ooh – ah – just a little bit, the DJ's garbled commentary obliterating the tail end of the conversation she had found herself involved in. She smiled politely, turning to survey the room.

She was clearly at a works party at some point in the recent past, the dimly lit interior of the function room alive with a celebration in full swing: yet the vibe was less than jubilant, the party-goers seeming subdued somehow, despite the music and dancing.

She nodded politely as the small-talk continued. Where the hell was Ravenna - and who on earth were the two women talking about? As the music pulsed and undulated she felt her thoughts begin to wander, trying to make sense of the mystery which had invaded her life - and the odd events which had taken place barely a few moments before.

*

'Special Collections?' the security guard had asked as she had paused on the threshold of the prestigious museum, trying to look as natural as she could with the heavy display case - but the guy on the door hardly seemed to notice. She had nodded, opening her mouth to mention her friend and the name she had been given but the guard was already ushering her through the metal detectors and into the huge cathedral-like hall.

As a tutor of the prehistoric past the museum was palaeontology heaven, but she had little time to contemplate the awe-inspiring exhibits as he led her briskly across the gallery. Eerie shadows flashed beneath harsh fluorescent lighting as they left the public parts of the museum behind, the guard leading her down a steep flight of steps and along echoing corridors, past rooms of goodness knew what treasures. The place was a warren – a crazy labyrinth of ancient curiosities – and despite her nervousness she felt a pang of jealousy at her friend's dream job.

They paused on the threshold of a large basement room while the man swiped inside, her gaze falling on the fossil skull of huge marine reptile sat amid piles of bubble wrap on the first of many tables. She shuddered involuntarily: a dream job but also a crazy calling - part of the same incredible secret which had changed her view of reality forever. 'Just through here,' the security guard said dragging her mind back from the waters of a Scottish Loch.

She passed the plesiosaur specimen without a second glance, overwhelmed by the scale of what she was seeing. The room before her was cavernous. Row after row of metal framed shelving units interspersed with table after table laden with finds - endless racks and boxes filled with fossil after artefact after treasure. She walked slowly, overtaken with fascination, but the weight of the heavy glass case was a reminder to press on, and rounding the corner of the nearest bay she stopped in her tracks, oddly surprised to find that she was not alone.

'Yes?' said a lean man in his mid-thirties, perched on one of the huge tables.

'Hi,' said Eve a little hesitantly.

The man put down the fossil he had been examining and rose to face her, hand outstretched. 'Dr Eve Wells I presume?'

Polly's superior was not at all what she had expected – a good deal younger for one thing – and a lot better dressed in his grey blazer and dark-wash jeans. 'Yes,' she smiled, struggling to shake his hand under the weight of the display case.

'Oh … sorry,' the curator replied, ducking forward to take the stuffed wild cat from her grip, 'and thank you – Vauncey must have an eye keeping on him at all times …'

Eve frowned, her gaze dipping instinctively to the long dead animal's snarling face, then back to the curator's, but he appeared to be deadly serious. 'You teach palaeontology at the University of the East Midlands I gather?'

'Yes,' she nodded, feeling a little confused.

'Miss Nightingale speaks highly of you Dr Wells … but I must admit I was already aware of your work - your palaeontological illustrations are truly astounding.' She returned a self-deprecating smile. 'And I have only heard good things about you from Polly – it is a joy to meet someone who is regarded as trustworthy by those you trust the most.'

'I … thanks,' Eve replied awkwardly, breaking away from his piercing grey-blue gaze. *Trustworthy.* She suddenly felt as if she had been left little choice – after all, who would believe what she had been through - who could she ever tell? A flood of questions lurched unexpectedly into her mind, longing suddenly to quiz him about the incredible secret his department contained.

'Look, Dr Speedwell ...'

'*There are more things in heaven and earth than can be accounted for,* and all that!' he interjected with an evasive smile.

She dropped her gaze to the stuffed cat on the table between them. 'What did you mean - about the wild cat –*Vauncey*?' But at that moment a figure appeared at the room's far end, bustling towards them along the aisle in a rush of Mediterranean flamboyance.

Ravenna Friere.

The dark haired young woman was dressed like an extra from a Shakespearean drama, tutting as she untied the lacing on the front of her voluminous outer gown and began to pull it over her head. Eve felt her heart sink.

'*Magna Mater* this outfit is near unbearable ...'

Eve just stared.

'Ah,' said the tall curator delicately, 'it seems I shall be able to leave you in Ms Friere's very capable hands – it has been a pleasure Dr Wells ...' and before she could respond he was making a hasty exit from the room.

'You are late Dinosaur Girl,' the diminutive time traveller began in her strange unplaceable accent, 'there is business in hand and I am between engagements …'

'What?' she replied incredulously, 'what do you mean, *late*?'

'Have you eaten – breakfast I mean?' she continued unabashed, 'you will need some food inside you, we have much to do …'

Then the penny dropped. 'No,' Eve replied firmly, 'no, no, no – I'm on holiday - up for the weekend to do the whole tourist thing and there's no way I'm …' She closed her eyes – it was clearly some kind of set-up. Hell, had Polly known this was going to happen - was that why she had sent her to the museum with the ridiculous package to deliver? The stuffed wild cat seemed to gaze at her mockingly from its place on the finds table.

'Where *is* Polly?'

The time traveller kept her face neutral as she began to change into a baggy Nirvana tee shirt and denim jacket. 'Ahead of us, preparing the way.'

'She knew about this didn't she – she knew but didn't say anything!'

'She did not want to spoil your Friday night Wells,' the dark haired girl continued lightly, 'and besides, we could not leave you out of this … we need you Eve Wells – need another pair of eyes, for what I have discovered is a serious matter – *really* serious.'

Eve felt her guts begin to churn, for in her limited experience Ravenna Friere's *serious* invariably meant mortal-danger-serious.

'But …'

'And don't worry about your clothes, you should be fine in the vintage puffer jacket and trainers.'

She had hesitated, struggling to make sense of the turn her day had taken...

Eve felt a hand on her shoulder and to her relief found herself gazing into the face of the dark haired girl who had summoned her, the athletic young woman moving rhythmically to the music at her side. As ever she looked immaculate and unruffled, her Mediterranean complexion giving her a vaguely exotic look beneath the pulsing disco lighting.

'Hi,' the time traveller said in a faux-West Midlands accent then turned to the woman who had been speaking as if she wasn't even there: 'So, any news?'

'I was just saying to your friend,' the speaker replied gesturing to Eve with her bottle of Diamond White, 'that they think it was some kind of chemical accident.'

'Just like Sayeed?'

The woman looked away awkwardly and Ravenna Friere made a sympathetic face. 'So I guess we won't be seeing her in the staff club any time soon?'

'Sick leave for the foreseeable future,' the woman continued, '– from what I've heard she won't be coming back to the department - I mean, after what happened to Sayeed ...'

The conversation moved on, and making her excuses Ravenna steered her towards the gyrating dance floor. 'Look, what on earth's ..?' Eve began as soon as they were out of ear-shot, but the time traveller held up her hand, straining to hear another conversation being yelled across the music.

'... *Some kind of reaction – exposed to something in the lab* ...'

'I'm serious ...' Eve whispered loudly into her ear, 'If you don't tell me what on earth's going on ...'

'Quiet Wells - that is what we are here to find out!'

Eve sighed heavily, turning to watch the revellers on the floor until at last Ravenna gave her full attention. 'So when ...'

'1997,' Ravenna replied briskly over the music, '13th October – this is an office party for the Queen Anne Teaching Hospital - a *leaving do* ...' She said it as if the concept was oddly alien to her.

'Right - so what are we doing here?'

'Just follow me and keep your ears open!' the time traveller yelled over the increasing beat. Eve let out an exasperated breath as she followed – mingling and eavesdropping - weaving their way towards the buffet before pausing to watch once more.

'This was no chemical reaction,' Ravenna mused grimly as she took a handful of crisps, then turned directly to Eve as if finally willing to provide answers. 'The young woman they speak of is a PhD student called Nicky Green - colleague of a man who passed away two months ago, a fellow researcher at this University Hospital. She fell ill two weeks ago and has been off work ever since – and she is not alone.'

Eve felt a strange sensation of dread begin to creep over her. 'Several of the research department she studied with have also taken voluntary redundancy and others left following the death of the man I speak of … like the woman this party is in aid of.' She glanced at a smiling middle aged woman opening cards on the other side of the room.

Eve turned her gaze away. The track had changed to *Professional Widow* by Tori Amos, and despite the seriousness of the conversation Ravenna seemed to be unable to stop herself from swaying rhythmically to the undulating baseline. Eve forced herself to focus, dragging her attention from the Brit-pop fashions and strobing lights to the time traveller's pensive gaze.

'So what are we talking about here?' she yelled over the pounding music, 'a radio-active leak or something?'

Ravenna looked at her darkly though her shoulders still bobbed. 'No Wells, nothing so easily containable.'

Her thoughts flew back to the women they had just overheard: *but you think she's going to be okay?* Eve swallowed. 'What exactly does the department these people worked for do ... what *was* her area of research?'

Disco lights strobed across Ravenna's dark irises as the music morphed into some euphoric dance tune. 'Come Wells...' the time traveller replied evasively, 'there is someone we must meet.' And knowing it wasn't worth arguing, Eve followed briskly, struggling to suppress her growing sense of concern.

Polly

Polly Nightingale smiled her thanks to the barman, hoping desperately that the man she sat with would offer to pay the bill. She sipped her drink, chiding herself for being so rash, suddenly aware that the plastic notes in her hip pocket would look like play-money while her cards would not be issued for at least another twenty years: hell, she was getting more and more like Ravenna! She smiled at her companion, preparing herself for what she was about to do. Never in a million years could she have envisaged that when she accepted the post at the prestigious London museum it would have led to this.

'Look,' she began, 'I'm really pleased you agreed to see me Dr Rembrandt - ever since the incident got into the news I've been worried about the implications for the medical school – and then when Nicky became ill ...'

The departmental manager who sat opposite her cupped his tall glass, regarding her thoughtfully through gold rimmed glasses. It suddenly seemed like madness – posing as a junior researcher at the university he worked at – but it had been the only way to organise an informal meeting. She forced a concerned frown, gambling that he was the kind of man to be honest with a vulnerable young woman in need of reassurance.

'No problem at all Miss … Rhodes,' he replied with a disarming smile. He spoke confidently, his tone calm and reassuring. She dipped her gaze to her drink. He had to be a good ten years older than her, one of those well-spoken people who bore a natural air of authority - and yet there was something a little intimidating about his thoughtful expression. 'And I can appreciate your concerns for your friend - but I can assure you that the incident is all over now, the four juniors who were affected are all on the relevant medication – and on the road to recovery'

She shot him a quizzical look. 'So they were infectious?'

'Please, don't mention that here,' the specialist said briskly, then seemed to regain his composure. Polly nodded.

'And the first case – Sayeed Mohala ... how do you think he contracted it?' She asked the question casually as she stirred her cocktail, 'to be honest I had no idea your department still kept live samples.'

Dr Rembrandt paused with his drink to his mouth, his expression guarded. 'I'm not at liberty to discuss that Miss Rhodes.'

'Sorry,' she nodded, 'I was just curious – I mean, I know you've worked with a variety of live viruses during your career?'

She saw his expression darken and felt a sudden pang of concern – she'd pressed too far. 'Look,' she continued with a disarming smile, 'I'm just worried about my friends – my colleagues – there's been so much negative press, and as several members of your staff have fallen ill ...'

He seemed to stiffen and put down his glass.

'Which department did you say you worked for Miss Rhodes?'

'I ...' her hesitation was a mistake. Rembrandt swore under his breath and sighed angrily.

'Look, who the hell are you really ..?'

'Sorry,' she said shakily, cursing herself as fear flared, 'look – I'd better go ...'

'You don't work for the university at all do you?' he said heatedly and to her horror made a grab at her wrist as she rose.

'Get off me!' she gasped instinctively and pulling free grabbed her jacket.

'Miss Rhodes,' the doctor continued heatedly – she could hear his stool scraping back behind her, 'listen, Miss Rhodes – or whoever you really are ...'

She quickened her pace, fear stinging the pit of her stomach – he was following – oh god, what should she do?

'For your information *Miss Rhodes*, I've had it up to here with reporters ..!'

She could hear his feet heavy on the floor behind her, forced herself not to meet the gaze of the concerned drinkers who sat nearby.

'Come back!' she heard him call angrily, but then the cool of the night was embracing her and daring to turn she saw a bouncer waylay him at the door.

She took a shaky breath feeling horribly light headed.

Oh god – what had she done!

Kebab House

'**W**hat *are* we doing here?'

They were sat on the faux leather benches of a greasy fast food restaurant where Ravenna was working her way through a huge sauce-laden kebab.

'Waiting,' the time traveller replied between mouthfuls, 'patience is a skill you must develop Eve Wells – and faith. You must have faith in me – and ask fewer questions ...' She took another large bite and Eve wrinkled her nose.

'God, how can you eat that?'

'You must try some Dinosaur Girl,' Ravenna enthused, 'the hot chilli sauce is to die for - and in my line of work you need calories – lots of them ...'

Her line of work. Eve's mind boggled at the very thought – the crazy life the dark haired woman lived.

The man behind the counter said something to a slightly drunk customer and the pair glanced in their direction and laughed. Eve leaned in a little closer her arms folded across her chest. 'At least tell me who the women at the party were talking about – who has died?' Ravenna looked at her steadily.

'A lab-tech who worked at the University Hospital called Sayeed Mohala, the official report says he passed away from chemical shock, but in reality …'

At that moment, the door opened filling the shop with the sound of rowdy post-club laughter. Eve turned, her question momentarily forgotten. It was like something from another world, like pictures from a photo album of her parent's university days.

'Man – everyone looks so frumpy,' she muttered as a gaggle of chatting students congregated around the counter. Ravenna just looked at her in a:*you-can-talk* kind of way, but as the bantering group loitered to place their order a girl gestured at Eve's vintage puffer jacket and said:

'Ace coat! Where did you get it?'

'On holiday in the US.' Ravenna replied on her behalf, adding: 'they did not begin to import in large numbers till '99,' in an undertone. Eve gave Ravenna a smug smile then turned her attention to the peg board menu above the heads of the laughing students, longing suddenly to know what on earth they had been called to deal with. Ravenna seemed to sense her question and putting down her food looked at her sagely.

'Go on - ask your question Eve Wells.'

She thought for a moment. 'Chemical shock?' she ventured in a low tone, '... but you're saying it was something else – a disease?'

Ravenna hesitated as someone behind her wolf-whistled at a passing gaggle of girls. 'This unfortunate young man died after being exposed to something at the university – but as we have just seen at the party, he was not the only one who was affected – and no-one is willing to publically admit that the incidents are linked – though they blatantly are.'

'But I still don't understand why this should concern us?' Eve frowned. Ravenna leaned forward, her expression serious.

'In 1978 a photographer from the University of Birmingham called Janet Parker contracted a virus being worked on in a sealed lab above her office.'

'Go on,' Eve prompted.

'The unfortunate woman passed away – and the method by which the disease passed from a sterile lab to her studio was seemingly inexplicable.' Something in Ravenna's gaze told her she was holding something back.

'And?'

'At first her death was blamed on chemical shock – exposure to an unknown substance.'

Eve frowned. *Chemical shock*. 'Like the young man who had recently died … but you said this is 1997?'

The time traveller looked at her with that perennial look of frustration. 'Indeed – twenty years after Parker's death - I had long had my suspicions that something out-of-time had happened, but this would seem to confirm it.'

'So you think that whatever happened to this Sayeed guy has happened before - that it's some kind of cycle?'

Ravenna looked at her darkly, then flicked her gaze to the young people walking out with their takeaway order. 'That Wells, I do not know, but what I can tell you is that over eleven thousand students currently study at this university, eleven thousand vulnerable young people …' Eve followed her gaze to the students who lingered outside the shop. She felt a shiver of unease run through her.

'So what do we ..?'

Ravenna took a bite of her kebab.

'Have patience Wells – *have faith* – everything will be revealed in its proper time … and - ah, here we are.'

Eve looked up to see a brisk moving figure push past the milling students, the shop bell chiming once more as someone hurried inside, and turning she felt her pulse leap - for something was clearly very wrong.

Revelation

'Have you spoken to him?' Ravenna asked briskly as Polly Nightingale swung around the door, but the anxious brunette seemed not to hear her.

'I'm sorry!' she said breathlessly, sweeping a strand of curling hair from her face 'I tried to find out what I could, but he's on to me - and sorry,' she added, turning to Eve, 'I should really have warned you ...'

'I ...' Eve began, then frowned, 'warned me of what? What's going on Polly – *who's on to you*?'

Ravenna spoke over her: 'No matter Nightingale, this may work to our advantage, yes?'

'Guys ..?' Eve interrupted, feeling utterly out of her depth; but even as she spoke the door swung open, once more dragging in the sounds of the city at night. 'And this is the one of whom we speak,' said Ravenna with a surprisingly casual inclination of her eyes, 'Dr Rembrandt I presume …'

'What on earth's going on – and who the hell are you?' the tall man who had entered said heatedly as he strode over to their table. Polly took an instinctive step away, but the Mediterranean woman just smiled, indicating that he should take a seat.

'Just someone who wants to help,' the time traveller replied with surprising calmness, 'now please – will you sit doctor?'

Eve swallowed. Dr Rembrandt was clearly less than happy to be joining them and stood pointedly, towering over their table. 'Look, if you're a journalist I'm not interested – I've already told the Observer I've nothing more to say – and I've a good mind to get the police involved - I don't take kindly to having my precious time wasted!' He turned his fierce gaze on Polly, 'Sayeed's death was an accident, plain and simple.'

Eve swallowed, but Ravenna held his gaze. 'But an accident in *your* lab all the same.'

The academic bristled, then broke off, realising the men behind the counter were watching him intently. Ravenna returned a confident smile. 'Perhaps if you'll take a seat and discuss this calmly I'll consider keeping my voice down about what happened at the lab you run.'

'*Ran*,' Dr Rembrandt replied grimly, then sighed and sat swiftly, the thick gold band of his watch clinking against the table top.

'So tell me what happened in your department Dr Rembrandt – how did a healthy young technician contract a seemingly deadly illness which he then passed on to others?'

For a moment Eve thought he was about to protest, but to her surprise he looked down and mopped his forehead.

'Sayeed was on a probationary placement – a lot of dogsbody work – spent most of his time in the stores making inventories of our old equipment in the basement, he barely went near the damned lab – our work was nothing to do with the virus he contracted!'

'And you'd swear to this – in a court of law?'

'What the hell do you think!' he exploded, making Eve glance away, 'that damned tribunal has already dragged me through the hoops – my whole career ...'

He broke off and ran his fingers through his hair. 'You can read the report of the inquest - it's all there in black and white.'

Ravenna sat back and gazed at him pertly. 'So what *were* you working on in the lab Dr Rembrandt? Something Sayeed came into contact with most certainly proved fatal.'

Eve found herself holding her breath, but to her surprise he let out a sigh and removed his metal-framed glasses.

'It's no secret what we keep – we kept – in the laboratory: a great many dangerous bacteria. We work with a number of highly contagious sub-tropical diseases, conduct research into the control and treatment of several highly contagious strains, but at no stage has our laboratory ever had anything to do with the *variola* virus.'

'But *variola* was stored in the facility at one time, was it not Dr Rembrandt – twenty years ago or so?'

'Yes, but ...'

'And to all intents and purposes it appears that Sayeed Mohala did die of ...'

Dr Rembrandt slapped the table with the palm of his hand making Eve flinch.

'Our facilities were quarantined two months ago – my research put on hold – but no trace of the *Variola Major* virus was found – not a trace! Nothing to link my work - my department's work - to Sayeed's death: as I have said from the outset, this was an unfortunate and inexplicable accident.'

Eve saw Polly glance away awkwardly, but Ravenna pressed him further, completely undeterred.

'Have you ever worked in any of the Eastern bloc countries Dr Rembrandt ... anywhere associated with the former Soviet Union?'

'What?' the academic frowned disbelievingly, 'what on earth has that to do with anything?'

'But you have worked across Europe?'

'What of it?' he replied defensively, 'my career is no secret, I've worked for several major European institutions ... look, what the hell is this?'

Eve found herself recoiling instinctively as he rose from the chair. 'Sayeed Mohala's death was a regrettable accident, caused by exposure to some unknown substance, as the report of the inquest states and I have nothing further to say on the matter – and if you ever try to contact me again, I assure you I shall press charges ..!'

'Listen, Dr Rembrandt,' Polly began placatingly, likewise rising from her seat, but Ravenna put a hand on her arm.

'Let him go,' she murmured, and then the door was closing noisily, leaving Eve staring after him in confused disbelief.

'Do you believe him?' Ravenna asked thoughtfully, likewise gazing at the place he had been.

Polly Nightingale shrugged. 'He was pretty intense – seriously concerned about what the whole thing would do to his department – and his career.'

Not for the first time that night Eve felt totally out of her depth. She turned her gaze to the pitch dark glass. Raindrops now spotted the window, glowing like incandescent beads in the shop sign's neon glow as the students hurried home. She felt again that sense of disorientation, trapped in a world which was so familiar – and yet so alien - dropped into a situation she didn't understand.

Polly spoke again, interrupting her thoughts.

'I managed to find a report online, here's the web address ...' She handed her a scrawled note torn from a ring-bound pad: no texts or WhatsApp here.

'So – what now?'

Ravenna traced a pattern with her finger on the table top. 'We find where Sayeed was exposed to the disease – and quickly – if this virus has somehow made its way into the twentieth century we must stop its method of transmission ...'

Eve, hesitated for a moment, then voiced the question she had been longing to ask: 'So this virus *Variola* – what exactly ...' At her side Polly shifted her weight uncomfortably.

'Come,' said Ravenna evasively, 'we are left with only one option.'

'Which is?' Eve ventured anxiously, but Ravenna and Polly were already getting up to leave.

Evidence

E ve shivered as she gazed at the figure crouched in front of her, watching with horrified fascination as Ravenna cursed softly in some long dead language. It was cold in the alley, cold and dark, and Polly's presence was doing little to negate the horrible reality that Ravenna Friere was picking the lock of the double doors in front of them.

'Tell me this isn't happening!' she whispered to her friend, but Polly did not reply, her gaze fixed on the sodium lit street just visible at the alley's end. Hell, what if someone spotted them and called the police!

Ravenna laughed softly and straightened her back. '*Nika!*' The lock clicked open audibly and Polly shot her a reassuring glance.

'There's no CCTV here,' her friend whispered, 'come on, let's get this over with.'

'So we're basically …'

'Breaking into a university medical school,' Ravenna whispered loudly from the gloom ahead, 'get over it.'

Eve shuddered as they entered a sizeable stairwell, lit dimly by light filtering through the double doors above. 'This part of the building should be deserted at this time of night,' Ravenna informed them reassuringly, 'but we must be alert, yes?'

They ascended cautiously, coming out on a wide corridor, long and dimly lit. Ravenna led them southwards for a few minutes then paused at a junction to take a hand-drawn map from her pocket. 'The labs are this way,' she said with a swift inclination of her eyebrows, 'while the basement stores where Sayeed worked are accessed off this stairwell.' There was a pointed look in her gaze.

'Toss for it?' Polly said with a shrug, '– I'll call heads.'

Ravenna took a handful of loose change from her pocket, of which at least one of the coins Eve guessed was Roman, and selecting a shilling flipped and cupped it on the back of her hand.

'Tails,' said Polly, '*I lose* – see you in a bit.' The dark haired girl nodded and without another word Polly headed for the staircase.

'Come,' said Ravenna and leading her into an adjoining corridor paused by the nearest door.

*

'Where the heck did you get that?' Eve whispered wide-eyed.

Ravenna was swiping an ID badge through a set of security doors leading to the first of a series of research labs. 'You do not live as many lifetimes as I have without picking up certain skills.'

Eve looked at her friend incredulously. 'What – *you stole it* - from Dr Rembrandt!'

'Think of it as a deft example of the ancient art of sleight-of-hand,' the dark haired girl replied as she pushed open the door, 'now come on – quietly.'

They entered a tidy office filled with dated looking IT equipment - massive CRT monitors and big cream coloured keyboards – and making for the nearest work station Ravenna began to manipulate the mouse to bring the screen to life. Eve frowned as the swirling geometric screen-saver was replaced by a series of unfamiliar icons on an aquamarine background. Ravenna clicked once more.

'Here we go,' said the Mediterranean girl and almost at once a strange intermittent frequency began to sound beneath the desk.

'What's that noise?' said Eve with a frown.

'Dial-up internet,' Ravenna replied, her fingers clicking on the keys, 'we're pre-broadband here – pre Wi-Fi.'

'Right.'

Eve blinked at the unusually blocky interface with mild fascination.

'And what are you …?'

Ravenna growled at the monolithic IBM in frustration. 'Web search of the person who died,' she replied pulling out the note Polly had given her earlier, then broke off and muttered under her breath, 'your phone is more powerful!' then glancing up said: 'Here – read this while we wait.'

She passed Eve a stapled document.

'You're kidding!'

'I never kid Eve Wells.'

She felt her heart sink as she realised what they were facing.

'But …'

'Indeed,' said the time traveller grimly, 'read it!'

Eve felt her mouth go dry. It was a copy of a medical article on the identification and treatment of smallpox. She didn't know much about the disease – but she did know that whenever it struck a virgin population it was deadly – and Smallpox had been absent from Britain for nearly twenty years. Ravenna's words leapt back to the forefront of her mind: *over eleven thousand students currently study at this university …*

She flipped the pages, lingering over an unsettling image of a little girl plastered head-to-toe in a mass of disfiguring flattened blisters. Her mind flew back to some documentary she'd seen. Facts about thousands dying in epidemics, the population decimated when it was introduced to the new world by the Spanish. 'So – this is pretty bad isn't it?' Ravenna gave an ironic snort. 'But wasn't smallpox eradicated years ago?'

'Indeed, the World Health Organization passed a resolution for its global eradication in 1959 through vaccination in developed countries.' She broke off and sighed darkly. 'It is a merciless disease – kills a third of those it infects ...'

The words seemed to hang in the air between them.

Eve glanced at her reflection in the flickering monitor– her eyes looked tired and anxious. 'It was Jenner wasn't it,' she said to distract herself, recalling a fact she had learned at school, '– Edward Jenner – who used infected matter from cowpox pustules to vaccinate against smallpox in healthy patients.'

'Top marks,' Ravenna returned, still staring at the screen.

'Hence vaccination, from *vacca* – the Latin for cow …'

'You can leave it there Dinosaur Girl.' Ravenna interjected, then sighed thoughtfully. 'Jenner was a really cute guy – so sincere … rubbish dancer though …'

Eve frowned in disbelief, but Ravenna continued oblivious. 'After Jenner's breakthrough the last naturally occurring outbreak of smallpox occurred in Somalia in '77 …'

Eve looked up to meet her gaze - Ravenna's pause told her that wasn't the end of it. 'The photographer who died in 1978,' she mused remembering their earlier conversation. Ravenna nodded.

'Like Sayeed Mohala, her death was blamed on chemical shock, for no-one could understand how the smallpox virus could travel through a sealed lab to her office. It was a mystery – inexplicable – and this is what first aroused my suspicions.'

'So you think the same thing is happening again, only two decades later …'

Ravenna fixed her gaze on the slowly spinning egg timer on the screen.

'No more questions Wells, I have been forced to intervene in the Dancing Plague of 1518 for the last three days, and my patience is wearing somewhat thin!'

Eve looked at her incredulously then let out a despairing sigh. 'Look - seriously, you drop me in the middle of a horror movie and won't even ...' But before she could finish, Ravenna slapped the desk in triumph.

'Here – the information Polly found about Sayeed's death. The report says he appeared to be delusional - seeing strange things – query mental illness.'

Eve leaned forward to gaze at the plain text on the screen. 'Seeing things – *what things*?'

Ravenna highlighted a block of text, quotes from the coroner's report.

The deceased kept speaking of "their filthy rags" and repeating that he was unable to understand "why they were down there" [last words].

Eve adjusted her glasses. 'That's weird – but I don't see how that helps us?'

Ravenna drummed her fingers on the desk as she waited for another page to load. 'Come on ...'

A thought struck her but the Mediterranean girl seemed to read her mind: '… and do not even think about suggesting I trawl social media Wells, Facebook will not be launched until 2004 …'

Eve glanced away, finding herself trying to imagine a world without the internet at her fingertips, wondering suddenly if it would be better or worse – less-informed, or simpler and more sincere a world? Ravenna smiled to herself as if yet again guessing what she was thinking. 'We now stand in the old world Wells, a world before everyone could share their opinions and their life continually … the last reaches of the analogue world – my world …' she tapped impatiently with the right-click button, 'this is a world in which you *learn* facts and do not *find* them - they are acquired through effort and wisdom – not effortlessly like fast-food!'

Eve found herself unable to reply, overwhelmed yet again by the improbability of where she had found herself; but as the time traveller worked an odd thought struck her: 'back in the kebab place – why did you ask Rembrandt about Russia?'

For a moment Ravenna was silent and when she spoke she never took her eyes from the screen. 'In 1947 the Soviet government established a biological weapons factory in the city of Zagorsk, seventy five kilometres outside of Moscow,' she began steadily, 'in '71 there was a minor outbreak after a research ship taking samples came too close to a remote test site in the Aral Sea.'

Eve felt an unexpected tingle of concern rush along her spine 'So what happened?'

'The outbreak was contained, but in 1991 the Soviet government allowed a joint British – US inspection of their research facilities and it was found the Russians had created around 20 tons of weaponised smallpox at Zagorsk.'

'So what happened to it?' Eve asked, her mouth feeling suddenly very dry.

'It was allegedly destroyed,' Ravenna said pointedly, her face illuminated eerily by the computer's screen, 'and the vaccine samples moved to an Institute in Koltsovo ...'

'And when did this happen?' Eve asked shakily.

Ravenna shot her an almost frustrated look. '1997 Eve Wells - earlier this year.'

'Oh.' The room felt suddenly airless.

'I am *putting two and two together* as your strange phrase has it,' the time traveller added lightly,

'Rembrandt is a renowned specialist who has worked in Eastern Europe ...'

Eve glanced anxiously at the research rooms which lay beyond the office, feeling panic grip her chest. 'You think he may have brought some of his work home with him?'

'It is just another angle Wells - no one knows what really happened to that weaponised bacteria, thus we must search this lab.' She clicked off the internet in frustration. 'Come on – this is getting me nowhere ...' But as she broke off a noise sounded from one of the rooms behind.

'Did you hear that?' Eve asked anxiously. They both stood listening but the only sound was the computer powering down.

'We had better keep moving,' Ravenna said seriously and with a shudder Eve followed, glad to be getting out of the room.

The Lab

They wandered through a series of characterless rooms all accessible with Dr Rembrandt's card. Hazard Warning notices festooned the walls, but Ravenna seemed utterly unconcerned, pausing by a bench to rifle through a pile of spiral bound documents before continuing. They passed a room through which Eve could glimpse chemical showers and racked air-fed suits, as well as a host of other decontamination gear.

'That doesn't bode well!' she mused grimly, but Ravenna wasn't listening. They had entered an unlit area of the department and pausing to examine her hand-drawn map, Ravenna swiped through another door to flick on a battery of lights.

'Woah,' Eve breathed as she stood blinking in the clinical brightness.

'The real deal,' Ravenna said triumphantly.

The sizeable room was similar to the others, but in comparison had been stripped almost totally bare. Where shelves had been stacked with books and benches lined with scientific equipment, the place was comparatively empty.

'I think we've found the disused lab,' Eve said glibly.

'You don't say,' her friend replied as she began to open cupboards and drawers.

'What exactly are you looking for?'

'I'll know it when I find it,' Ravenna replied enigmatically.

Eve sighed.

Double doors with reinforced glass windows lay ahead, and pushing one she found it open. Inside the air was stale and musty. She wandered, fascinated in a shop-of-horrors kind of way, taking in the long forgotten microscopes and abandoned centrifuges. To her right lay a glass fronted room with a bundle of discarded warning tape lying beside it on the floor.

Quarantined – it was like something from a low-rent B-movie, only this was horribly real. She paused, glancing back to see Ravenna examining a file in the previous room through the tiny window. She turned her attention back to the door. The rooms had clearly been locked down after the investigation, but the discarded tape squarely suggested there was no longer any real threat - and despite her concerns curiosity got the better of her.

She turned the handle and to her surprise found the door opened. It was oddly cool inside, lit dimly by the light of the room she stood in. She paused on the threshold, squinting into the gloom - this place hadn't been used for months. She moved into the open doorway. There was neatly stacked equipment on the desk below the plate glass window and microscopes covered with polythene bags; a row of sterile booths was set against the far wall.

Intrigue took hold of her and she took a step forward letting go of the door as she did so, her feet making prints across the dusty floor. She could almost imagine the place brightly lit and alive with activity, filled with researchers working quietly as they concentrated on their dangerous test subjects. She thought again of Nicky Green, the PhD student put on permanent sick leave and Sayeed Mohala who had died – surely if the cause *was* smallpox there was no way they would have been able to gain access, even with Dr Rembrandt's card?

As she stepped forward something caught her eye. Hers were not the only footprints to mar the dusty floor; someone had clearly entered recently, leaving a discernible trail toward a locker by the sterile cabinets. She felt her heart skip, wondering suddenly if this *was* where Mohala had been infected, but as she did so heard the door click shut behind her.

She gasped, her musings forgotten, and turning briskly glimpsed a figure flash past into an adjoining room.

'*Ravenna?*'

But the time traveller was still examining documents, just visible through the double doors. With a sting of concern she lunged for the handle, then swore under her breath. It wouldn't budge.

Ravenna

R avenna put down the file she had been flipping through, stepping forward to examine the heavy double doors to the sterile lab. They had clearly been taped closed at some juncture, but the tape had been recently removed.

She frowned thoughtfully then pushed inside. The room itself contained much more scientific equipment than the last – clearly the business end of the laboratory's research. It made no sense. It had been easy enough to gain access – too easy – and there was little if any sign of an attempt to decontaminate the office facilities.

She sighed and ran her fingers through the dust on the nearest bench. Some instinct told her that this was not the place – that she had been wrong about the source of the contamination and yet …

'Wells?' she called absent-mindedly, but there was no answer. She sighed in frustration glancing into the musty room ahead, but there was no sign of the palaeontologist anywhere. Just silent work benches and glass fronted sterile cabinets. She moved forward with a frown, switching on a bank of lights as she stood surveying the lifeless space.

'Wells, what on earth are you ..?'

An inter-com began to ring and she glanced up sharply. There was a large grey telephone unit attached to the wall to her left and a green light was blinking intermittently in time with the ring. She lifted the receiver.

'Hello?' she began, frowning as she knotted her fingers into the connecting spiral of wire.

'Ravenna!' exclaimed a familiar voice, 'it's me ...'

'Eve?'

She became aware of a dull knocking sound, mirrored on the window to her side, and with a sinking feeling turned her gaze to the glass fronted chamber to her immediate left. Eve Wells was stood with her left palm pressed against the grimy glass. 'Ravenna ... I'm trapped in here – someone just locked me in!'

*

Eve heard Ravenna swear softly in ancient Greek.

'Wells?

'The door,' she replied shakily, '– I can't get the door open!' She knew she was starting to panic, struggling to control the fear rising within her.

'And you say someone locked it?'

'Yes – I … I mean I think I saw someone.' She saw Ravenna take a step to her right and heard the mechanism rattle violently. 'Can you pick it?'

The dark haired woman shook her head.

Eve took a shaky breath, 'someone's been in here before us – the tape's been removed and …'

Ravenna's look silenced her and when she spoke her tone was serious: 'Wells - listen … someone clearly does not wish us to know about this place.' She shot a glance towards the door to her left.

'You don't say!' she returned bitterly, 'just get me out of here before someone finds us!'

Ravenna seemed to hesitate. 'Wells – listen to me … I cannot.'

'What?'

Ravenna hesitated. 'Someone clearly wanted something from this room … and if I am right about my Russian connection, I'm afraid there is a very real chance you have been exposed to the virus.'

Eve just stared open mouthed. 'You don't seriously think ..!' She felt her skin begin to crawl.

'If so, minor symptoms will manifest themselves in a handful of hours … the worst will appear in twelve days - a fever, the blisters - you will be dead in three weeks.'

'Don't sugar-coat it!' Eve shot back, unable to take it in. *Exposed to the virus.* Her hands were beginning to tremble, but she ignored the sensation. 'At first it will seem like you have a cold – a fever …'

'So what do we do?' she cried desperately, running her fingers through her hair, 'just sit here for twelve days waiting to see if I'm going to die!'

The line was silent for a moment.

'I must think Wells … consider …' Eve felt terror lurch in her chest. 'You say someone else was in the lab?'

Eve looked at her anxiously. 'I think so - yes …'

Ravenna's voice was strained when she spoke again. 'Wells … though there is no certainty you have been exposed I cannot take the risk … believe me, I would give anything for it to be me in that room instead of you, this should not have happened.' Eve swallowed, unable to reply. 'I have failed you Eve Wells, my time here is long over-due and I have no-one – but you …'

Her thoughts leapt to Adam … her family – her parents. Still words evaded her. A part of her wanted to yell at the dark haired woman, another to break down and cry, but she felt only numbness, a strange detached weariness as if she was watching a documentary: her mind totally unwilling to believe the horror of the situation she was trapped in. She closed her eyes.

'So I'm stuck here?'

'For the moment.'

Eve took a shaky breath, trying to think clearly. 'And there's a good chance this isn't the source of the infection?'

'A very good chance Eve Wells, but I cannot take the risk ...'

'There's nothing in the historical record about a smallpox outbreak in 1997!' she insisted desperately, 'Hell, how did you even know this Mohala guy had died?'

She heard Ravenna take a measured breath. 'Eve Wells, there are some things which for your own safety you can never know - but I *can* tell you this: that the shape of reality is continually changing – that unexpected anomalies forever present themselves - off-shoots and side-alleys of what you perceive as reality ...'

'But Ravenna ...' She broke off, the question dying on her lips as she failed to frame it. It was all too much for her to take in – the total incredulity of it - and yet the horrifying certainty that what was happening was mortally real. 'So the guy who died – the researcher Sayeed – he may have been alive in our time, and then suddenly reality changed: there was a leak in this lab and ...'

'Maybe.'

'And Dr Rembrandt, his supervisor, perhaps he..?'

'Perhaps yes,' Ravenna replied, her voice tinny through the telephone's receiver, 'Perhaps Rembrandt is involved – maybe he has connections with Soviet Russia and Mohala discovered it? Maybe he was in possession of smallpox from Zagorsk – but maybe not. Perhaps he was infected in another place entirely and bought it back to this hospital?'

Please God! She willed then forced herself to consider the problem. 'But I still don't understand his crazy last words - what filthy rags? This place is dusty I guess, but it was left empty – sterile when it was quarantined - there are no rags anywhere?'

The line went silent and for a moment she feared they had been cut off. She stood briskly, panic flaring.

'Ravenna - are you still ..?'

The dark haired girl was still watching her from the other side of the glass, brows knitted.

'Yes Wells, that's it!'

'What?' she replied, her own face wrinkling with confusion.

'*Their filthy rags … unable to understand why they were down there!*'

'Maybe he was just hallucinating, some kind of feverish comments …'

'No Wells, that's it! That is why the room in which you are trapped is so clean - there are no rags here …' She turned and glanced briskly towards the door.

'What – *Ravenna!* I don't understand?'

'I must go Eve Wells – *now* – but I will be straight back for you, yes?'

She felt terror sting her gut. 'Ravenna, please, what on earth …' She began to rattle the handle violently.

'Sorry, there is no time!' And to her horror she saw the time traveller let the receiver drop to dangle against the wall.

'Ravenna!' she yelled, thumping her palms against the window, but the athletic figure was already making for the doorway.

'Ravenna!'

With a sob of frustration she pressed her forehead against the glass.

*

Eve slumped against the wall and sat staring.

Though she tried to breathe evenly, her mind was racing, her breath coming in swift unsubstantial gasps. What if she had the disease - was there a retroviral cure? Her thoughts shot forwards, accelerating at the speed of light – and what if she was discovered trapped in the lab – or worse, what if she could never leave the room - not without professional medical help! And if she did would she spread it to her own age?

Her mind returned to a documentary she had seen about Cortés and the New World – how the Spanish Conquistadors had bought Western diseases to the Aztec kingdoms which had wiped out thousands, a quarter of the population – including the emperor Cuitláhuac succumbing to the smallpox epidemic their presence had unleashed.

Some instinct made her push back her sleeves, terrified she would see some rash or blistering, but there was nothing. She suppressed a sob of despair - and what about Adam? She reached for her phone instinctively, but knew that it was impossible. Decades separated them – realities. The horror of it seemed to leave a vacuum inside her which she could barely stand to face. She'd never see him again, never be able to touch him ... she forced herself to get a grip – there was every chance she hadn't been infected - and yet ...

She tried to distract herself by studying the tiles of the wall in front of her, neat rows of clinically white squares about the size of her palm. She let out a troubled sigh. Was this it? Was this all she would know for the remainder of her short life? A strength sapping weariness seemed to take hold of her, more worries gnawing at her frightened mind: and if she were found, their secret would be discovered, the dangerous truth of where they had come from would be revealed.

She took a breath to clear her head. Where the hell was Ravenna? She sat, listening, straining her ears.

Silence.

She let out a long breath, trying to pull herself together, running her eyes along the line of sterile cabinets with their built-in protective gloves. It looked like it had been disused for weeks – if not months. She thought again of the technician who'd lost his life: what on earth *had* he meant by filthy rags – it made no sense – and even if Dr Rembrandt had brought smallpox from Zagorsk, then how had Mohala contracted it?

She sat listening to the odd noises which echoed through the huge building, the creaks and groans of air-conditioning pipes and twisting heating ducts. Something seemed to echo in the distance – footsteps perhaps – and the sound of voices – or was it just her tired imagination? She lay her head against the wall and closed her eyes, trying not to think of Adam, trying not to think of what would happen when Ravenna *did* return – and then she saw it.

The shadow moved neatly across the strip of floor in front of her, pausing as if someone had stopped to look inside.

'Ravenna?'

She twisted, craning her neck to squint through the grimy glass, but before she could make eye contact the figure had turned away.

'Oh God!'

The face vanished, disappearing from the window as if satisfied the situation was under control. She hesitated, blinded by panic, then recovered herself and rose to bang on the reinforced glass.

'Hey! Stop …' but the door ahead was already swinging closed. *Oh god – Ravenna!*

She began to pound on the reinforced glass with all her strength, hoping she was close enough to hear.

'Ravenna!'

Confrontation

At 5'2" the man's size 'L' hazmat suit Ravenna Friere had found was a poor fit, but her mind was elsewhere, oblivious to the discomfort. There were portable breathing apparatus racked in a steel locker, visored gasmasks and thick sterile gloves. Her mind was racing, darting and spiralling between the two women she had endangered, lurching between the questions and the possibilities – and yet whatever the outcome she needed to protect herself from the virus – *whichever way she decided.*

Scanning the last page of the ring-bound contamination protocols she left the lab, discarding the folder as she headed for the basement. Again she cursed her own stupidity, angry at her own lack of foresight. Yet this building was clearly the source of the infection – and someone was here – someone who was well aware of that fact. Her thoughts flew to Polly Nightingale, praying that she was not already too late.

She made for the stairs, cursing the encumbrance of the uncomfortable suit, but as she passed through the fire door an unexpected sound stopped her in her tracks.

'Hey!' called a voice which echoed around the stairwell she'd entered. She twisted, tensing. A figure stood behind her, backlit by the corridor's amber glow. *Dr Rembrandt.* 'Stop right there!' he continued, his voice muffled by her suit's protective hood - his expression an unsettling blend of anxiety and indignation, 'What the hell are you doing? You shouldn't be in here after business hours … nor should your friends!'

Panic flared – she had to get to Polly, ' … 'and take off that damned suit - this hospital is virus free – I'd stake my life on it.'

'Would Mohala have said the same?' Her voice sounded overly loud within the confines of the mask. He took a half-step towards her, the door closing noisily behind. 'What are you really up to Doctor,' she continued loudly, 'what did you come back into the lab to find?'

He hesitated. 'Who the hell *are* you?'

'That is irrelevant,' she replied,' – if you want to live, leave this place … leave now.'

He took another step, his face etched with tension. He was *not* going to leave. 'I don't know who the hell you're working for, but this ends right *here*.' Her gaze fell to the torch held truncheon-like in his tensed right hand. There was desperation in his eyes – the look of a man on the brink. He was not about to go to the authorities.

She sensed him tensing, saw the look of deliberation as he considered the line he was about to cross: she readied herself - she had brought down bigger men in the amphitheatre of the city whose name she had taken – used her speed and agility to the astonishment of the roaring crowd: she was already three moves ahead, subconsciously calculating the speed and force of the strike which would disarm him.

'Don't!' she called firmly, 'walk away or this will end badly for you.' He was an academic – a medical man. 'I am here to help you – to stop this thing and save my friends …'

He swung at her and she lashed out with her arm - but to her surprise he sidestepped. She grunted, realising her mistake too late. The suit's bulk was a

247

handicap she had not accounted for, her perception clouded by her concerns.

She jerked back clumsily, struggling to keep her weight centred as he rounded on her. He swung again and she blocked with her elbow - but he was ready for her and with a shove sent her thudding against the banister. She gasped and twisted, kicking out with her left foot but he barged again and then she was falling, stomach lurching as her shoulder smashed into a step, twisting head-over-heels as she fell - and then the world went black, the sound of a swinging door filling the stairwell as heavy footsteps disappeared into the darkness.

Polly

Polly Nightingale paused, listening.

Every sound seemed amplified in the dimly lit corridor, the noise of her own breathing discernibly loud within the echoing strip-lit space. She swallowed, straining her ears, still unable to shake the unsettling memory of the moment Dr Rembrandt had grabbed for her arm in the bar. She forced the thought away. Some instinct told her he was clearly involved in Sayeed's death, but in what way she could not fathom. He was clearly troubled, confused by what had happened within his lab – and yet … Her thoughts turned to the miles of twisting corridor ahead. She could easily imagine the young man wandering the lonely walkways, lingering in each room as he checked and ticked off each box and piece of equipment.

She sighed. If Sayeed had somehow been infected down here then where? She walked a little further, her boots tapping noisily, then paused again, sure she heard someone behind.

Nothing. Just echoing emptiness and the bright reflections of the corridor lights. She took a breath to steady her nerves. More than once she'd felt certain she had heard footsteps in the cavernous network of corridors – heard voices even – and yet she'd found not a trace of another soul either in her own moment or the past. She shook her head – just her mind playing tricks.

She stood listening, closing her eyes. The space around her was as quiet as the grave and yet … she frowned, straining her mind, sensing as much as seeing, knowing something was not as it should be. A year ago she would have decried Ravenna for following hunches, but of late she had learned to trust her instincts more and more. She felt her attention drawn to the room to her right, the wooden door ajar. Swapping her torch to her left hand she reached for the handle, hesitated for a moment, then pulled it open with a thudding heart. Nothing – just dust and empty boxes. She shook her head – it was a wild goose chase. She turned her gaze to the corridor with a sigh. Up ahead the ceiling lights had failed leaving a ten foot stretch bathed in shadow.

She frowned.

There was something different about this empty stretch – more than just the gloom - something she couldn't put a finger on. It was as if she could see Sayeed emerging from the darkness, pausing on the threshold, panicking as he struggled to understand what he had seen. She laughed softly – she'd been hanging around Ravenna too long - had become too used to the madness of what she did and yet ... she turned to glance back along the well-lit section behind her, unable to shake the sensation that it somehow felt *different*.

A low sob seemed to come from one of the rooms ahead.

'Hello?' she frowned.

She listened for a moment longer then stepped forward, filling the corridor with her echoing footsteps, watching as her shadow crept out in front of her - a long and spectral form. A room lay to her right opposite a stack of disused chairs. She lifted her torch, pausing before shining it into the doorway. 'Hello?'

Just blackness. She sighed, chiding herself for letting her imagination run away with her, wishing she had a map or some reference point to go by. Aside from the untidy stack of plastic chairs and a few stacked boxes the corridor was empty – completely unworthy of note - and yet, as she took a last look at the open doorway, something made her hesitate - sure there was something unusual about the room. She shone her torch in a wider arc - certain that she could hear a muted groan deep within. The back of her neck began to prickle.

'Hello?'

Something fell to rattle noisily in the corridor behind her and she whisked around, torch beam jerking – but there was no one. She stood breathing rapidly, straining her eyes and ears, but the length of corridor was utterly empty. She let out a breath and turned towards the door, struggling to shake the sense that someone was watching her, bracing herself as she concentrated on the gloom - preparing for what she sensed was about to happen.

She clicked off her torch, and with a last glance at the silent world of incandescent lighting stepped into the cloying darkness, allowing the blackness to envelop her mind.

*

It was a warm spring morning, the low sun creating a halo of diaphanous light where it broke through the morning mist. She passed between green-budded hawthorn hedges, animals lowing somewhere close at hand: the air was painfully fresh. Almost out of nowhere a building loomed into view, low thatched eaves and a rickety door, the muddy ground around it well-trampled. Swallows darted in and out of a tightly woven nest.

She paused, heart thudding – again that sense that someone was following her – she turned her head, glancing back through the hazy dew soaked morning, but there was no-one. She swallowed, turning her attention back to the tumbledown dwelling, somehow knowing she had to enter, and bracing herself stretched out a hand.

Gloom engulfed her and it took a few moments for her eyes to adjust.

She stood in a low plastered space, light filtering through shuttered windows and cracks in a steeply thatched roof. It could have been any time from the sixteenth century to the nineteenth – just ragged people in ragged clothes in a dark and stinking hovel. *A breach in time*.

'Mercy mistress,' a voice called from ahead of her, 'in Jesu's name, give us succour!'

Several people lay within, bundled shapes on low straw pallets. 'Please Miss in God's great name!' The place stank foully.

She stepped forward covering her mouth, compassion momentarily overriding her concern.

'The red plague,' a woman muttered from beside the hearth, her face lit dimly by a rush-light stuck into the wall, 'bring the physic Miss, pray Jesu for us ...'

Her eyes fell on a pitiful bundle at the bottom of the nearest bed - a child shivering by an adult's feet. She knelt, her instinct to comfort the girl, but as she pulled back the blanket she realised her mistake.

'Oh god!'

The girl's face and arms were disfigured by a mass of pustules, the spots pressing in so close as to make her body seem swollen. *'Oh hell!'*

She stumbled back, horrified. It *was* smallpox – the most virulent airborne infection on the planet - the corner of the threadbare blanket fell from her grip.

'I beg you help my girl, young mistress, I beg you if you have a heart – if there's any mercy in your spleen!'

She felt her breath begin to come in quick ragged gasps. This was what had killed Sayeed Mohala – this was what the unfortunate young man had found - stumbling into the past as he had inventoried the stores, he had been exposed to the disease, bringing it back to the twentieth century. That was why there was no trace of smallpox in the lab.

'Water Mistress, *I cry you mercy* – bring water from the well to quench us.'

She turned, horrified, her mind reeling, knowing she had to get away. Chinks of light revealed a rickety side door and she stumbled outside in a daze, trying to steady her breathing. She was already as good as dead. Her mind raced – desperate to be home, desperate for the safety of the present, but even as she thought it, she knew she couldn't go back – knew she could never see the others, would never ...

A figure stepped out from behind the blackthorn ahead of her and she gasped with the shock of it.

'*Polly!*'

Ravenna stood barely twelve feet away in the hawthorn's shade haloed by brilliant sunlight. Hope rose only to be crushed almost instantly by the impossibility of going back to her own time. She was exposed – infectious.

'Don't come any closer!' she yelled desperately, '– get back – keep away!'

'Polly!' the Mediterranean woman repeated urgently, 'don't go inside … this is what Sayeed found – the smallpox did not come from the lab!'

'It's too late,' she replied desperately, taking a step away from her friend, 'I've touched their blankets … *their filthy rags.*'

'Nightingale …' Ravenna said bleakly, but Polly shook her head.

'You're hurt,' she observed. The time traveller touched a hand to the livid cut across her lip.

'Rembrandt confronted me – I fell …'

Polly swallowed anxiously, fear flaring. 'He's here in the building? You have to stop him!' But the time traveller shook her head.

'It is too late Nightingale ...' she said taking a step towards her, the protective hood of the suit she wore held loose in her hand.

'No!' she yelled, beginning to back away, 'don't come any closer!'

'I am committed now,' the time traveller said resolutely, 'he tried to harm me then fled, my suit was compromised in the fall – there is every chance I have the virus already.'

Polly shook her head. 'No! You've got to stop him - close the rift.'

Ravenna took another step.

'Go!' she forced herself to yell, 'If anyone finds out about this we're looking at a widespread epidemic – hundreds will die ... thousands!'

'*Polly* ...'

She felt the inevitability of it lie heavy in her gut like a stone – a physical knot of dread and despair. 'You've got to seal this rift and get Eve out of here,' she said, forcing her voice to be calm.

Ravenna shook her head. 'No Nightingale – we must get you out - I know a specialist who can help – a team in Zurich – they have all the necessary equipment.'

'You can't!' she called back urgently, 'we can't take the chance that Rembrandt might …' She broke off and closed her eyes, feeling dread overwhelm her, blinking away the tears which stung her eyes. She felt tired now, weak and nauseous, '*you can't* – the more people we have to involve – the more who know …'

'We will lie!' her friend replied with uncharacteristic desperation, 'create a plausible story tagged to the death of Sayeed Mohala.' She took a couple of paces towards her.

'No,' she implored, '– *please* … we've got to stop Rembrandt … if he even suspects how Mohala really contracted smallpox …'

Ravenna paused, and in that heartbeat of momentary hesitation Polly felt hopelessness overwhelm her. Her friend would leave her – would follow Rembrandt and do the right thing - and she would die. It was the only way and both of them knew it. The rift had to be sealed and to do that her life would be forfeit. When Ravenna spoke it was little more than a whisper. 'Polly …' The time traveller took another step across the dew laden grass, her boots leaving dark footprints against the silvery fronds.

'Please - don't come any closer!' They were barely four yards apart, bathed in the warmth of the still spring morning. It was beautiful, painfully so. Polly swallowed and took a shaky breath. 'It's funny,' she said mustering an ironic smile, 'I'd always feared we'd be the ones who'd carry some infection back into the past, some modern bacteria which would cause havoc ...'

'I will fix this Nightingale Girl!' the Mediterranean woman replied resolutely, 'I will make things right!'

Polly suppressed a sob. 'Just ...' she took a shaky breath, 'just close this rift.'

Her friend nodded. 'But not quite yet ... you will wait for me, yes?' She began to turn away.

'Don't!' she called almost angrily, 'do it now!' Her pulse began to race as she struggled with the memory of what she had seen in the cottage – the memory of what awaited her: disfigurement and delirium – maybe blindness and death. She would never see her home again – never return to the present. 'Seal the damned rift Ravenna!'

The time traveller continued to walk away.

'*Ravenna!*' The blood was hissing in her ears – her heart thudding out of control.

The Mediterranean girl paused and turned towards her, framed by the sun's bright aura. 'I will close this rift, Polly Nightingale – but not yet ... I will go now – and you must stay alive! Stay alive to stop anyone walking through this door until the time comes for it to be sealed.'

'*Ravenna!*' she called desperately, but her friend was already vanishing into the blinding light of the future – centuries away.

She sat heavily, wiping perspiration from her brow with the back of her hand as her thoughts raced out of control. *Just stay alive*. And then, as the swallows chirruped above her, she wept.

Eve

Eve jerked awake with a start. She had clearly been sitting against the wall for so long her despair had turned to exhaustion and she had slept.

She sat stiffly nursing sore limbs then remembered the full horror of where she was with a sickening rush. *Smallpox!* She pulled up the sleeves of her jacket with a desperate jerk and almost sobbed with relief. No rash, no fever - *she was safe!* She almost laughed out loud – but then she frowned as two thoughts struck her at almost exactly the same time. The air was fresh and cold – and the door was open. With a groan she pulled herself upright and stood trying to clear her head. So where was Ravenna?

The building was silent as she left the lab – deathly so - her feet echoing horribly as she trod cautiously along the empty corridors, her shadow casting strange shapes across the highly polished floor. Where the hell were Polly and Ravenna? And who had opened her door - and then a horrible thought struck her – what if they were dead? What if they'd stumbled across the source of the infection and …

She'd come to a broad crossroads of corridors and a brightly lit room lay before her, visible between open double doors. Long rows of chairs were arranged either side of a central aisle which terminated in a colourful geometric mural. It was clearly some kind of meeting room – no, a chapel – and a solitary figure was sitting mid-way along the right hand side.

'Hello?' she called nervously, but the figure didn't move. She stepped forward and was bathed almost instantly in a sense of quiet and space – an utter emptiness.

The solitary figure was sitting head bowed - praying perhaps. *'Hello?'*

As she continued forward she slowed her pace, feeling her face wrinkle into a confused frown. It was Ravenna. The time traveller was sitting forward, hands clenched in front of her mouth as if in prayer, but drawing nearer, Eve became aware of the audible hiss of pounding dance music. She paused by her shoulder and frowned. 'Ravenna?'

Sensing her presence the Mediterranean girl glanced up, popping out one of her ear buds.

'You're hurt?' Eve observed with a frown, seeing the cut across the time traveller's lip, '... what's going on?'

Ravenna coughed into her hand then looked up at her slowly. 'I am meditating Dinosaur Girl.' She seemed agitated – distant.

'I saw Rembrandt,' she began urgently, 'he locked me in the room.'

'I know,' the time traveller replied impassively, almost as if it was irrelevant. Eve hesitated.

'Where's Polly?'

Ravenna seemed to ignore the question. 'You are still alive, yes?'

Eve frowned, 'yes, I woke up in the room and the door was open ..?'

Ravenna seemed unmoved by this detail. 'You do not appear to be symptomatic Eve Wells – no feverishness, no blisters in your mouth ... so happily, you are alive.'

Eve just looked at her. 'What about the rift – the virus?'

Ravenna hesitated. 'I have been exposed to the virus Wells.'

'What?' She stepped back instinctively.

'I made a foolish mistake Dinosaur Girl, it should have been me who investigated the basement, my wits were slow.' She broke off and sighed bitterly. '*It should have been me* – I have already lived more days than any should be allowed …'

Eve felt an unexpected wave of dread wash over her, a cold thrill of terror.

'Where's Polly?'

'Polly is in the hospital stores below us,' Ravenna said neutrally, 'and she will soon be dead.'

The silence of the chapel seemed momentarily deafening.

'What?' Eve exploded, feeling utterly horrified, '– what on earth do you mean?'

'You were right Eve Wells and so was Sayeed Mohala. There were no filthy rags in the lab, because they were "down there" – down in the basement – he had discovered an intermittent rift and that is why he could not understand what three ragged people were doing *down there* in stinking rags.'

Eve swallowed, feeling suddenly weak as her mind made the connection – Polly had just found them too. She had found them and had been exposed to the disease. 'Though technically she is no longer in this hospital – she is in some point centuries away, but ...'

'So what the hell are you sitting here for?' Eve exploded, 'Can't you just shift time around - do whatever crazy thing it is you do?'

'No Eve Wells ...'

Eve carried on regardless. 'Go back before this even began and make sure Polly never ...'

The time traveller glared up at her angrily. 'This is not some choose-your-own-adventure game, Wells,' Ravenna said in a tone which silenced her instantly. 'There are only so many times I can intervene – fewer and fewer trusted people I can call upon ...'

Eve stared at her in horror. 'But we can't just leave her – we can't ...'

265

'Rembrandt clearly knows something Wells … and I have lost him.'

She hesitated, barely able to take it in. 'But we can't just …'

The look in Ravenna's ancient eyes silenced her instantly.

'Do you think I do not know this Wells! Do you think my heart does not break for all I cannot do – that I do not weep for all those I could not save – for the family I left in the Warsaw Ghetto, for the child in the well before Hardrada's men came ..!' She looked away angrily, wiping her hand across her eyes. Eve felt her chest rise and fall. But they *couldn't* leave Polly!

'The die is cast Wells, our course set … I cannot just …' She broke off and sighed as if wracked by indecision and once more coughing into her hand. 'But there is a man I know – a physician from your time – a trusted friend with contacts.'

'So use them!' she shot back desperately, 'hell Ravenna, we can't just leave her!'

Ravenna turned her gaze to the prominent cross beyond the altar rail. She seemed to think for a moment then closed her eyes. 'The picture is bigger than you or I or Polly Nightingale, Eve Wells, infinitely bigger - an intricate web – and the slightest mistake …'

'You can't let her die!' Eve replied adamantly, unable to shake the horror which gripped her. Ravenna locked her with a fierce gaze.

'I must consider Wells … I must listen! The direction I receive is a lamp unto my feet not a 30,000 watt spotlight! I must tread where I am bidden … walk by faith …'

'But …'

'Leave me Wells – I must think. This is not a decision to be made by reason alone.'

Eve just stared, a part of her wanting to rant and yell – to scream at her that she had to get up and help Polly - to demand how she could even consider … but as she watched the time traveller put in her ear buds, gaze fixed firmly on the modernist steel cross, she knew it would be useless. The music began to hiss once more – a tiny sound amid the emptiness – and swallowing away the sting of desperation in her chest she turned towards the door.

Discovered

Polly wandered in a daze, exhausted beyond caring. She had lost count of how many days she had lived by the tumbledown farm – if it could be called living – keeping out of sight as she kept her lonely vigil. She shuddered, fighting weariness as she contemplated another night of broken sleep, torn between the mouse-infested hay loft and the discomfort of the hedge, hardly daring to go near the now-silent hovel. The pitiful moans had long since ceased and the world was all birdsong and lowing cattle. She wiped her eyes with her hands.

How long would it be she wondered: how long 'til she too succumbed? Her appetite had long since vanished, and she had abandoned her meagre subsistence from the farmstead's stores - no taste for salted meat and apples – keeping herself alive with water from the well. She took a shaky breath; her symptoms were worsening, the fever making her shiver away the darkness hours - *how long?*

She pushed the thought away. At least she was alone - the farm was outlying and isolated - and save for the occasional wagon on the road no-one had appeared in the fields nor darkened the track which led to the lane. That at least was some consolation. But they would come. How long before some neighbour arrived to find out why the cows were not in pasture or some parson called checking his parishioners? She turned her gaze to the hayrick longing suddenly to be home.

Swallows swooped playfully before the setting sun; flies buzzed lazily. She took a breath, weakness overwhelming her - but somehow she didn't care. Tomorrow she would check the rift again, see if it was sealed. She sighed. Until now she had been able to keep her sanity by forcing that question from her mind, half longing half dreading that Ravenna would return. She slumped down in the long grass beside the hedge, the tranquillity somehow unbearable. Her existence was a dream, her former life – her modern life – like a fondly remembered story; a childish memory tinged with nostalgia. She closed her eyes but as she did so something skittered in the orchard beyond the hedge.

She took a breath, hardly daring to move. The cattle were lowing noisily and the geese were hissing by the pond. Someone was approaching the farm, boots crunching loudly across the dry yard – and there was movement behind - muffled voices. Her heart began to pound: a whole group of people. With an effort she pulled herself upright, edging forward, hoping to keep step with them; squinting out from the shelter of the ditch below the hedge just in time to see a figure disappear into the hovel. Her heart skipped. There were two of them at least, and as she blinked against the dazzling sun, she became aware of more dark figures fanning out from the gate - ghostly silhouettes amid the tumble-down buildings. She shuddered. The men seemed huge and monstrous to her exhausted mind – almost inhuman. She took a breath, afraid she was becoming delirious.

Movement sounded close at hand and she flattened herself into the foliage. Someone was in the orchard behind her. She lay heart pounding, hardly daring to breathe as heavy boots passed close by then stopped barely a few feet from where she lay. She held her breath, pulse racing, aware of the rustle of clothing and the buzzing of flies. The seconds passed, and then, to her relief, she sensed the person move away to her left.

She lay, wheezing, peering out with bleary eyes. The figures were moving, two of them pausing to exchange some words - strange shapes against the darkening yard - monsters in the twilight. She took a breath, feeling suddenly exhausted. With luck they would miss her – find the dead in the hovel and hurry away to avoid the red plague. Sweat stung her eyes: she was shivering, struggling for breath, and as a third figure joined them, the urge to cough began to grow steadily within her. She cursed, clamping her mouth shut, but the pressure began to build within her chest, the impulse becoming overwhelming.

If only they would move on! She had to hold it together – but it was no good, and unable to supress the urge any longer she doubled as the reflex wracked her shoulders, struggling and gasping as a fit of coughing overwhelmed her. Movement sounded almost immediately to her left. There were voices, feet running. She knew she had to do something – knew she had to get away - but the darkness seemed to pluck at her, the twilight growing dusky as she tried to crawl away.

'*No!*' she coughed, '*please!*'

Shadows fell across her, but she was sinking, descending into the blackness of her fatigue, struggling feebly in her exhaustion as she sensed them crowd

271

around. 'Stop – get away from me!' Then there were strong hands grasping her, shapeless figures silhouetted against the dying sun.

She moaned, feeling herself slipping into nightmares as they lifted her.

Eve

E ve forced her emotions into check as she dragged her eyes from the tangle of medical equipment which surrounded her stricken friend. Polly Nightingale lay motionless, a fragile figure beyond the reinforced glass of the isolation booth, head rolled to one side as she slept.

'Is she going to be okay?'

Ravenna blinked long lashes over her dark eyes.

'She is stronger than she looks Eve Wells – as are you.'

Eve swallowed. She didn't feel strong. Barely five hours ago she had expected to be the one in ITU – had known she'd never see Adam again. She took a breath, fighting an upwelling of emotion. She had tested negative to smallpox but had been given the vaccine and put on a course of anti-viral treatment as a precautionary measure. She shuddered, hugging her arms around her body as she watched her friend stir and murmur. Polly's mouth and stomach were blistered, but beyond that her symptoms seemed to be lessening by the hour.

'She is indeed strong Miss Friere,' said a warm voice behind them, 'treasure in earthen jars.'

'Rashid my old friend,' Ravenna said warmly, twisting to embrace the tall man who had joined them. Eve glanced away as they said a few words in Arabic. The last few hours had been a blur in which she had lost track of both when and where she was – long past caring who knew of their secret and how. 'I can never thank you enough.'

The thoughtful specialist gazed back at Ravenna seriously. 'No Miss Friere, it is nothing compared to all you have given over time,' then smiled and turned towards Eve. 'And how are you feeling today Dr Wells?'

'Good thanks.' She nodded self-consciously, feeling suddenly like a very small part of a picture of which she knew only fragments, 'just tired.'

'As is to be expected,' the tall doctor smiled. 'Eat well, rest – make the most of the pool and the gymnasium. I'm afraid we must test you for the virus daily, but I'd estimate we could give you the all-clear in six weeks.'

Six weeks!

She forced a thankful smile, fighting the instinctive urge to reach for her phone. Eve hardly noticed him leave. *Over a month without Adam.*

'You'll see him soon enough Wells,' Ravenna grinned as if reading her mind, 'and as you know well enough, upon your return almost no time will have elapsed.' Eve bit back the response which shot to her lips. 'Don't even think it Wells,' the time traveller continued, turning to gaze at Polly once more, 'I have not so much as looked at a man for over ...'

'I get the picture,' Eve sighed, 'but the vow you took was your own choice ...'

The time traveller chose to ignore the comment. 'A six week spa break at this Swiss facility – and when you return it will be as if you have never been away,' she said lightly, 'It is win–win, yes?'

Eve nodded grudgingly, still unable to get her head around the fact: the insane truth that however much time she spent in the past she would always return to the same point she had left at that exact moment, no older - *unchanged*. She shot Ravenna a sidelong look. Each time they met she seemed rejuvenated – more perfect than she remembered. 'The longer you live Wells, the more you realise that sometime, the things we cling to are not always what we need.' She turned and put an unexpected hand on her shoulder. 'Take heart Wells, all will be made right in its proper time.'

Eve looked at her for a moment then let out a long sigh, struggling to get a grip on herself in the face of what had just happened. 'And thank you,' the time traveller added deliberately. Eve looked at her questioningly, 'for forcing my hand ...'

Eve held her gaze for a moment, then looked away, hardly able to believe how rash she'd been - lost in the visceral memory of that nightmare walk to the stairwell, the crazy snap-decision she had made.

'It was monolithically stupid of you to rush down to that basement room Wells, but it seems that in forcing my hand you led us on the better course.'

Eve said nothing, remembering Ravenna's searing anger as she had caught up with her in the dark corridor of the museum's basement. 'So what made you change your mind – about intervening?'

The time traveller stared fixedly at the prone form of their friend.

'You Eve Wells – *as* ever your naïve compassion cut through to the heart of the matter - as it is written: *love conquers all* – it is all we really have.'

Eve kept her gaze on Polly, unsure what to say. After a moment a question popped into her mind: 'And Doctor Rembrandt – did he really have something to do with the Soviet experiments at Zagorsk?'

Ravenna shrugged. 'He was concerned enough to come back for something in that lab.'

'And do you think he knows about the rift in time?'

Ravenna gazed at the reinforced glass in front of them, her reflected expression deeply troubled. 'That, Eve Wells, I do not know …' and as she looked down Eve saw genuine concern in her face, 'I pray that he does not.'

Beyond the glass Polly murmured and began to stir. 'I shall go now,' the time traveller said softly, disappearing as their friend opened her eyes.

'Morning,' said Eve pressing her palm to the glass, 'sleep well?' Polly yawned and sat stiffly, taking a breath before pressing the inter-com to reply.

'Pretty good – hell of a headache …' she paused to take a drink, '– you okay?'

Eve laughed and looked down. *What a question.* She managed a nod. Polly sipped her water then shot her a crooked smile. 'How's Vauncey?'

'Sorry?'

'Vauncey – the wild cat – did you manage to drop him off okay – at the museum?'

'Yes,' she replied with a puzzled grin, 'but why …'

'You don't want to know,' the curator replied, but continued before she could comment: 'did you find Rembrandt?'

Eve sighed. 'No – there was no sign of him by the time Ravenna got to you – but there hasn't been another case of smallpox since 1997 … as far as we know.'

Polly held her gaze then nodded. 'How's Ravenna?'

'Her usual self,' Eve grinned looking behind her, but the time traveller had gone, '- off again.'

Polly sat back and closed her eyes. 'I'm kind of glad I've got six weeks of enforced recuperation – I seriously need a break from this!' Eve returned a reluctant smile.

'Until the next time she needs us.'

Polly nodded. Until the next time.

Anomaly

'I see you're good to your word.'

The young woman's tone was casual and a little mocking. She looked cold in her smart black coat, despite her prominent fur hat, clearly a little frustrated to be where she was – exposed - out of place. She was gripping the rail tightly, he noticed, as the deck pitched beneath them, momentarily struggling to keep her composure as the vessel dipped towards the horizon. 'You still have it in your possession?'

Dr Rembrandt hesitated. Despite her disarming North American accent, there was something deeply unsettling in her penetrating gaze. He took a step forward, indicating the briefcase he had brought with a downward glance. The girl nodded. She wore red leather gloves, he noted, her fingers long and slender. He hesitated, glancing out across the near-empty deck of the cross-channel ferry before closing the distance between them.

'Don't look so worried,' she grinned as she took the briefcase in her scarlet-gloved hand, 'it's all over for you now.'

An icy wind had begun to pluck at the young woman's hair, stirring the fur of her hat as she pressed a small package into his hand. He tried to shake off the horrible misgivings which now tugged at him – the rash decision he had made. 'And the young woman you encountered ..?'

'Three women,' he replied, '– one of them called herself Rhodes, I didn't catch ...'

'No matter,' the girl cut in with a smile, leaning into the rail as she compensated for the roll of the ship.

'But the sample is intact, it doesn't explain how Sayeed ..?'

'Let it rest Dr Rembrandt,' the girl continued in her disarming tone, 'it's my problem now, not yours.'

'And the women, how on earth did they ..?'

The girl turned her gaze to the leaden waves. 'Like I say, it's my problem now Dr Rembrandt.'

He paused nervously, his gaze darting towards the lounge door. 'You can go now Doctor,' she added disarmingly, 'and don't worry about the woman you encountered, I've been aware of her and the help she receives for longer than you could imagine.'

Rembrandt nodded, then turned, mopping at the sweat which now beaded his forehead as he pocketed the package.

'God speed Dr Rembrandt,' the woman called lightly. He nodded, glad of the chill spray on his face, his vision beginning to blur as he staggered towards the cabin door.

Part 5

Valley of Dry Bones

God's Mirror

She paused, squinting, unsure if she was seeing correctly.

From across the valley the mouth of the cave shone like burnished glass - a hollow shimmer of blinding light, like a lens high up in a rocky cleft.

'*Here* – here *mademoiselle*, this is it – *ici, ici*!'

The dark-haired young woman frowned, downing her backpack as she gazed at the glittering point of light, unable to make sense of what she was seeing. She had spent enough time in this arid wilderness to know every nuance of the desert climate, every shimmer of heat, every trick of the light - but this was something different. She took off her cap to fan her face, pushing her sunglasses onto the top of her head.

'What is this Yusuf? What *am* I looking at?'

The local man seemed to ignore her comment, nodding and gesturing as he beckoned her to the lip of the rise on which they stood. 'Come – *ici mademoiselle!*'

She took another couple of steps, then stood staring, one hand shielding her eyes. If the patch of light had been horizontal she would have sworn that it was a sunlit pool – some kind of oasis – or at least an optical illusion of one, but this was high up against the steep and crumbling rocks, rippling way above the ground. A heat-haze perhaps – a mirage? But this pool was facing her – a great mirror of light. *God's mirror.*

'Like *Moise, oui?*'

She frowned at the grinning man, then realised.

The Jews and Christians spoke of a burning bush in the wilderness, a holy place where God had met the prophet. 'Ah, yes – *oui – shukran Yusuf - like Moses.*'

Sunday school stories flitted through her mind – long hours spent listening to those strange old tales, kicking her heels against the pew of the old Baptist church her grandma had insisted she take her to. The encounter of Moses in the wilderness – the deeds of the people of Israel. Ahead of her, Yusuf made the sign of the cross, then wrapping his robes tighter around his body began to descend.

'But Yusuf ..!'

'Come,' the guide replied with a gesture of his fingers, 'come *mademoiselle - Le Miroir de Dieu – viens ...*'

The guide was taking off his sandals, carrying them loosely in his left hand as he began to descend the hill on which they stood. She hesitated for a moment, surprised by his seeming lack of concern, his unexpected eagerness to visit the place renowned for mysteries, but as she donned her backpack a voice made her turn.

'*Wait!*'

She frowned, shielding her eyes with her hand, confused to see a tall figure silhouetted against the rocky outcrop behind her.

'Tarek?' she said pensively, confused by the unexpected presence of her colleague. It was barely 7 AM and she had left at the first light of dawn - he must have left camp almost immediately after her – had he been watching?

'Hey,' she laughed nervously, 'what's up - were you following me?'

'I was worried,' the tall palaeontologist said neutrally, 'it is early and when Mohammed said you had left with Yusuf before dawn ...'

'You don't seriously think I'd pass up an opportunity to see this?' she replied forcing a confident grin. 'When Yusuf said it had been seen again ...' the tall man returned a gentle smile which she could tell was equally fake, 'I mean, it's not every day you get to see a real-live miracle ...'

'Come, this is madness – old wives tales as you say – a trick of the light ...'

She shrugged. 'But it's a pretty cool story, right?'

The tall palaeontologist seemed to regard her thoughtfully. 'Mohammed says you are asking too many questions – unsettling the local volunteers. You know they regard this as a holy place?'

'I know,' she returned lightly, 'and I mean no disrespect.'

Tarek looked past her, his expression pensive as he gazed at the dusty valley, the shadows drawing back from the rocky outcrops as the sun rose steadily upwards. She followed his gaze, putting on her cap once more as she frowned at the silvery point of light, still visible across the narrow gorge. To all intents and purposes it appeared to be a literal wall of water – like the window of an aquarium – rippling slightly in the morning breeze.

'It's a hell of a phenomenon,' she breathed softly, 'you can see why so many stories …'

'But in light of what we have found?' her colleague warned.

She stared for a moment longer, gazing deep into the point of light, unable to drag her eyes away. She sighed, watching Yusuf's thin frame as he ambled towards the gorge. 'Let the man go – let him make his pilgrimage - it is not safe for you here.'

She turned sharply to meet Tarek's eyes then shifted her gaze to watch the figure picking his way towards the rocky cleft.

'I'm going,' she said firmly, setting her pack squarely onto her shoulders, 'I didn't get up at the crack of dawn for nothing!'

'Look, you must stop – do not follow this man, please Miss Wiedermann - in the light of what we've found …'

'Hell, that's exactly why I *am* going down there!' she laughed back adamantly, 'Don't be such an old woman Tarek – don't you want answers?'

But as she looked back to the gorge the point of light was gone – and the guide was nowhere to be seen.

Eve

'Hang in there – you're doing fine ... try to keep calm!'

The prone young woman groaned and shivered, moaning as the dark haired girl who crouched over her mopped the sweat from her brow.

'What ... where on earth ...'

'We are safe now,' the crouching woman said gently, 'we have water and shade and you can rest.'

The sandy haired woman groaned and tried to sit, but as she did so her stomach rolled once more. She lay back, aware of a tent-like structure above them, a jumble of equipment stacked at her side – but the light beyond was almost blinding - she felt her vision swim.

'What's happening ..?'

'It is heat stroke Eve Wells,' the dark haired woman said with a hint of frustration entering her voice. She was about her own age, maybe twenty-five, confident and athletic - and her presence inevitably meant the impossible was about to happen. 'You have a migraine – a little rest and some time to cool off and you will be fine.'

Eve turned her head and vomited again. It felt like her skull was splitting, her body grasped by an almost overwhelming weakness.

'I am not fine!' she moaned bitterly. At her side Ravenna Friere wrinkled her nose in mild disgust. '… I think my body's going into some kind of shock!' She wretched again, grasping her stomach as another heave of nausea wracked her guts. Barely three hours before she had been swathed in her parka, crunching through the snowy grounds of the University of the East Midlands' ornamental gardens, discussing a palaeontology conference paper with one of her eager post-grads, yet within moments of the young man's departure, Ravenna Friere had appeared and …

'Come on, drink some water, we must replace the fluids you have lost.'

Eve stared at the flapping awning. Whenever Ravenna Friere called on her she knew the world was about to be turned upside-down.

'It must be like forty degrees in the shade,' she gasped, 'and when I left the university it was skirting zero … I'm not sure I …' She vomited again, then gasping propped herself on one elbow to sip gingerly.

'I will concede that your system is struggling to adjust,' the enigmatic young woman said lightly, 'just try to rest – rest and drink …'

Eve took a shaky breath. One minute she had been shivering in the depths of an English winter and the next she had been bidden to step into … 'where the hell are we?'

'All in good time Wells.'

Eve looked at the dark haired girl indignantly.

'And how the hell did I get here? The last thing I remember was …' Hazy images of a blazing wind-blown desolation flitted through her mind, the sensation that she had been conveyed straight to hell.

'You fainted,' the Mediterranean woman replied a little disdainfully, 'I carried you over the rise and by God's grace we found our destination.'

Eve closed her eyes, trying to clear her head. 'You carried me … and what is our destination?' Some memory flashed back to her: struggling across a stony landscape carrying the bundle of her winter clothes, noisily lamenting the lack of a sun hat and factor sixty-five as Ravenna Friere marched ahead of her.

'All in good time – rest first, yes,' the time traveller said coolly, straightening into a ready crouch, 'you must sleep – now I know that you are not about to expire …' and with that began to get to her feet.

'No!' Eve demanded indignantly, 'no you don't - for the love of god will you please tell me what's going on?'

'Later Wells,' Ravenna Friere said lazily, slinging her rucksack over her shoulder, 'I have work to do – meantime you must sleep, yes?'

'Please! *Ravenna!*' But she hadn't the strength to sit.

'Just sleep Wells!' the enigmatic woman called from beyond the awning. She could hear her boots crunching away across the sandy ground. *Just sleep.*

Eve closed her eyes, praying that contrary to all the other insane experiences she had had with Ravenna Friere this would all be some crazy dream.

*

It was dusk.

Eve shivered as she crawled from under the sleeping bag which had been laid over her, blinking as she stooped out from beneath the flapping tarp. She felt utterly drained but otherwise recovered. She rubbed her eyes, trying to make sense of the world around her.

Long shadows lanced across a vast and table-like landscape, thrown by strange wind-weathered rock formations, mushroom like protrusions against a vast and endless sky. It was utterly captivating, but lonely and a little unsettling – an almost alien landscape. She shivered in the evening cool. Where the hell was she?

Her thoughts flashed back to the last time she and Ravenna had met, the sinking feeling as she had realised her knowledge would be called upon again.

'Hell, have you seen that girl over there, she's just climbed the new 8a ..!' Even at the climbing wall of the UEM's sports centre she was not safe – glancing up dumb-struck to see the athletic twenty-five year old pull off a ridiculously explosive lunge for a hold five feet above her.

'I greet you Wells,' Ravenna had smiled moments later - now hanging upside down, her feet hooked into an over-hanging hold. 'You are enjoying this pastime your man has introduced to you? It is good for your skinny frame, yes?'

'You are not having anything to do with Adam!' she had shot back instantly, but the dark haired girl ignored her, beginning a set of free-hanging sit-ups as she spoke.

'Fear not … Dinosaur Girl … your private … life … is your own sacred … kingdom …'

She had folded her arms across her chest in clear frustration, *'Look - what ARE you doing here?'*

Ravenna lowered herself onto the crash-mat below. *'There is trouble afoot Wells and for once I thought I would give you warning – and besides this is a good place to hang out and meet ripped guys, yes?'* Her gaze drifted to a couple of young men who were ambling past them.

Eve had rolled her eyes in despair. *'What do you mean - trouble ..?'*

'I have learned of a discovery – a most unsettling one.'

'And?' she had replied, already beginning to stack up her objections, but the dark haired girl had said no more.

'Just be ready,' the time traveller had warned as she had headed for the lockers, *'I will come for you when you are needed.'* And three days later, as she had been trudging through the drifting snow, Ravenna had indeed come for her.

The breeze changed direction and she became aware of voices to her right, laughter carrying on the wind. Four people stood framed against the last amber rays of the sunset, dark silhouettes against the purple landscape. One of them was Ravenna.

'Dr Wells!' her friend exclaimed in an enthusiastic Oxbridge accent at odds with her usual Mediterranean tones, 'how are you feeling?'

'Fine,' she shivered as Ravenna jogged over to join her, registering her bulky silhouette with mild confusion, 'but I'd be better if you'd tell me where on earth … hey, you're wearing my coat!'

The dark haired girl returned an unconcerned shrug, the breeze dragging languidly at loose strands of her hair; she looked comfortably snug in the down-filled expedition parka. 'It is proving most adequate for these plummeting night-time temperatures,' she said innocently.

Eve shivered again. 'Will you please stop *borrowing* my clothes!'

Ravenna raised an eyebrow, then slipped off the coat and handed it to her. 'As you wish Wells – but as I recall I bought you this jacket.' Eve made to protest, but Ravenna continued undeterred, 'and do not call me Ravenna, here I am …'

'Dr Wilding?' she said tersely as she struggled into her jacket, used now to the alias the time traveller used whenever she posed as a palaeontologist, 'what's your first name this time?'

'Something cute, yet refined – Beatrice,' she mused thoughtfully, 'Bea Wilding – yes, call me Bea, Wells - *Bea* will do nicely.' Eve rolled her eyes - and as ever she would act as her advisor, the scientific muscle to provide credibility to her cover story.

'So why are we here – in this desert?'

Ravenna retreated a few paces to pull a body-warmer from their makeshift shelter.

'This is Egypt,' she said, 'about one hundred miles from Cairo - but we are not here to see pyramids and pharaohs - nor raid tombs,' she added with a glint in her eye.

Eve sighed despairingly, following as they began to walk back towards the centre of the camp.

'And when ..?' It was hard to fathom if they were in the present or at some point in the past – the tents and equipment looked relatively modern, but out in such a wilderness it was difficult to tell.

'April 2014,' Ravenna replied casually, 'and somewhere you will feel right at home ... inhospitably barren landscape notwithstanding.'

A number of faces looked up at them expectantly as they neared the campfire around which the people now sat – three Westerners and about five locals in long robes and tightly wrapped head-gear.

'Look,' she whispered from the side of her mouth, '– just for once, will you please give me a heads-up ...' But as she spoke a good looking man in his late thirties rose to offer his hand.

'Dr Wells,' he began expressively in accented English, 'I hope you are feeling a little better, the desert sun can be harsh on the uninitiated.'

She smiled awkwardly. The speaker was dark haired and deeply tanned, his smile as charming as it was concerned. 'Forgive me, I am Professor Renato Saraceni of the Gardellino Institute in Milan.' She nodded warmly, leaning in to shake his outstretched hand, wondering suddenly if she was supposed to know who he was.

'It's a real pleasure to meet you at last,' she began, dreading he was going to question her about her own background, but to her relief he gestured to the girl at his side.

'And this is Brenna Wiedermann of the Maston Foundation, Illinois - she is on loan to us here and her forensic skills are proving invaluable.'

'Hey,' said a petite brunette little older than one of her PhD students, her dark eyes thoughtful in the firelight – a little guarded, Eve thought as they shook hands.

'And Dr Tarek Zalmoud our local expert – a true genius at interpreting this site - a specialist from Cairo working on …'

'You're too kind Renato,' said the slender man who took Eve's hand. He had a thoughtful expression for such a young man she noted, almost melancholy.

Behind them the fire crackled.

'You are up to some food Dr Wells? A little goat stew – fava bean puree?' She felt her guts begin to churn. 'Some flat bread perhaps?' She took some and nibbled gingerly.

As she ate, Professor Saraceni sat back and cocked his head to one side. 'So, you must tell me more about your research Dr Wilding, your interest is somewhat particular – as is the mystery we have unearthed.'

Ravenna smiled demurely, her teeth white in the firelight, and for a moment Eve wondered what on earth she was going to say – suddenly dreading that she would be forced to come up with a hasty backstory - but to her relief Brenna Wiedermann cut in.

'Come on Renato - it's getting late for site talk,' she said with a grin, 'tell me about life in the UK - I hear that funding is being cut real tight at English universities?' Yet something in her eyes told Eve she hadn't the stomach to discuss whatever it was they were here to help with.

As they made polite conversation Eve felt her thoughts begin to drift. She was cold and exhausted – and found herself longing suddenly to be at home with her fiancé. She turned her gaze to the star punctured skyline. Man, what would Adam say to see this – to be in such a remote place? She frowned as a sound met her ears. The breeze was getting up and the animals in the corrals behind them were starting to stamp and bray in agitation. She shot Ravenna a concerned look, but as if in answer Tarek Zalmoud began to collect the plates.

'Come friends, it's getting late …'

'Yes, we had better retreat to the safety of our beds!' Professor Saraceni added with a wry grin.

'Safety?' Eve repeated without thinking. Tarek Zalmoud paused as he took her plate.

'Because of the dragons,' Brenna Wiedermann cut in and the party laughed – but the young woman looked away briskly she noted, her smile clearly forced, and Eve tried to hide her own unease.

'It is because of what we are excavating here,' Zalmoud explained, reading her troubled expression, 'prehistoric remains weather out of the dry desert so readily that the locals have long since called this a place of dragons – the valley where the basilisk roamed …'

'*And* because of the strange stories,' the girl cut in pointedly. Eve felt Ravenna straighten at her words and forced her expression to remain calm. Saraceni was gazing at her thoughtfully, she noticed, his features eerie in the firelight, despite his amused smile.

'Yes - if it is strange stories you are after Dr Wells then you have come to the right place – this valley is notorious in its own way, and has many legends attached to it in both local Muslim and Coptic tradition – so I am sure you will not be disappointed!'

Ravenna laughed and Eve smiled politely, feeling suddenly chilled despite her coat. There was a strange look in his eye – something unsettling. She saw Brenna the research assistant look away anxiously.

'And so to bed.'

*

'What did he mean, strange stories – and why notorious?' Eve asked urgently as they stepped away from the fire.

Ravenna walked in silence for a few moments then stopped to look at her directly. 'Notorious because this Wadi is famous for unexplained disappearances Eve Wells – herders and explorers alike vanishing without trace - a place of dragons and demons.'

Eve just looked at her, then shivered as the breeze stirred her hair.

'Great,' she replied glibly, 'I'll sleep really well now.'

'My pleasure,' said the time traveller and without a word slipped inside their tent.

Nightmare

Eve awoke with a start, feeling utterly disoriented.

The sound of running feet and urgent voices filled the darkness beyond her shelter – someone was screaming.

'What ... what the hell's going on?'

Ravenna was already dressed, pushing through the flap of their tent, and bundling on her coat she followed in a daze, heart pumping.

Star punctured darkness filled her senses, the first grey slit of dawn separating land from sky across the horizon, and in the light of several torches she could just make out the troubled features of both Brenna Wiedermann and Renato Saraceni surrounded by a gaggle of anxious local men.

'I saw it!' the girl was exclaiming almost hoarsely, 'I was NOT dreaming!'

'Please Brenna, be calm,' she could just make out Saraceni replying, but his expression was less than consoling, gripping her tightly by both arms as he spoke.

'What's going on?' whispered Eve, anxiously, but before she could answer, the tall Egyptian – Zalmoud - appeared, speaking briskly with the local men, before steering the pair away towards the dark shape of the mess tent.

'Come on!' whispered Ravenna leading her a couple of steps closer and as the wind changed Eve heard Zalmoud's voice, annoyed and clearly disappointed.

'Tell me you did not go there again! Brenna, you must let this madness go!'

Eve walked in a daze, shivering as she focussed on the girl's troubled features. The girl was still trembling, clearly freaked out by whatever she had experienced, 'What were you thinking – you swore you would not go back there!'

'How could I let it go,' she shot back, '– not after Yusuf …'

But Saraceni put a hand on her arm, glancing towards them as he noticed their approach. 'Brenna! Calm yourself.'

She broke off, likewise noticing the approach of their lancing torch beams, and swallowed as if brought suddenly back to her senses. She shot the professor a troubled look before glancing quickly in their direction.

'What happened?' Ravenna began, adopting her Oxbridge accent.

Brenna was breathing erratically, her face pale in the moonlight.

'Nothing,' she said after a moment, 'just a bad dream ... too much sun and too many bones I guess.'

Eve blinked at her sceptically as the wind sighed around them, bringing with it the chatter of the local men and the braying of mules. Behind her Zalmoud glanced away, his expression hard to read.

'Come, you need rest Brenna,' Professor Saraceni said gently, but his tone strongly implied that refusal was not an option, 'we have all had enough excitement for one night. I am sorry we have woken you, ladies, my deepest apologies.'

Ravenna smiled.

'Not a problem Professor - Brenna ...' and catching her eye said, 'if you need company you can always ...'

'No, I'm good,' the girl replied briskly, 'just a crazy dream,' and with that disappeared towards her tent as Saraceni and Zalmoud bid them goodnight.

Ravenna sighed. 'If only we could speak to her alone ... something is not right here.'

They returned to their own tent in silence, but as Eve began to slip off her coat Ravenna caught her arm. 'What on earth are you doing Dinosaur Girl?'

'Going back to bed?' she whispered tersely, 'though I don't think I stand much of a chance after ...'

'Come, follow me,' Ravenna said gathering her backpack. 'We have to investigate while the trail is still fresh, yes?'

Eve frowned. '*What* – what trail?'

'Why the trail our young friend just made on her way to and from the creature she just saw.'

'What!'

'Come on Dinosaur Girl we have no time to lose!'

Eve shuddered as her gaze drifted to the dark world beyond the canvas – suddenly horrified by the thought of venturing into the night after what they had just witnessed. 'What creature – you still haven't ..?'

But Ravenna was already leading her out of the tent, tightening the straps of her pack as Eve struggled after her, wrapping her parka tightly round her body. 'Listen, Ra ... *Bea* ...' Her voice had become a whisper, breaking off as she saw movement to their right - a host of local men were just visible in the firelight and she ducked left, sure that one of them had looked her way.

'Come Wells, follow me,' said the time traveller briskly, 'and keep to the shadows, we do not want to be seen.' Eve swallowed away her fear.

Above her the desert sky was a vast and star-punctured vault, but the horizon was growing lighter – they hadn't got long - and shivering she quickened her pace, heading for the nearest rocky outcrop: a great bulwark of sandstone stark against the lightening sky. A part of her almost laughed at the madness of it: yet again they were tracking a monster.

'What?' Eve whispered, fearful their voices would carry back to the camp, 'what have you spotted ..?'

Ravenna just gestured to the rocky outcrops which towered above the camp with an inclination of her head.

'Did you see her boots?'

Eve frowned. 'Her boots – what ..?'

'The girl Brenna's walking boots - they were dark Wells, dark with something and at first I did not understand ...'

'What?' Eve ventured, 'what on earth are you talking about?' But the Mediterranean girl was already pulling ahead of her, ponytail bobbing briskly as her dark silhouette merged into the shadow of the nearest monolith.

Eve shuddered as she stepped into the blackness. The narrow canyon they had entered was as cold as the day had been hot, the narrow passageway of rock dark and claustrophobic. She reached a hand towards the rock wall, willing her eyes to adjust, then yelped as she walked straight into Ravenna.

311

'Nice work Dinosaur Girl,' the time traveller hissed back tersely. She sighed and as she stepped back Ravenna knelt to draw something long and slender from her pack.

'What's that?' she ventured nervously as steel glinted unexpectedly in the moonlight.

'It is a *falchion*, Wells – a medieval combat weapon – I find it most effective for dealing with arthropods and other thick skinned species.' Eve felt her concerns leap off the chart.

'Ravenna – what on earth are we ..?'

'And it is easier to conceal than a shotgun yes?'

Eve found that her mouth had gone utterly dry, watching in horror as the long machete like weapon glinted threateningly in the Mediterranean girl's hand. 'Focus Wells, with luck it will not be needed.'

Eve fought to still her thumping heart. 'So what are we ..?'

'Tracks,' Ravenna said briskly, 'footprints. Brenna Wiedermann set out specifically to come to this place in the dead of night – she was clearly looking to find something unusual.'

Eve tried to blank out the brooding darkness of the rocks around them. 'But what?' she whispered back, 'it's black as night down here and ...'

'Look at the ground Wells ...'

She frowned, then watching as Ravenna stooped down, did the same.

'Footprints,' she observed, 'lots of them.'

She saw Ravenna nod, her eyes flashing bright in the gloom. 'The prints of those who came running when she screamed, but that is not all Eve Wells ...'

She frowned as she took in the churned and mired ground – and then she realised. 'The darkness on her boots!'

Ravenna ran her fingers through the cold earth beneath their feet and nodded.

'Mud – her boots were caked with mud. This earth is wet, yes?'

Eve likewise ran her fingers through the churned dust which – though drying – was damp and even clumped as mud in places. 'Highly unusual in the middle of a desert ,yes?'

313

Eve swallowed. 'So how on earth ..?' But Ravenna had straightened and was beginning to walk softly into the depths of the canyon. Eve followed hurriedly, 'look – shouldn't we ...' But then she froze, sound registering to her left – turning in time to sense movement and the soft trickle of pebbles and sand as something above them moved away.

'Ravenna!' she hissed urgently, but the Mediterranean girl was frowning into the gloom where she had come up against a rock wall.

'There are many caves here – many fissures in this ancient stone,' she was saying softly, but Eve's mind was on other things, scanning wildly to either side, sure that someone or some-thing had been watching them from the overhanging walls.

'Ravenna!' she hissed again, but the dark haired girl was stooping to examine the floor once more, sniffing at the mud in her hand.

'The ground is wetter still here, Wells, it is like a bog yes?'

'Look Ravenna, I think someone is ...'

Ravenna stood to gaze at the strip of star punctured sky between the night-black walls of rock. Eve waited, her heart pounding, certain that someone had been watching them. Nothing. The time traveller sighed.

'The earth here is churned and saline – come and see.'

She hesitated then obeyed, her feet squelching unexpectedly on the damp ground. 'What on earth can this mean?' she whispered, still wary of the shadowy canyon behind, 'and what was Brenna Wiedermann looking for when she came here?'

Even in the shadows she could see Ravenna frown. 'I do not know Wells – but there is clearly something *wrong* about this place … and the question is whether this Brenna knows its secrets or has merely stumbled upon …'

A sound behind them made Ravenna turn.

Eve followed her gaze, wrapping her arms around her body as she shivered in the morning cool, her tired eyes drawn to the shadowy walls - sure she saw movement amid the folds and crevices of the wind-worn stone. 'Did you see that?' she hissed urgently, 'there's someone – something – watching us.'

Ravenna turned her hawk-like gaze to the gully's mouth, weapon ready as she scanned the gloomy walls, but as the moments ticked on it was clear that if anything had been there it was not about to put in an appearance now. Eve shuddered. 'Just my mind playing tricks I guess.'

'Perhaps,' Ravenna said darkly and sheathed her weapon. 'Come,' the time traveller continued grimly brushing her hands on her trousers, 'there is little more we can do here - let us get back – we will need our sleep.'

Eve shuddered, knowing with a grim certainty that a good night's rest was the last thing she was about to have.

Morning

Eve's head was aching mildly as she dressed and reached for her shoes.

'Ah – ah - ah!' exclaimed the dark haired girl sharply.

Eve froze, her right boot held ready below her foot. 'What?'

'Have you checked your boots for scorpions yet Wells?'

Eve's face wrinkled in horror: 'You're kidding?'

'Nope,' said the dark haired girl, taking the boot from her to shake it briskly outside the tent. Eve's pulse began to thud as something scuttled away across the sand.

'Just a baby – now come Dinosaur Girl, there is a lot for you to do today.'

Eve stared at her other boot in horror, taking it gingerly to the tent's mouth before urgently beginning to shake all her folded clothes.

'Come Wells,' the time traveller called from beyond the tent, '– the local fauna are the least of our worries.'

Eve followed with a sigh. Ravenna looked as cool and collected as ever, dressed in casual walking clothes and a borrowed broad-brimmed hat.

'So tell me about the era this landscape preserves,' she asked lazily. 'I need facts to give Bea Wilding some credibility!' Eve groaned, trying to cover her arms and neck against the blazing warmth. It could barely be past 8 AM but already the sun was fierce on her skin and she sighed as she shielded her eyes.

'It would help if you'd warned me where we were coming to in advance,' she replied tersely, pulling up the collar of the bush shirt she had borrowed to shield her neck.

'And where would the fun be in that?' Ravenna grinned back coolly, 'here ...' She removed her hat, giving it to her before putting on her aviator sunglasses. Eve mumbled her thanks, finding herself trapped half way between annoyance and admiration – still barely able to believe the confidence the dark haired girl possessed to turn up to a palaeontological dig posing as an expert with almost zero knowledge of palaeontology. She chose to shoot her the disdainful looks she reserved for undergrads who indulged in last-minute cramming.

'Come, you must cut me some of your proverbial slack,' the dark haired girl grinned calmly from behind her sunglasses, 'I have little time to delve into the intricate technicalities of the problems I am called to – and I *have* given you my hat.'

Eve shook her head, letting her eyes rove across the sandy landscape. Below the hazy azure heavens, the ground was a flat and endless plain, punctuated by the writhing weathered forms of what remained of a long eroded sea bed – yet it was not the sculptural monoliths and twisting canyons which caught her attention, but the dry dirt beneath her feet. 'This was once a vast ocean,' she said thoughtfully, 'maybe thirty-five or forty million years ago … you can see the evidence all around us.'

'Oh?' said the time traveller thoughtfully.

'Well, the eroded layers of sandy sediment in the rocks around us for one thing, but look at the floor ...' She stooped to pick up a pointed rock a little darker than the rest. 'A shark tooth,' she said pointedly, turning the serrated fossil over in her hand, 'and look here – a sea urchin spine ...'

'I get the picture,' Ravenna shot back, 'give me some clever sounding names I can quote.'

Eve sighed despairingly, slowing her pace a little, aware that the mess tent was drawing near. 'From what I can remember the ocean which covered this part of the world was called the *Tethys*, it stretched from India to Gibraltar during the Eocene epoch ...'

'My thanks Dinosaur Girl,' Ravenna returned briskly, and without warning stepped ahead of her, raising her hand as they drew near the flapping canvas.

'Look,' she said hurriedly, 'before we go in, can you just tell me what it is they've unearthed ..?' But Ravenna was already two paces ahead.

'Good morning Professor,' she began in her prim English accent, 'it looks like another lovely day for it!'

'Please, Ravenna!' she begged in an undertone, but the time traveller only shot her a grin and turning back to her whispered:

'You will have a whale of a time, yes?'

*

The mood in the mess tent was congenial but subdued. It was as if there was an unwritten rule that no-one would mention the events of the night before, and while Ravenna stood making small talk with the site director, Eve found her attention drawn to where Zalmoud and Brenna Wiedermann were stood talking in troubled tones. The Egyptian palaeontologist put his hand on the young woman's arm she noticed, but she shook it away.

'... And you are looking forward to seeing what we have found Dr Wells?'

She turned briskly, smiling awkwardly to see Professor Saraceni standing at her side.

'Yes, I ...'

'It's just a massive privilege to have been invited out to look into this matter,' Ravenna cut in jovially in her enthusiastic academic tone, 'Eve's practically over-the-moon to be here!' She fought not to make a face.

'Good,' the Italian palaeontologist beamed as she tried to force an enthusiastic smile, 'then let us take a little breakfast – and then we must be away to the site before the sun is at its fiercest.'

Eve nodded and as they turned towards the table shot Ravenna a sickly smile.

'Thanks *Bea* – thanks so much.'

'My pleasure,' Ravenna returned coolly as she pulled back her chair, but her attention was clearly focussed on Brenna Wiederman, who was now gazing pensively at the rocky canyon they had visited the night before.

*

The find site was a short truck ride from camp across uneven ground.

'This whole area – approximately thirty square hectares – is a giant slice of eroded sea-floor,' Saraceni was telling them as they jerked along the uneven track, 'the rock we stand on is the lowest level, and the great monoliths sedimentary layers which wind and time have stripped away.' She followed his gaze to survey the almost blinding landscape, imagining the eroded monoliths as part of continuous strata – rocky layers laid down as silt and decaying creatures, decade after decade. 'This is a snap-shot of a long-gone ocean … and a graveyard of extinct species of whale.'

Eve looked on in wonder. 'There are finds literally everywhere,' Saraceni continued, gesturing with his hand, 'weathering out of the rocks all around us.'

Eve gasped to see the crumbling lower jaw of some huge creature protruding from the sandy cliff they were passing and Zalmoud laughed softly at her wonder.

'It is impressive, yes,' he chuckled, 'but in this valley dragons are a dime-a-dozen.'

Eve's smile faltered, her mind drawn back to the troubling events of the night before.

'Outstanding!' Ravenna replied over-enthusiastically in her twee tones, but Eve was now oblivious, her mind filled with shadows and footprints, lost in the dank claustrophobia of the lonely canyon. To her left Brenna shifted in her seat. She looked thoroughly preoccupied, Eve mused, gazing pensively out of the truck's open window.

'Goodness its warm!' said Ravenna as if to lighten the mood.

'Indeed,' replied Saraceni with a winning smile, 'and I would recommend you do not touch the vehicle's doors as we exit, the metal will be scorching!'

Ravenna nodded her thanks, holding the Italian's gaze for what seemed to Eve to be a little too long.

As the vehicle drew to a halt something clicked. 'The Wadi of Whales!' Eve exclaimed to herself as she remembered the pop-science headline about the site famed for its ground-breaking mammalian finds, then smiled as Dr Saraceni caught her eye. 'I've always longed to see it,' she added quickly to hide the fact she had only just made the connection.

'Then I am glad I have been able to make your dream come true Dr Wells,' the Professor said expressively, stepping down to open the door for her. Eve nodded her thanks, then gasped as the heat of the desert hit her – it was as if she had stepped into a bread oven. At her side, Ravenna was likewise fanning her face, but her mind seemed to be on other things, smiling as she allowed Saraceni to help her down.

She tried to catch the Mediterranean girl's eye but Ravenna ignored her, nodding her thanks to the Professor who was directing her towards the nearest shade.

*

'It is incredible to think we are less than 100 miles from Cairo, yes?' Professor Saraceni remarked as they trudged across the sun scorched ground. Eve nodded, watching as Ravenna ambled casually in front of her, pausing to pick something from the ground.

'This is remarkable,' she mused, holding up a small fragment of fossilised bone to examine, before showing it to Eve, 'just to be able to walk along and pick up a …'

'Dorudon toe,' Eve finished briskly, knowing full-well the Mediterranean woman hadn't a clue what it was.

'This place is just something else,' Brenna Wiedermann cut in, 'may I?' She examined the find then stooped to investigate the area in which it had been found.

'The Valley of Whales,' Eve said thoughtfully, shielding her hand with her eyes.

'Indeed,' Saraceni replied ruefully, 'this place is a crucible of evolution – a test case for Darwinian theory.'

Eve saw Ravenna frown.

'A real kick in the gut for the creationists,' Brenna added thoughtfully, 'a crazy anomaly that just didn't seem to fit with Darwin's theory – the whale I mean, an animal which appeared in a class of its own, to have no direct evolutionary link.'

'Yes,' Renato added thoughtfully, 'as I'm sure you are aware - the whale is a mammal which appeared – at the time Darwin was formulating his theory of natural selection - to have no evolutionary link: it fitted no existing order or cohort of mammals and thus appeared as if God had created it in an instant.' He took the bone from Brenna and produced a polythene bag from his pocket.

'Until an evolutionary link was found, people who wanted to invalidate Darwin's theory of evolution still held up the whale as evidence of its impossibility.'

'Until these kinds of finds were unearthed, 'Eve said thoughtfully, 'evidence of whales evolving from land dwellers to fully aquatic forms.'

Ravenna held her gaze, expression thoughtful.

'But come,' said Saraceni briskly, '- over here is our little conundrum – and the real reason you have travelled across the world, yes?'

Eve caught the Mediterranean woman's eye but her expression remained neutral. They were in a valley of ancient whales – a melting-pot of evolution - but what on earth did that have to do with Ravenna's concerns for the integrity of physical time?

'Come on Dinosaur Girl,' the time traveller muttered, falling into step with her as she walked, 'and keep an open mind, yes?' Eve shot her a look – *an open mind!* But before she could question her further, Saraceni gestured to a sun baked patch of ground.

'So this is it?'

They had come to a halt in an exposed spot and stood fanning their faces at an area which had clearly been dug many times before. It was now witheringly hot, the heat of the sun like a palpable weight pressing down on every part of her body –yet Eve found every fibre of her mind focussed on what lay before them.

Saraceni pulled back a tarpaulin which had been weighted over the dusty remains.

'*Wow,*' said Eve almost reverently.

A length of huge vertebrae – half foot high tubes, with great sail-like projections to attach muscles – lay half-buried amid a jumble of huge two foot long ribs.

'You know what this is?' said Renato Saraceni in a tone close to amusement. Eve nodded.

'Basilosaurus,' she breathed, 'a massive ancestor of the modern whale.'

'Thirty-seven million years old,' the Italian smiled, 'a real-life sea monster which could grow up to sixteen metres in length – about fifty feet.' Eve nodded. She'd seen reconstructions of its massive many-toothed jaws and elongated almost snake like body. 'The ancient Egyptians have a story about a sea monster enshrined in their hieroglyphics …'

She noticed Ravenna shoot her a serious look. 'Tales of monsters.'

'And dragons,' Zalmoud interjected, probing gently with his trowel, 'this place is renowned for monsters – though doubtless the stories go back to these bones, stumbled on by herders and camel trains.'

'Doubtless,' Ravenna smiled, but Eve saw a pointed look in her eye.

'But of course old stories are not the mystery that have drawn you here Dr Wilding.'

Ravenna smiled. 'So – can you show me ..?'

Renato gave a brisk nod and the young man pulled back the tarpaulin even further.

Eve did a double take.

Belly of the Whale

'**B**ut that's not possible.'

Even as she said it Eve knew with horrifying certainty that it was.

'The sign of Jonah,' said Saraceni thoughtfully and Eve shot Ravenna a frown.

'So – what do you think we are dealing with here?'

'Dealing with?' Saraceni said lightly, 'why a mystery of almost biblical proportions - the utterly impossible.' Eve swallowed as the Professor weighted the tarp down against the breeze and began to point at the jumbled bones he had revealed. Eve closed her eyes: unmistakably human bones.

'Essentially this man – or woman - is in the belly of the whale,' Tarek Zalmoud interjected, 'whether he is within or *below* the basilosaurus' gut it is as yet to be established.'

'Impossible, yes?' Saraceni said almost delightedly. Eve returned a nervous smile, 'when you e-mailed to say your department researched such matters ...'

Ravenna smiled demurely. '... So your first impressions?'

Eve frowned, caught mid-way between horror and curiosity. 'Well, logically, there's pretty much no way this could be an early human – not out in the middle of an ocean ...'

'And the age of these bones?' the Italian academic continued pointedly. Eve said nothing as she ran her gaze along the contorted jumble, fully aware of where he was going. They were slender, gently tapering – she was no expert on human evolutionary forensics, but the bones didn't look like those of an archaic human. The Italian grinned. 'We have unearthed a fragment of the jaw – the muscle attachments are slight – I would have expected something much heavier – more jutting – in a human who had lived nearly fifty thousand years ago.' Eve gave a non-committal nod.

Zalmoud loosened his neckerchief and leaned in a little closer. 'Maybe the basilosaurus and the human remains were buried separately,' he ventured, 'some freak geological action confusing the sedimentary layers - the burrowing of rodents jumbling the bones, perhaps?'

But Eve could see that the matrix of sandy rock within which the bones lay was utterly undisturbed. Both human and animal had perished at roughly the same time – if not the same moment – and been buried together. But that was impossible. *Utterly impossible.*

'So, this guy was eaten by an ancestor of the modern whale,' Brenna said almost flippantly, 'and we've got a hell of a story on our hands.'

Eve shot Ravenna an urgent look.

'Does the media know about this yet?'

'Of course not Dr Wells,' Professor Saraceni replied with a reassuring nod, 'why if the truth of this were to get out before we had chance to properly investigate it ...'

'Come,' said Zalmoud, turning to Ravenna as if unwilling to dwell on the implications, 'you wish to conduct your own study?'

'That would be great,' the Mediterranean girl replied, '- maybe you'd like to make some notes Eve – do some field drawings?'

They all stood, fanning out as Saraceni pointed out other noteworthy features of the site, speaking animatedly about what they had found as Ravenna did an adequate job of hiding her almost total ignorance of the era in question.

Eve paused to make a few notes, and sketch the relation of the bones to one another.

'Have you lifted any of these?' she ventured as she stowed her notebook.

'Not yet,' the Egyptian palaeontologist smiled '– that is our job for this afternoon – you are happy to help?'

'I'd love to,' she smiled, but almost instantly felt her sense of enthusiasm doused by the terrible madness of what had been found.

'You are okay Dr Wells?' Zalmoud frowned.

'Just tired, aren't you Eve?' Ravenna interjected warmly, taking her arm to steer her away from the others. 'Do you mind if we get our bearings Professor,' she called to Saraceni, '– field walk the area?'

'Be my guest,' the Italian replied casually, 'though I and my colleagues have been over it a thousand times, - just do not stray too far Dr Wilding, and drink lots of water.'

'Will do.'

Eve wiped her forehead, a dull headache seeming to register at his words. Her shirt seemed pasted to her back and she fanned herself briskly, suddenly concerned at how much moisture she was losing.

'The valley of dry bones,' Ravenna said thoughtfully as they walked away across the baking plain, '– a vision given to Ezekiel … have you ever read the Bible Eve Wells?' Eve hesitated but the time traveller continued before she could reply. 'It is the weirdest story – the mass resurrection of the body … long dead soldiers reanimated – I must investigate it some time.'

Eve shuddered. 'And what bearing does it have on this dead guy in the whale's stomach?'

'Absolutely nothing,' Ravenna replied distractedly, 'it just came to mind – and as we have discussed many times, to slip through reality is nothing unusual – to be dead and reawakened, yes ..?'

Eve swallowed. Or to step back from life into death. Whoever now rested amid the jumble of whale bones had slipped through to the bottom of a primeval ocean and most likely been devoured by a huge marine mammal. 'I need some shade,' she said feeling suddenly nauseous.

Ravenna sniffed, though whether with amusement or disdain she couldn't tell.

'And this creature – this sea-serpent ...'

'A mammal actually,' Eve replied pointedly, 'like a modern whale it would have lived its life in open water, never coming to land as their ancestors had done.'

'But they ate flesh, yes – not krill?'

Eve looked away, fully aware of what she was implying.

'Yes – this species at least ...' She broke off, taking a few deep breaths as a wave of sickly warmth swept through her.

'Wells?' Ravenna ventured, 'you are like a lobster, yes - overheating? I see this climate is not good for your barbarian complexion.'

'Thanks,' she muttered, making for the shade of the nearest rocky overhang, 'I'm going to sit down for a moment.'

'As you wish,' the Mediterranean girl replied, 'you will need all your strength for this afternoon's forensic work – I need your mind to be clear and your ears open.'

Ravenna

R avenna sat alone in the tent, listening to the flapping of the awning and the hiss of sand as it skittered across the hard-baked ground. It was now late afternoon and the party had long since returned with the jumbled human bones.

She sighed with frustration. The wind seemed to moan and sigh, singing its ancient songs as she contemplated, trying to relax her mind as she let go of all that they had seen and heard. She needed direction – needed a clear path, but her mind was so distracted.

The open door, the mud of the gully, the scream in the night ... bones in a belly.

She growled with frustration, unable to let go – unable to see clearly amid her own imaginings and impulses.

337

'*Pater*,' she whispered softly, searching for the place where she could simply be – to wait, to listen – but the wind continued to mutter and sigh. '*Pater!*'

The tent flapped violently and she broke off with a curse, turning her gaze to her flask. She drank slowly, revelling in the cool of the water, then let out a sigh as she closed her eyes once more, the vessel still clasped in her hands.

The canvas continued to flutter, the wind still sighed, and now in its songs she sensed a mischievous brooding – the old and silver-tongued whisper. She swallowed, forcing herself to concentrate, but the wind sang on, conjuring pictures in her mind. *Her face - her name*. She tried to breathe evenly, trying not to give in to her imagination, but the voices kept whispering, seductive and flattering. The things she had done before – the roll-call of her triumphs and her glories. The things she would do again … the fulfilments she craved. She screwed her eyes tighter, teeth gritted now as the voice seemed to whisper deceit in her ear, the soft and tinkling incitement to vanity.

She heard again the roar of the crowd and the clink of gold, felt the power she had experienced - the freedom she had earned in a world where such freedom was impossible. She fought the whispers – fought the imaginations – but the voices made it clear it could be hers once more, that she had every right – the things she could do with her knowledge … flattering her skill, needling her pride, caressing her aches.

She gritted her teeth, but she was lost in her imagination, laughing as she enjoyed what suddenly seemed hers to take, feeling the power which she had once known. *Just a little* the voices seemed to whisper - not a compromise but a just reward. And then she realised – conscience prickling.

She howled, feeling the tug of it like a physical wrench in a gut – she saw one face before her mind's eye – then another. Surrender, the voice seemed to whisper, just once – just in this moment …

She yelled angrily, throwing her flask at the flapping material with all her physical strength.

'Are you okay?' said an anxious voice from the doorway.

It was Eve.

*

Eve stepped back as Ravenna stepped out of their tent to stand gazing at the busy camp before them. She looked distracted – guilty.

'I feel so close to an answer, Wells, but cannot see clearly,' she said without looking at her, 'I am frustrated – my apologies.'

Eve looked away feeling strangely troubled.

'Your operation went well – this lifting of the bones?'

Eve nodded. It had been a tiring five hours, working in the scorching heat to free the bones encased in the creature's gut, but the joy of field work – of photographing and drawing the position of the finds - had been a satisfaction she hadn't known for a long time. 'We got him out and have the remains over in the finds tent – Brenna's working to clean them up now.'

Ravenna nodded.

'So this sea creature – basilosaurus ..?'

Eve rifled in her bag for her sketchbook, remembering a drawing she had doodled earlier. 'Here – look – it was big … darned big, like a massively elongated killer whale, but bulkier.'

'Like a serpent,' Ravenna mused, frowning at the unusual creature, which did indeed look as if an orca or dolphin had been ludicrously stretched and elongated.

'It must have been a real top-predator in its day.'

'A monster,' Ravenna mused, pushing back strands of her wind-blown hair.

Eve swallowed.

'Come,' Ravenna said briskly, 'I will walk with you to see the finds,' then added: 'I seem to remember you have an affinity with these early whales, yes?'

Eve's mind flashed back to the first trip she had taken her on – the tropical gloom of the Eocene Messel rainforest and the horrifying moment she had seen a crocodile-like snout break the water through which she had been wading. 'She was rather fond of you?' the time traveller grinned, 'twice she tried to taste you Eve Wells, this Ambulo ...'

Eve shuddered.

'*Ambulocetus*,' she finished with an effort, the moment the early whale had pulled her feet from under her, dragging her beneath the murky surface leapt vividly to the forefront of her mind, her horrified screams as

Ravenna had pulled her free, forcing her to remain in the water to overcome her fear ...'and why do you think it was a she?'

'*She* was a she, Wells – I know it in my gut ... a badass who would not give up!' She turned away with a wry smile. Eve forced herself to concentrate on the present. 'So these mammals in this long dry sea – they will be like the Ambulocetus, but bigger, yes?'

Eve shook her head.

'The animal we ... *met* – in the Eocene swamp lived about ten million years before Dorudon and five before Basilosaurus came on the scene. It was still a land mammal – but with webbed feet, evolved to cruise the shallows – but by this time ...' she gestured to the dry world around them, 'its descendants had evolved into much more familiar forms, with flippers and tail flukes – though Basilosaurus still retained tiny, useless back legs.'

Ravenna laughed ironically. 'And Darwin was mocked for this yes?'

Eve shrugged. 'His theory that animals like shallows-swimming bears could one day evolve into whales was ridiculed so much he left it out of his *Origin of Species*.' Ravenna gazed at her thoughtfully. 'I mean, why would an organism make an evolutionary u-turn if all life came from the sea in the first place. It made no sense and to sceptical scholars the whale fitted nowhere in the big scheme of life.'

'Until the remains of your friend Ambulocetus were found.'

Eve laughed. 'No - its ancestor Pakicetus – discovered in Pakistan in 1979. The team that found it knew they had something special when they unearthed what appeared to be a wolf's skull but with sails of bone to secure massive neck muscles.'

'I believe your modern phrase "smart arse" is appropriate here,' Ravenna replied tersely.

'If you live in the nineties,' Eve returned, '- and if you weren't impressed by that kind of knowledge you wouldn't have brought me.'

Ravenna laughed. 'A point to you Wells.'

Eve slowed her pace as they drew near the flapping canvas of the large tent ahead of them. 'Does it bother you – evolutionary theory I mean? You know, I know you ...'

Ravenna came to a halt, an enigmatic smile playing across her lips. 'Eve Wells, I do not particularly care which medium the creator used to make his great and mighty master-piece – all I do know is that his pallet of colours is truly astounding ...' Her gaze drifted to the interplay of dusty ochre and burning azure where land met blazing sky; but before Eve could respond a voice made them both turn towards the tent.

'Dr Wells? We are about to proceed with processing the remains if you wish to join us?'

It was Zalmoud, the Egyptian specialist.

'Go,' said Ravenna, 'find out what you can – see if they suspect anything unusual – particularly this Brenna girl, yes?'

Eve nodded. 'And what are you ...'

'The gorge,' she said after a moment's hesitation, 'I will go to the gorge and explore it once more.'

Analysis

'What have you found Eve Wells?'

It was almost evening and Ravenna's shadow lay dark across the specimen Eve stood examining. She looked up from the finds tray, stretching her back as she placed the fragment of bone on the low trestle table.

'Conundrums,' she replied with a sigh, wishing she didn't have to reveal the blatant truth she'd discovered, 'there's no way this is a hoax or an accident of geology – there really *is* a human body inside the basilosaurus' stomach.'

Ravenna nodded sagely, glancing up to where Brenna and Mohammed Zalmoud were stacking polythene wrapped plaster casts into the back of the team's truck.

'And they too are aware of this?'

Eve sighed, likewise watching as they stacked the basilosaurus bones. 'It's pretty obvious – the way the bones are trapped together in the matrix of sediment … I've been trying to steer them away from the idea.'

'And what does Renato think?' There was a strange look in her eye, Eve noted.

'*Renato?*' She couldn't help but grin, 'So *he's* your type … I have been wondering!'

Ravenna shrugged. 'He is attractive, yes, in many ways – but that is of no consequence.' Eve shook her head.

'And Brenna?'

Eve hesitated. 'Yeah, she's kind of passionate for the whole unexplained angle.'

Ravenna sighed darkly. 'She worries me Eve Wells, she is idealistic – headstrong … she knows that she has found something incredible here and I suspect that she will not let it rest.'

Eve felt a frown creasing her brow. 'So what will you do?'

Ravenna side-stepped the question.

'So, tell me about this body in the whale's gut?'

Eve shuddered. 'Well, I'm no expert on human forensics, but we think the remains are modern human from the femur we have, not prehistoric – probably Caucasian – but putting together the fragments is a bit of a jigsaw,' she swallowed, 'they were in a pretty bad shape.'

'Eaten?'

'Crushed,' she corrected feeling suddenly light-headed, 'like the bones have been pulverized by some huge force.'

'The weight of sediment before fossilisation?' the time traveller wondered picking up one of the ancient fragments.

Eve shook her head. 'No – the other bones – the whale bones – show no such signs … and please, put some gloves on if you're going to touch the fossils!'

Ravenna set it down casually. 'Ah - then?'

Eve gestured to one of the huge ribs which lay on the adjoining trestle table. 'A whale's physiology is evolved to survive both the cold and the pressure of the deep ocean. Blubber, huge bones, massive muscle attachments. As whales evolved from shallows-swimming four legged animals, their bodies became flattened, more streamlined, their necks flatter and more muscular ...'

'And humans have no such evolutionary adaptions,' Ravenna said flatly. Eve suppressed a shudder.

'Somehow this man sank to the depths of the deep ocean.'

'And was crushed to a pulp,' Ravenna observed, turning a fractured femur over in her hand.

'Thanks for that,' her friend replied glibly. 'So how on earth are we supposed to ..?'

'You have found something Dr Wells?'

They broke off as Renato Saraceni came striding towards them, wearing his perennially perfect smile.

'Only questions,' Ravenna smiled in the voice of Bea Wilding, then shot her a glance which seemed to say: *tell him nothing!*

Eve smiled nervously. 'Personally I'm still gunning for it being some kind of elaborate hoax,' Eve ventured, '- weirder things have happened - sights being rigged to give credence to a theory or make some kind of statement ...'

Renato Saraceni frowned. 'But if that was the case, who would do such a thing – some local party who wished us off this land?'

Eve felt her thoughts leap to Zalmoud, then dismissed the impulse out of hand. 'And have you been able to ascertain if our enigmatic friend was a male or a female ..?' But footsteps made them turn – it was Brenna.

'Hey,' said the palaeontologist brightly, 'I've bagged up the samples ready to ship back to Cairo for carbon dating – from there we should be able to get them over to the US for more tests - we'll be able to confirm the origin if there's any DNA present.' Saraceni nodded as if satisfied, but something told Eve that she was holding something back.

'Come Dr Wilding,' the Professor ventured, then turned to Eve, 'you can spare us for a while Dr Wells, there is something I wish to discuss with your colleague?'

'Of course,' she nodded as Saraceni gestured towards camp with his left hand, placing his right on the small of Ravenna's back. To her surprise, her friend made no effort to pull away.

'Looks like your colleague Dr Wilding and the professor are getting on okay,' said Brenna as she put down a number of empty boxes on the table beside the finds.

Eve hesitated, still surprised by their seeming familiarity. Where had Ravenna been all afternoon, she wondered suddenly, she'd said nothing about exploring the canyon? Pushing the thought away she laughed and directed her attention to the tray of bone fragments.

'Come on, we'd better get these bagged up.'

But still, as she watched the time traveller and the site leader walking away together, uneasiness began to stir within her.

Evidence

'So what do you make of all this?'

Brenna Wiedermann's voice was casual as they bubble wrapped the last of the finds, yet there was something deliberate in her pointed tone.

Eve looked at her thoughtfully. They had worked closely together all afternoon and though it had been refreshing to spend time working with a fellow professional she had not had the chance to speak privately with her about what she had seen at the canyon. She found herself snatching glances at the men who stood some way away discussing the remains.

'It's just bonkers,' she replied as casually as she could, 'I mean, I've never seen anything like this before – if it's some kind of prank, it's truly spectacular.' She forced a disbelieving laugh. Brenna smiled in reply then seemed to hesitate.

'Look,' she said glancing around before slipping something from her pocket, 'I found this – on the day we first uncovered the specimen.'

Eve did a double take.

A tooth! Eve marvelled as she unwrapped the small parcel of paper towel the girl handed her, a human tooth still lodged in a fragment of fossilised jaw.

'But where ...' The girl broke off and closed her eyes before taking a sharp intake of breath.

'You okay?' Eve frowned.

'Just a crazy headache – been bugging me all afternoon.' Eve looked at her sharply and the girl shrugged. 'Started when I began to handle the finds.' She slipped the tooth back into her pocket. 'Look, I've not told anyone about this,' the palaeontologist continued guardedly, 'I don't ...' she took another glance to where Zalmoud and Saraceni stood talking by the truck with Ravenna looking on sagely at their side, 'look, I'd rather get this checked out myself – get it sent to a specialist in Michigan I know ... they should be able to confirm when and where this girl lived from the shape and ...'

'Girl?' Eve frowned. Brenna held her gaze.

'Length of the femur,' she returned, '– it's just a gut-reaction, but ...'

Eve glanced up as she broke off to see Zalmoud looking at them thoughtfully.

'Look, anyway,' the girl continued quickly, 'I just want to get to the bottom of this myself – there's something not quite right here and I know that some of the local guys would rather see us all out of this place – both the Muslims and the Coptic Christians revere it ...'

'But why ..?'

The American looked at her pensively as if assessing her trustworthiness. 'Look, I know this will sound crazy, but I have this theory ...' there was an awkward, almost apologetic look in her eye and she looked down briskly as if plucking up the courage to voice the idea she was about to confess. Eve swallowed, almost knowing what was to come. 'What if ... well ... what if there was a way you could slip into another place– another time – some kind of gateway or doorway to the past ...?' She broke off. 'I mean, I know it sounds totally ridiculous, but this man – or woman ... I mean, what if they found a door and stumbled into it?'

Eve found herself momentarily unable to reply. 'Time travel?' she replied in a voice she could tell sounded far from natural, '... *wow.*'

'You must think I'm totally nuts!' Brenna replied awkwardly, briskly stacking away the plastic trays they had been examining.

Eve hesitated, 'No ... I – I mean ...'

'I just can't think of any other explanation for how this could have happened,' the girl continued. She looked deeply troubled, her face etched with confusion, '... and then there's what happened the other night.' She picked up one of the trays and began to stack it with the others.

'What did happen that night?' Eve cut in a little anxiously. She'd been both longing to know and dreading to hear what the girl had experienced since that horrifying moment she had been awoken from her sleep - but some part of her couldn't bring herself to ask.

Brenna put down her trays. Above them the tarp was slapping in the desert breeze.

'I saw an animal,' she said without hesitation, 'a large one ...'

'Go on,' Eve swallowed, feeling the hairs on the back of her neck begin to prickle.

'I had this hunch ... this crazy idea about walking into the past – I mean, the local guides tell stories about men and beasts vanishing here all the time ... and about monsters ... slipping through to our world.' She found herself unable to reply.

'So the other night after you arrived I just couldn't sleep. I took a walk, threading my way back to the canyon – it was moonlit but the ground was dark.'

'Dark,' Eve interjected, 'how do you mean?'

The girl hesitated. 'Wet,' she replied briskly, 'it was water like a spring had burst and flooded from the caves – and there were tracks ...'

Her thoughts returned to the moonlit canyon and the disturbance they had seen.

'Tracks?'

'Prints and impressions in the sand ...'

'What kind of prints?' Eve asked hoarsely. The girl hesitated.

'I mean … no-one was going to believe me, and by yesterday morning the wind had scoured them away – but there were huge prints and impressions … flipper and tail prints, marks where a huge belly had marred the sand as something lumbered forwards.' She broke off and gazed towards the distant skyline.

'And what do you think ..?'

'Hell – you must think I've been working too hard,' she laughed a little defensively, 'letting it go to my head …'

'No!' she cut in urgently; terrified she'd clam up, 'no – not at all, I … look, Brenna, I've seen some weird things too in my time, things which couldn't be explained …'

The American girl gazed at her for a moment, her brows dipping into a delicate V as the wind stirred her hair. 'I've been studying these animals for five years,' she continued almost passionately, 'researched how they lived and moved – examined a host of comparative modern species – the locomotion of seals and crocodiles … you don't believe me do you!'

Eve caught her arm as she began to turn away.

'No! Brenna, please – tell me what you saw ... I've ...' She hesitated, knowing it would be madness to confess what she knew and had experienced to the girl, but longing to confide in her, to put her mind at rest.

The young palaeontologist swallowed and ran her fingers through her hair.

'There was a light,' she said distractedly, 'at the base of a rocky overhang.'

'Moonlight?' Eve ventured.

The girl hesitated.

'The local guides call the phenomenon God's Mirror – some say that it's just a mirage – but I saw it ... at night ... the reflection of the moon.'

'The reflection?' Eve frowned.

'On water,' the girl replied hoarsely, the desert breeze plucking at loose strands of her hair, 'on a literal wall of water – like a sheet of silver ... and then I saw it ...'

'Saw what?' Eve replied in what emerged as a whisper.

'A monster,' the girl replied her eyes suddenly wild with the memory of it, 'and then I ran.' She turned briskly and Eve saw she was close to tears.

'Look, Brenna ...'

'Please don't tell me I'm going mad!' the American said almost desperately, 'I just couldn't ... it was so real!' Eve placed a hand on her shoulder.

'Look, I've learned ... I know that in this world almost anything is possible. We write legends off as something of the past, but there's often a germ of truth in them ...' She broke off, stifling the urge to tell her about Ravenna's work. 'What did it look like Brenna ... the animal you saw ..?'

The girl swallowed her eyes suddenly wide and anxious. 'Look, Dr Wells, I ... maybe I was just hallucinating, the heat and the pressure – I live, breathe and sleep what we do here twenty-four-seven ...'

'Maybe,' she replied gently, 'but what if you did see something ... I mean, we have these bones,' she continued, gesturing to the neatly bagged finds from the basilosaurus' stomach, 'and don't you want to get to the bottom of this?'

The girl hesitated for a moment as if sensing that would be dangerous, then nodded. 'So go on,' Eve prompted once more, 'what did you see ...?'

'Well,' the young woman replied, after taking a breath, 'it was dark and I didn't really ...' she swallowed, 'but it was big – big and lumbering, lolloping forward like an elephant seal ... and its ...'

But at that moment a noise rang out which made them both turn briskly, panic flaring as she realised what was happening.

Ravenna

Ravenna cursed, unable to believe how stupid she'd been, her mind shooting back to the moment before the conversation had turned, feeling again the mild elation as Professor Saraceni had pulled out a bottle of white from the mess tent cooler.

'I wish I could offer you something more appropriate, but crystal travels so badly in my experience.'

They had both laughed.

'*To answers*,' Ravenna said demurely, raising her tin mug to his, '- and new discoveries.'

Dr Saraceni tapped his mug against hers with a soft laugh. Behind them the sun was a blaze of gold, highlighting his hair in a glowing halo. '*To answers*.' There was a knowing look in his eye and though she knew she should not allow herself to feel the rush of attraction she had long since learned to suppress, she allowed it to take her as if she was a young girl again. 'Dr Wilding, you are one of the most beautiful women I have ever met.'

'Quite probably,' she replied, revelling in the quickening of her pulse. He looked down, his expression hard to read. She had taken her vow so long ago, but sometimes – just sometimes someone came along who stirred her, and for a few precious moments she would allow herself the pleasure of those feelings, the power her physical form had over others.

Dr Saraceni looked up from the surface of his wine with a thoughtful grin. 'Though I guess that's not strictly true,' he continued, eyes twinkling as he paused to take a sip of his wine.

'And why is that Renato?'

He held her gaze, eyes smiling with a look close to triumph.

'Because you are not Dr Wilding,' he continued in a casual tone, 'because we have met before – if fleetingly – and then you called yourself Miss Bartoli.'

Time seemed suddenly to coagulate around her – reality crunching to a halt as she realised her mistake - how could she have been so stupid! 'Rome,' he said lightly, 'three years ago – a press release about a dig in the Subura ... I would never forget a face as engaging as yours.'

She hesitated then nodded slowly, knowing the next few moments would be amongst the most pivotal of her life. 'Who are you really Miss Wilding?' he continued in Italian, 'In Rome you were a journalist writing about the inexplicable find of what appeared to be a bullet casing in a Third Century grave - and here you come to investigate *homo sapiens* remains in a place they could not possibly be.'

The desert wind stirred her hair. 'I am a woman of many talents,' she replied calmly in the same language.

Renato laughed. She kept her expression neutral.

'You contact my office out of nowhere – a mysterious expert ... a seeker of impossible things.'

Her mind was racing – struggling for the way ahead – he knew about the secret – perhaps they all did – and that could never be allowed! 'Professor

Saraceni, for your own sake, you must let this go!' she said pointedly in English, but at that moment a commotion made them both glance back towards the darkening canyon.

'God help us!' she exclaimed in a horrified whisper.

'We shall continue this conversation later Dr Wilding!' the academic said grimly, and then he was leaving her, breaking into a run.

The Basilisk

The camp was in panic, the local guides yelling and gesturing as they argued with Tarek Zalmoud, who was clearly trying to placate them.

'What the hell's going on!' Ravenna yelled desperately, grabbing at Eve's trailing arm as she caught up with her in the finds tent. Around them mules were being loaded, tents taken down and equipment dismantled as the locals made it clear they would not stay. Her mind was in a whirl, struggling with the weight of Saraceni's words, but the look on Eve's face brought her thoughts rocketing back to the moment.

'Brenna ...' Eve began urgently, clearly struggling to order her thoughts, 'she ... the local men are in a state and ...'

'Slow down,' the Mediterranean girl ordered, 'take a breath Dinosaur Girl!'

Eve swallowed and glanced towards the empty mess tent.

'I was talking with Brenna … and then we heard a load of yelling – one of the local men had come out to find the guides … he says he's seen something – back at the gorge near camp,' the palaeontologist broke off and swallowed nervously, 'they're in a hell of a state – talking about dragons …'

'Dragons?' Ravenna frowned, then swore. 'So they have seen something, yes – seen a creature from the past?'

Eve hesitated, screwing up her face momentarily as the wind sent sand blasting against them. 'I – I don't know exactly, they kept going on about the legend of the basilisk … apparently one of their party, a guy called Yusuf, vanished while showing Brenna the gorge a couple of weeks ago … she's gone to speak with them.' But even as she said it the junior palaeontologist ran out across the strip of ground ahead of them, hurrying over to grab Tarek Zalmoud's arm before pointing in their direction. They both knew.

Ravenna closed her eyes in despair: the situation had slipped right out of her control.

'What?' Eve said worriedly, 'and what on earth were you talking to Saraceni about?' Ravenna glanced up, but found herself unable to meet the palaeo-artist's gaze. She had surrendered to her own path and her focus had slipped: she had failed them both because of her stupidity.

'What?' her friend pushed, 'Ravenna – what on earth did he say to you?'

She swallowed, turning her gaze from where the academic and his young assistant were now speaking in animated tones, watching as the encampment was broken down around them.

'I have made a mistake,' she said softly, 'a terrible one …'

Eve

'What's going on?' Eve demanded, 'what on earth do you mean? Brenna suspects there's a rift in time – that's why she went up to the canyon alone – and ...'

Ravenna let out a despairing moan.

'Pater parce mihi!'

Eve felt her shredded nerves give way to a whole new level of panic. 'What – what on earth did Professor Saraceni ...'

And then she realised.

'What ... you two weren't ..?'

Ravenna slumped onto the nearest chair, covering her face with her hands. 'This is the biggest disaster since I was caught on camera at Glastonbury in the year 2008!'

Eve looked at her in shock, hardly able to take in the implications. 'So while I was slaving away in near fifty degree heat you were ..!'

'He is very good looking, yes? Erudite – *a gentlemen!* But that is not the worst of it Wells – he has met me before – in Italy – he knows I am not Dr Wilding …'

The implications of it hit her like a physical blow. She stared at the Mediterranean girl incredulously, caught somewhere between the two revelations. 'Oh god! And, you made a play for him – *seriously!* What about your crazy vow?'

'Technically, *he* tried to hit on me Wells …'

'What difference does that make!' she shot back, 'you let him … I mean … and now look where we are!' She shot a glance at the rapidly emptying encampment, knowing with certainty that the truth about the discovery was about to be blown wide open.

'Regardless of my romantic intentions he already knew I was not Dr Wilding!' the time traveller replied heatedly, then dropped her gaze. 'You do not know what it is like Eve Wells – you could not even begin to imagine this loneliness …'

Eve made as if to answer then looked away. 'In those first days, when I had realised the magnitude of what had been asked of me I swore to commit myself body and soul - to seek purity from material things,' she sighed bitterly running her fingers through her hair, 'but even with decades of practice …'

Eve looked at her quizzically, the chaos momentarily forgotten.

Ravenna took a shaky breath. 'I was little more than a child when I awoke from the sleep which had been imposed on me – but at that point I did not fully understand why I had been called.' She looked up and caught her eye. 'You know that I became a slave when I left the cave … you know that they trained me …'

Eve nodded, still hardly able to believe the truth which Ravenna had once confessed.

'My fame spread throughout the East … and in the barracks I had lovers …' She closed her eyes and sighed remorsefully.

Eve dared to frame a question which she had often considered. 'Was there ever anyone ..?' she broke off.

Ravenna gazed up at her and for a second she felt sure she wouldn't answer.

'Yes, but that was long ago Eve Wells – when I was another person.'

Eve glanced away. She couldn't imagine being without Adam – couldn't imagine a life of self-imposed singleness. 'Ravenna, how long is it since ...'

Her friend looked up at her then laughed sharply.

'Sometimes, Eve Wells, I love your foolish questions – only a person of your age could ask this!' She let out a thoughtful sigh. 'And I did love him Wells ... he was the best of men - and you will not ask me what happened to him.'

'Of course,' she replied quickly, 'sure ...'

Ravenna was getting to her feet, gazing out over the sun scorched ground. 'Look, I didn't mean to ...' but the time traveller was clearly now focussed on something else, hand shielding her eyes. 'What?' she said nervously, 'what's going on?'

'*No*,' the dark haired girl said bleakly, '*oh no!*' And then she was running forward, heading out into the rapidly emptying camp.

'Wait! Eve called desperately, following briskly as the Mediterranean girl grabbed for the bridle of a mounted local man, yelling at him in Arabic as he tried to push her angrily away.

'What's happening?' Eve called as the pair exchanged animated words.

'Water is flooding from the gorge,' Ravenna called back fiercely as the guide pulled free, 'they say God's Mirror has broken!'

'*God's Mirror?*'

Eve just stared, what on earth … and then she realised. 'Oh god!'

'The team!' the Mediterranean girl was calling as she pulled away from her, her features now filled with concern as she gestured out across the dusty encampment. Eve frowned.

'What – I can't see any of the team …'

'Exactly,' the time traveller replied, stooping to grab her hat and pack, 'the guides are not the only ones to break camp ...'

'What?' Eve gasped, gazing at the flapping canvas of their abandoned tents, realising with sudden concern that Zalmoud and Brenna were nowhere to be seen - but at that moment an unexpected noise broke the silence, carried clearly on the gusting wind.

'Oh no!' exclaimed the dark haired girl breaking into a string of curses in ancient Greek.

'Ravenna ..?' she yelled as she tried to process what was happening, but the time traveller was already grabbing at her arm.

'Come Wells – we may already be too late!'

Pursuit

The roar of the truck's engine filled the stuffy interior as Ravenna floored the accelerator of the 4x4, grimacing as she struggled with the heavy gears.

'I can't believe you just ...' Eve began, then broke off – for she could, in fact, easily believe that Ravenna had just hot-wired the short-wheelbase Land Rover, and was now coaxing it out of the sandy depression in which it had been parked. Ahead of them, the team's six seater Hilux was just a smear of dust on the horizon, a dispersing cloud as it raced towards the canyon they had investigated the night before.

'He knows about the rift,' the time traveller said grimly as they bounced along the rutted earth, 'if he did not already suspect that something like this was possible – Brenna's confession of her experiences has convinced him ...'

Eve felt her blood run cold – and Brenna was taking him to the place she had seen the creature. 'But they may find nothing,' she ventured trying to reassure herself, 'after all it's not like the rift is always open.'

Ravenna said nothing – clearly she did not agree. Eve yelped as the truck sped over a rocky outcrop, grabbing desperately for the door handle. 'Can you go a little slower?'

'No!' Ravenna said darkly, her expression grim as she followed the twisting track, muttering as she pushed the accelerator yet harder. Eve fought not to close her eyes. 'The guides have gone,' the Mediterranean girl continued after a couple of heartbeats, '– spooked by all this talk of ancient sea monsters and have left the Westerners to their crazy quest.'

Eve winced as a bump made her leave her seat, almost smashing her head into the roof of the vehicle. 'How much do you think they ...'

'Know?' Ravenna shot back, her gaze still hawk like on the tracks ahead of them, 'most likely everything Dinosaur Girl – and that inquisitive American girl is not going to let it rest!'

Eve felt her heart sink as she realised the impossible situation they had been put in – the more people who knew that gateways to the past were a reality … 'Oh god – Brenna!'

Ravenna sighed darkly. 'And it is clear that at least one of her colleagues does *not* wish her to investigate this revelation – this is not a good combination, yes?'

Eve closed her eyes as she clung on for dear life, unsure if the nausea in the pit of her stomach was due more to travel sickness or the horror of what lay ahead.

'This is the opposite of a win-win, yes?'

Eve turned her mind to the bumpy track ahead, the discomfort of her teeth rattling in her skull preferable to the horror which awaited them.

The Gorge

'So what do we do now?'

They had found Saraceni's truck parked hard up near the entrance to the narrow gorge, the sand marred by tracks which congregated in the narrow cleft.

'They are spreading out,' Ravenna said as she jogged to a halt and crouched to examine the ground, 'searching for a way inside.'

Eve shuddered as she stood to catch her breath, fighting the nausea which still dogged her. Somehow – if it were possible – the gorge seemed more intimidating than it had done in the depths of the night, silent shadows and rasping breeze-blown sand giving it a lonely, haunted feel. She swallowed and put out a hand to touch the glistening rock: it was wet – damp from where water had flowed down to churn the dusty earth below.

She lifted her gaze to the rocky face, shielding her eyes from the glare above the east wall's fractured rim. '... So where?'

'This rock is like a sponge,' the time traveller returned grimly, likewise gazing up at the crags around them, 'porous and crumbling – riddled with fissures and caves - some no bigger than a fist sized pot-hole, but others ...'

Eve frowned, 'But how do you ..?'

'I explored it earlier today Wells - as I said I would.'

'Oh ...' She felt her cheeks flush at the assumption she had made about what her friend had been up to that afternoon. 'So where do you think ..?'

'There,' the Mediterranean girl replied, pointing to a more substantial opening a few yards ahead of them, 'but we must climb to it, yes?'

Eve nodded, forcing away her uncertainty, 'So you think this is where they've gone in?'

Ravenna shot her a frustrated look.

'Judging by the footprints and coupled with the fact this is the only cave big enough I should think so Dinosaur Girl, yes,' and with that she began to climb, using the tapering wall as a staircase of neat holds to traverse up to the opening. Eve followed, glad of the easy going, drawing some consolation from the sandy prints which clearly showed several boots had made the climb before them – they were on the right track at least.

'Here,' said the time traveller taking a torch from her backpack, 'you will need this soon.'

'Thanks,' said Eve tersely, taking the heavy light, which looked distinctly like a Second World War G.I.'s flashlight.

'Apologies, it is my spare,' Ravenna replied taking out a powerful palm sized L.E.D torch, then ducked straight into the cramped space. Eve followed with a sigh.

The cool was utterly surprising, pleasant at first in contrast to the near-painful heat of the desert sun, yet as Eve pressed deeper, she soon began to wish for its warming touch on her skin.

'This is odd, yes?' said Ravenna directing her attention to the ceiling and wall of the cave with her torch beam. Eve frowned.

'The walls are worn smooth, looks like water-action,' she mused running her palm along the cool rock wall, 'but there's got to be virtually no rainwater run-off here and no natural spring?'

'These were my thoughts also,' Ravenna returned grimly, 'and yet a large volume of water has sluiced through here with some degree of regularity ...'

'Carving the solid rock and wearing it smooth.' Eve broke off and swallowed as a horrible thought struck her. 'So ... what the hell are we going to do? If we do find a breach into the Eocene past we'll be at least a hundred metres under the sea!'

'How remiss of me that I did not think to pack a submersible,' Ravenna returned tersely, 'if only I had known!'

Eve took a shaky breath. 'So what the hell do you intend for us to do?'

'We find this rift and close it,' Ravenna replied, neatly swinging her torch back to the passageway ahead, 'If you wish to step through it when we find it, then be my guest Eve Wells, but I for one will not.' Eve glanced briskly away.

They walked in silence for a few moments, stooping as the passage narrowed. It was cold now, Eve's breath misting in front of her, an eerie cloud in the glow of her torch. *Hell, where were the others – had they already found a doorway into the past and been dragged into the primeval ocean?* The passageway dropped yet lower and as she resorted to her hands and knees she began to question the time traveller to distract herself.

'So why – in this place, this desert – does the rift lead to the same point geographically, whereas ...'

'Whereas once or twice before we travelled further?' Ravenna cut in. Eve swallowed, trying not to muse on the La Brea Tar pits of North America or the Chinese Jehol Biota where she had been stranded in a world of feathered dinosaurs.

'Yeah – why does a rift lead to a point hundreds, or even thousands of miles from where it begins?'

Ravenna grunted as she pressed herself yet lower to the freezing floor.

'Sometimes when we enter a place where the fabric of time touches, we follow a twist which carries us thousands of miles as well as thousands of years –' she grunted as her pack snagged on the rocky roof, 'yet sometimes it is little more than seconds and millimetres where one era rubs against another.'

'Okay,' Eve grunted, trying to ignore the fact that the space was narrowing yet further.

'Twists and knots, Eve Wells, twists and knots – that is what makes this interesting yes?'

'*Interesting!*' Eve echoed disbelievingly then grunted as the crown of her head thudded against the hard ceiling. *Close places* – it hardly seemed to make logical sense, yet she knew that it was true – that the framework of reality was both flexible and could coil back upon itself – even break when it touched another twist.

She turned her mind to the caves ahead, the claustrophobia of the narrow squeeze giving way to a wider space from which other passages clearly led.

'It is a system, yes?' Ravenna mused as she swept her torch around the damp space, 'carved by water …' Eve shuddered feeling a sudden sense of hopelessness grip her – at least five passages of varying sizes led off the sizeable chamber.

'So which way ..?

'Turn off your torch,' said Ravenna with a brisk gesture of her hand. Eve frowned, but obeyed and was plunged almost instantly into complete blackness.

'But what are we …'

'Listen,' the time traveller hissed back, '-perceive …'

Eve forced herself to stay calm, trying to focus her mind on the distant world of caves and passages – but the blackness around her seemed almost alive and though she had never thought of herself as claustrophobic, the weight of the darkness around her and the cold which seemed to seep into her from the rocky floor made terrors prickle within her; fears which whispered and pulled at her, threatening to become a panic if the torches were not put back on soon. And then she thought it: what if the torches failed? What if they pressed deeper and became lost in the blackness – entombed in a living night – or worse, stumbled into the waters of a long dead sea before they could stop themselves?

'Do you hear that?' said Ravenna, her voice unnaturally loud in the echoing darkness. The sound of another's voice had never felt so good.

'No,' she said briskly, her own voice shaky in her ears, 'I can't ...'

'Keep calm Wells,' the Mediterranean girl said reassuringly, 'open your senses.'

She swallowed, trying to slow her breathing as she strained her ears – nothing – she felt the impossibility of it begin to seep into her once more, the panic nagging at her as the darkness pressed in; but just as she was about to apologise, flick on her torch and revel in the light she craved, something registered on the periphery of her hearing. She turned her head, straining – and then she frowned, sure she could see a change in the shape of the rocky chamber. 'There,' she said excitedly, 'up there, do you see it?'

For a moment Ravenna was silent, but then she too laughed in triumph. A couple of metres above them, the blackness was discernibly lighter, and as she stared Eve began to make out the texture of weathered stone, the edges of a passage illuminated by some distant light. 'Yes Wells – I see it, well done!'

Relief filled her as the light of Ravenna's torch flooded the blackness bringing life and hope back to her formless world. 'This one,' she said, pointing with her beam as Eve flicked her own light back on, 'it is an easy climb,' and with a nod they began to ascend.

*

Eve just stared.

They stood in a stepped chamber, the floor ahead of them dropping steeply to a lower level where a water-worn passageway clearly led to another larger cave in which lights bobbed. Torchlights – and the distant sound of echoing voices! Yet as her subconscious mind worked on all these details it was another feature of the chamber in which they had found themselves which occupied the greatest part of her mind.

'My god,' she whispered as Ravenna shone her torch to the glistening opening some metres above,

384

which was disgorging a steady flow of water into the trough of the passageway just below them. 'What's going on?'

Ravenna stooped to lean down and dip her hand into the water collecting at their feet. 'Salty,' she said briskly, but even as she straightened the volume of water rushing through the hole began to increase, filling the echoing cavern with a power-hose like rushing.

Eve stood, momentarily lost in awe, trying to get a grip upon the fact that she was most likely seeing the run-off from an ancient ocean, leaking through the porous rocks. 'The rift must be way above us,' she said breathlessly, 'and it's opened again, letting the water seep through.'

'It is like a valve, yes?' Ravenna mused, then grabbed for Eve's hand as she began to reach out towards the bubbling flow, '– do not touch it Wells, there is every chance it will suck you in!'

Eve felt a shiver of pure horror run right through her. Had Brenna and the others already found the sump and ... 'Hell, do you think ..?'

Ravenna shook her head, 'they are still alive – there are torches ahead – now come Dinosaur Girl, we haven't long.' Eve found her gaze drawn back to the foaming jet. It was probably less than a metre across, but water was blasting through the sink-hole like a firefighter's hose, filling the passageway at their feet so that it was now almost at the level on which they stood.

'We have to move!' Ravenna yelled over the roar of the waters, 'now! Get to the lower level before both chambers are flooded!'

'I ...' Eve hesitated, realising the implications with a sudden jolt of terror. They had to get to the next cave before the connecting passageway was filled – but if they did, then what guarantee was there that they would be able to get back to the chamber from which they had come!

'Ravenna!' she gasped desperately, 'but ...'

'Have faith!' the time traveller said firmly, 'a way will be made for us - come on!' but Eve found herself unable to move, her eyes glued to the rising waters as panic flooded her mind, lost in the horror of going forwards with no guarantee of being able to get back. There was barely a foot between the flooding channel below them and the roof of the passage now, the water flowing and spreading to fill every available nook and fissure as it rose inextricably towards them.

'Now Wells!'

Eve fought debilitating panic. They were already as good as dead. Even if they could swim against the surging flow, there was every chance they would be dragged away by the churning current, sucked back into the cave system and into the primeval Tethys. They'd be battered and drowned, their bodies crushed to jelly by the pressure of deep-ocean. Panic gripped her.

'No!' she gasped desperately, 'no, no, no! I can't ... I just ....' She shot her gaze to the hole they had climbed through, her body turning instinctively - she was finding it hard to breathe, knowing she was gulping at the air in the cavern too quickly, her head beginning to spin.

'Calm yourself Wells,' the time traveller said gently, but Eve could see the concern in her dark eyes. 'Be calm – we can do this ... together.'

The water was a seething mass of darkness and foam, barely a couple of inches between the channel and the roof of the lower passageway, the tide now lapping at the ledge on which they stood.

'God ... oh god!' She was fighting not to hyperventilate.

'Wells!'

'I can't!' she gasped, 'please ...' The cave behind seemed to beckon to her, screaming at her to retreat and climb back through and descend to safety before their chamber was flooded – to get outside, to scrabble down towards the light and warmth of the distant world.

'We cannot go back!' Ravenna growled at her firmly, 'Wells – listen to me – the safest place for you in this entire universe right now is with me! Now come on – you must trust me!'

Somehow, her logical mind knew that she was right, but her body would not move – watching transfixed as the spray began to splash up to lap against their boots.

'Come,' said Ravenna, 'we have to go ...' but as she turned the flow began to lessen, 'what on earth?'

They both yelped as a large creature shot flailing through the sink hole in an explosion of movement and noise.

'Wells - what was that?'

'Giant catfish of some kind ...' Eve stammered in a daze, 'an extinct giant catfish.'

'Are they dangerous?' Ravenna swallowed as they watched it thrash on the surface for a moment before disappearing beneath the foam.

'How should I know?' Eve shot back hysterically, 'fish aren't my specialism!'

'Then let's find out,' Ravenna said briskly, turning towards the rising flood.

'No!' Eve gasped, 'no – you're nuts if you think I'm getting in …'

'Do you want to die Wells?' Ravenna returned sharply, 'then do nothing and let the water rise.'

They both stood, breathing hard as they looked into one another's eyes. Eve took a shaky breath then nodded. There was no other option. 'Take my hand.'

'Are we going to count to three or something?' she stammered, then screamed as Ravenna grabbed her other arm, yanking her swiftly into the freezing pool.

*

Eve kicked and flailed feeling hysteria beginning to grip her, adrenaline stinging her body as the pressure of the water crushed her chest – and all the while the knowledge that the fish was somewhere below them – darting and prowling, its silvery body twisting through the murky passageway.

She forced her eyes open, fighting the salt sting as she struggled forwards, grabbing desperately at the rocky walls as she followed in Ravenna's wake. And all the time the fear – the horrible knowledge that at any moment the catfish would make a grab for her - dreading the sensation of its teeth clamping around her hand or heel.

She fought onward, lungs burning, dimly aware of Ravenna kicking powerfully just ahead of her, longing for the light which had manifested ahead - knowing that air and warmth were only seconds away. And then she felt it. An unexpected tug which pulled her whole body – and then, to her horror, she saw Ravenna dragged rapidly sideways, caught in the same sucking current which had grabbed her, pulling her towards the left hand wall.

There must be another passageway she thought – another passage to the flooding Tethys - but this undercurrent was dragging them down, sucking them into the depths of the primeval ocean.

And then the world became chaos, her body impacting with Ravenna's as the current dragged her sideways, and Ravenna was flailing her arms, eyes wild, arching her back and limbs as she braced herself against the cave into which the current was dragging them. *Go!* her wide eyes seemed to scream, and understanding, she pushed upwards, fighting the flow with every ounce of her strength, pushing off Ravenna's shoulder as the time traveller wedged herself over the sucking hole.

Her lungs were screaming, arms burning as she fought against the current - and then she was breaking the surface, gasping desperately, filling her lungs as her terrified mind struggled to make sense of the echoing space above her.

Ravenna

Ravenna closed her eyes as the elemental current tugged her downwards, lungs burning as her mind grew dark and for a second she was drifting – breaking free of her body – longing suddenly for the eternal flow to take her: and yet she knew that she could not surrender – knew that without her Eve would die.

She fought the agony in her chest, blotted out her screaming limbs, but the silky sonnet of death kept tugging at her, and with it the blackness of self-recrimination – the ache for it all to end.

Your foolishness is worse than physical death, the bubbling current seemed to whisper, *there is no forgiveness for what you have done …*

And then she was in Prylix' yard again, her expression hard and proud as they led her into the main building, blinking in the shade and cool of the high plastered space. She whimpered in her spirit – *so proud*.

There were men waiting for her, many standing, several seated on folding stools like she had seen politicians and officers of the law use. They were proud – but she felt prouder, proud and angry despite her youth and gender.

Her *Lanista* was stood before them, but he did not look her way as the fighters who escorted her brought her to a halt.

'So the girl is ready?'

The seated man spoke with that arrogant confidence she had always despised. He was a master – a leader – and the situation was his. 'You appreciate that Domitius was taking a gamble when he agreed to allow her training … the women are a mere side-show after all on the wider circuit – and you know how much the church disapproves.'

She felt her gaze drawn to the man who had trained her – worked with her and counselled her since the day she had been snatched from the arena floor where she had been condemned. 'In which category will you enter her?' the seated man continued, 'Do the women even fight within the categories?' A murmur of laughter ran around the waiting crowd.

Her *lanista*, she noticed bore an expression as calm as the freshest dawn, but a flushing in his neck told her what he felt – and she felt it too: felt that anger, that indignation. She forced herself to remain as calm as he. Expressionless.

'As you say, my lord, the women have no categories,' he replied without expression, '… they fight in a class of their own.' She felt a burning pride begin to swirl in the pit of her stomach – a flame which would sustain her. 'But she is swift and skilled – she would be a *retiarius* if she were a man – and yet she wields the sword like a *secutor* also.'

'Like a *secutor*!' the seated man retorted mockingly, eliciting more laughter, 'then Prylix, let us see what this little dove can do!'

A signal was given and two men entered via the wide double doors behind the seated party – men from another school. *Murmillo*: heavy armour. 'A swift bout,' the seated man said lazily, 'practice swords – we wouldn't want to damage the merchandise after all.' Again the party laughed. A shield and wooden sword were pressed into her hands; but her weapons mattered little compared to Prylix' approving nod: she was ready. The baton was raised.

The show fighters circled forwards as she dropped into a ready stance, blades protruding over the rim of their shields in the proscribed way of their class.

Surprise, she heard the old man say within her mind, *speed and surprise – that is your greatest weapon Eudoxia*.

They were big men, strong but slow, and with an explosive sideward feint she opened the first man's guard discarding her shield as she threw herself down and forwards, whipping upwards with every ounce of her strength and agility to send his weight cartwheeling over her back: and he was out; then the second was upon her – her limbs were a blur as she flicked aside with gymnastic agility – parrying and thrusting as she fought him off, shocking him with her speed and ferocity, using her size and speed to outwit him. Time blurred, the hits on her own body barely registering as she parried, and then the second man was on his back, gasping in disbelief. She tore off his helmet, discarding her wooden sword, punching and punching with every ounce of her strength till the blood flowed from her knuckles.

'Stop now girl.'

She withdrew, breathing hard, oblivious of her broken hand – and the dead silence in the room – for all she heard was the pride in her master's voice.

You are a weapon girl – a killer …

'*No!*' she sobbed, as the salt stung her eyes. She saw the olive groves of her childhood home, saw the farm once more, the simple pastoral life which had been stolen from her. '*No!*' but the waters seemed to mock her: *yes selfish, heartless girl – a killer … that is all you are …* And then they were grabbing for her – dragging at her shoulders, rough hands jerking her as her body was pulled upwards.

Eve

'Help us!' Eve screamed as soon as she had the breath, staring wildly at the three shocked faces which gazed down from the water's edge, 'she's being pulled under!' And the world became a blur as strong hands took her, Zalmoud and Brenna Wiedermann bracing themselves across the flooding passageway as Professor Saraceni hauled her onto the ledge on which they stood.

Though it all could only have taken a matter of seconds, it seemed an eternity to Eve's exhausted mind, watching numbly as they fought to pull Ravenna upwards, tugging and struggling with all their strength against the elemental flow.

'Oh god!' Eve gasped, hurrying forwards as they lay the sodden form of her friend face down on the floor of the cave. She was battered and blue, her elbows bleeding where she had braced herself against the jagged wall, 'Ravenna?' she whispered desperately as she twisted her over, 'oh hell – Ravenna!'

But even as she said her name the time traveller began to cough and groan, clawing at the cold rock floor, fighting to pull herself upwards. She was gasping and trying to speak, moaning in some long forgotten language. 'I am not ..!' she groaned, then seeing the faces staring down at her exclaimed: 'we must go!'

Eve put her arm under her shoulders to support her, dimly aware of the panic in the chamber as she pulled her friend upright, the disbelief and the questions.

'What the hell are you doing here … who are you … what is going on ..?' But Ravenna ignored them as she struggled to recover herself.

'We have little time, we must …'

'No,' said a soft voice, 'no – it is certain death – it is not a place we are meant to be.' The look on Tarek Zalmoud's face was far graver than Eve could ever have anticipated.

'So what the hell are we meant to do?' Brenna Wiedermann shot back desperately, 'just sit here and wait for the water to rise?'

'We *must* go on,' Ravenna breathed as Eve helped sit her against the rocky wall – 'there will be another way.'

'Will there?' Professor Saraceni interjected grimly, 'how can you be so sure *Dr Wilding*?'

The time traveller turned fierce eyes upon him.

'You must trust me Professor – trust me and you will live ...'

But at that moment a great rushing sound made them all turn to the passageway behind. 'It is flooding,' Zalmoud said grimly, then shook his head. 'Come, she is right, we must continue upwards.'

'Upwards?' ventured Eve, then swore as she realised to where he was indicating. The only way out of the sizeable chamber was a cave at least seven metres above the cold rocky floor.

Climb

'We should never have come to this place,' Zalmoud said grimly as he and Saraceni gave Ravenna a boost onto the shallow rocky ledge about three feet above, a neat platform from which to begin their brisk climb. Eve shuddered.

The Egyptian palaeontologist's face looked eerie in the torchlight, strained with something more than fear. At his side the Professor said nothing, his expression grim as he glanced up to meet Ravenna's tired gaze. If he had told his team of his suspicions about her then none of them were willing to show it, concentrating on getting the exhausted woman out of the flooding chamber.

'Look, I'm sorry,' said Brenna weakly as they turned to help her upwards, 'but I couldn't just let this go – I mean … I was right! This has to be like some kind of gateway to the ocean which was here – which *is* here … hell this is crazy!'

The tall man looked away sadly, his features grave in the bobbing torch light, 'there are some mysteries which should be left well alone …' he broke off and glanced at Eve, who swallowed nervously – it was as if he knew full-well of the crazy secret to which they were now all party.

'Dr Wells?' ventured Professor Saraceni, gesturing to the ledge above, but she shook her head, No – you go: help Ra… I mean Dr Wilding.' The academic held her gaze for a moment then turned and began to climb.

She swallowed, casting a glance at the water bubbling up to flood their chamber.

'Your turn next Dr Wells,' the tall Egyptian said calmly, but as she readied her foot on the rock she felt his hand on her shoulder. 'Brenna must never be allowed to speak of this to the outside world Eve – do you understand me? This secret is far too important.'

'What?' she frowned, surprised by his sudden candour.

'She is naïve and headstrong,' he continued in the same low tone, 'her inquisitiveness began this madness and she does not realise the implications ...'

She took a shaky breath. 'Look, how do you ..?'

He stooped and said no more, cupping his hands to take her heel, 'here – quickly Dr Wells, the waters are rising.'

She nodded, her mind racing as she clawed at the dripping rock, gasping as she allowed Brenna and Saraceni to pull her onto the ledge. What the hell had he meant – what lengths would the man below her go to in order to keep the secret of the cave?

'Come on,' said Brenna who crouched at her side, 'we'll get through this.'

She forced a smile then glanced away as Zalmoud appeared at her side.

Eve realised that she was shivering. It was cold in the cave – far colder than in the desert beyond – and her sodden clothes were now chilling her to the core, her fingers numb and trembling.

'Your turn,' called Brenna from above. She had just topped the entrance to the cavern above and gazed down anxiously from the torch lit aperture, Ravenna's pale face just visible behind.

Taking a breath she nodded, and putting her hands to the frigid rock began to pull herself upwards.

'My hands are freezing!' she called in frustration, 'I can hardly grip the wall!' She forced herself to fight the panic which dogged her, blotting out the sound of lapping water as the cavern flooded below.

'Adam takes you to the climbing wall all the time does he not?' called Ravenna's disembodied voice from above her.

'Yes – but ...'

'You can do it!' Brenna called encouragingly.

Tentatively, she took a step, but her foot slipped out from under her and she smashed her elbow, clutching at the rock with all her strength, breathing hard. 'It's so damned slippery – I can hardly see the holds let alone feel them!'

403

'Come, Wells,' called Ravenna's frustrated voice, 'just imagine this is the University's indoor wall!'

Eve baulked at the comment. 'Yeah, like a sub-zero, soaking version of the university's indoor wall!'

She grunted, struggling for suitable holds, making slow progress with only Zalmoud's direction and the helpful glow of his torch beam allowing her to find suitable holds. She felt her strength beginning to fail, frustration and fear vying with the growing numbness in her straining fingers as her hands fluttered fruitlessly at the freezing rock.

'I'm stuck,' she called up loudly, 'I can't find any more holds guys!'

'You can do it,' Brenna called again – Saraceni had appeared at her side, his features hard to read in the wavering glow of her light.

'Climb the damned wall, Wells!' Ravenna yelled down in desperation.

Below them the waters were surging, sloshing and foaming as they gurgled up to the shelf on which Zalmoud stood.

'Go on Eve!' he called up with surprising calmness '– here, I will guide you with my flashlight.' She took a shaky breath, watching as the misty beam flashed incandescently beside her.

'There!' called Brenna encouragingly as the yellow beam fell on a sizeable ridge of stone, 'and there – near your right knee.'

She nodded nervously and following the patch of light got her foot another few inches higher. 'Come Eve,' Zalmoud called up reassuringly as she reached for the left hand hold he indicated. 'Like a ladder yes? Nice and steady.'

She made another couple of holds, then paused again, panting desperately, her body trembling now with the effort and the cold. The waters were lapping over the ledge upon which Zalmoud stood and the lip of the cave above felt miles away.

'I don't think I can hold on!' she exclaimed desperately, her fingers feeling numb beyond anything she'd ever felt – but she had to – her life depended on it.

'Go on Eve – we haven't long,' Zalmoud called up briskly from below, his voice echoing loudly as the others called encouragement, 'my light will guide you!' She nodded then closed her eyes for a moment, readying herself to push the last two metres.

'Come on Tarek!' Brenna yelled past her, 'the water's rising – you've got to get going ...' But Zalmoud drowned her out.

'Follow my torch beam Eve, here – now here ...' She obeyed, forcing out her trembling left arm to be rewarded with a neat almost handle like hold. She moved her right foot, gasping with relief as it also found a solid step and allowing it to take her weight took a ragged breath.

'Keep moving Wells!' Ravenna called from above, her eyes wide and anxious as she craned down to see her, 'Zalmoud, you have to ...'

Eve twisted her head to see the tall man just visible in the glow of his own torch, the water now swirling round his thighs. 'Just climb Eve!' he commanded brightly, 'all your strength yes!'

'Tarek!' she heard Brenna call from above, but Eve obeyed him, following the welcome patches of light he created, swearing under her breath as she forced her aching limbs up the last couple of metres, horribly aware of the way Brenna called his name over the rush of the rising flood.

'Reach for me Wells!' exclaimed Ravenna as she and Saraceni leant over to grab her hand, and before she had a chance to look back Ravenna's fingers had connected with her own and the pair were grunting as they pulled her up - and then she was half-climbing-half-flopping over the lip, feet scrabbling as she hauled herself into the cave – and Brenna was screaming Zalmoud's name. She twisted, breathing hard, desperately scanning the blackness below.

The torch light was gone.

Reckoning

'They walked in silence, Eve's breath misting as she listened to Brenna's sobs, wiping the tears from her own eyes as she avoided Ravenna's gaze.

She tried to blot out the memory of the darkening pool, the frantic cries and the desperation as they had raked the rising waters with their torch beams – but the tall palaeontologist was gone without trace. She cuffed at her eyes, still hardly able to process it – he'd waited till the last moment – too long: sacrificed himself to make sure she and the others made it …

'Do not dwell upon it,' Ravenna whispered at her side, but Eve hadn't the strength to reply.

Up ahead Saraceni swore, his torch beam dipping. The cave was large and echoing, but every twist seemed to lead to another dead end. Fear began to prickle Eve's scalp – it was yet another fruitless turn - and always the echoing sound of the gurgling flow to remind her of what was to come, the unstoppable rising sea percolating through every fissure and passageway. They rounded another hopeful-looking buttress of rock, torch beams lancing eagerly as Saraceni led them forward – then sighed bitterly – yet another false hope. She stood, breathing hard, turning her gaze to the inky waters which pooled in one corner of the large chamber – a gently rippling lake of icy blackness. Yet another rising sump which threatened to flood the diminishing cave.

'This is madness,' said the Professor, his torch beam lashing wildly. To all intents and purposes there was no way out.

'I'm sorry,' said Brenna despairingly, 'I ...'

'Quiet girl,' the Italian said briskly, 'you are not to blame ...' His gaze flicked to Ravenna, who held his steely glare for a moment before looking away. Eve cuffed her eyes, her nerves strained near breaking. They were trapped.

They slumped by the edge of the sloshing pool which seemed to ebb and flow along the cavern's furthest edge. Eve felt her breathing begin to race out of control and had to fight to slow it, concentrating on Ravenna, who was tracing the left-hand wall of the chamber where the floor tapered away to meet the rippling pool.

'Why is this happening?' Brenna asked shakily as she nursed a bleeding elbow, 'how can it even be possible …?'

But Ravenna spoke over her – her voice sounding unnaturally loud in the echoing space. 'This is a way out,' she said firmly, 'we can swim through to the next chamber.'

Saraceni looked up at her sharply then got to his feet. 'And how in heaven's name do you know this *Dr Wilding*?'

Ravenna held his gaze for a moment, then turned towards the pool. 'I will dive down, see if there is a way.'

Eve looked at her, horrified.

'You can't!' she exclaimed desperately, her mind filling with brooding gloom and swirling bubbles, '– I mean, the currents could pull you down.' But at that moment Brenna gasped, making them all turn.

'The cave!' the American exclaimed desperately, getting quickly to her feet, 'the cave is flooding!'

Eve twisted, then did likewise, realising with horror that the waters in the cave they had left had indeed risen to the level they had reached.

'It's flooding more rapidly,' Saraceni said darkly, 'filling the whole system - and we are trapped ...' his gaze shot to the rocky ceiling, their own shadows looming eerily above them in the torch light. *And soon we'll be out of air*, Eve thought with a sting of panic.

'I will go!' Ravenna interrupted determinedly, and before Eve could stop her she had dropped into the glistening pool, disappearing beneath the briny waters in a rush of bubbles and foam.

'Oh god,' she gasped, gazing at the place she had been, then turning felt the breath catch in her throat as she saw the look in Professor Saraceni's eyes.

'Who are you really Dr Wells?' His voice was calm and deliberate.

She hesitated, the echoing chamber seeming suddenly vacuous, a dark place where all hope had been sucked away – and all that remained was the horrific truth that he knew of their secret – know about the breach in time.

'I ...,' she stammered, raising her hands pleadingly, 'please, look – I'm just a palaeontologist – I teach reconstruction techniques at an English university ...'

'Renato –' Brenna frowned, 'what's going on?' but the academic ignored her pointedly.

'When your friend Dr Wilding first contacted me I was a little confused,' he continued in a level tone, '– I did some checks - some research – and then my suspicions were confirmed.' Eve felt her blood run cold. 'There are those who have seen her Dr Wells – for that *is* your real name isn't it? Those who suspect what she really is. Online conspiracy vloggers who have taken her photograph, even a department of your own ...'

There was a noisy splash behind them as Ravenna broke the surface with a desperate gasp.

'There is another chamber!' she yelled triumphantly over the sound of the gurgling water, 'it is a short swim – Brenna, you first!'

'I ...' the American, began, then hesitated, shooting a brisk look at Professor Saraceni, but the

Mediterranean woman seemed oblivious of the tension as she paused to wipe water from her face.

'Come on, we must be quick – take a breath …' and with a reluctant look, Brenna took the hand she offered, lowering herself into the pool with a grimace, and was gone.

Eve turned slowly to meet Renato Saraceni's gaze.

'Please,' she began, but without a word he rose and shook his head.

'Don't do this,' Eve said shakily, feeling despair sting her chest. Saraceni was stood before her, blocking her view of the pool, his expression grave yet calm.

'Your friend's true identity is less pertinent than our current predicament,' he said darkly, 'we are trapped like rats with no food and little light,' he dropped his gaze to the sizeable torch in his hand, 'and soon the air in these chambers will be gone.'

She swallowed, hardly able to take in what she was hearing. 'We have limited resources ... battery power ... air to breathe ...'

She began to back instinctively away, longing suddenly for Ravenna to break the surface of the pool once more. 'Please, Renato ...' she managed, but he was already rounding on her, edging her back along the cavern, back towards the rising waters which had filled the chamber they had climbed.

'You of all people should understand the logic of this,' he said steadily as he walked towards her, his heavy torch held menacingly in front of him, 'the stark lessons of this crucible of evolution.'

Eve dared to break eye contact, glancing briskly over her shoulder at the water now ebbing at the edge of the smooth-worn entrance – barely six feet away.

'Survival of the best-fitted,' he continued with an unsettling smile, 'Darwin's stark revelation - ultimately we are just animals, are we not Dr Wells? For all our pretensions we are just highly evolved organisms ... and yet still ruled by our primeval needs and fears.'

Water was flooding across the floor behind her now, trickling and flowing over her boots as the chamber began steadily to flood. She took a breath, glancing once more at the flooding entrance: it would be madness to go back – she thought again of Tarek – then shot her gaze to the sump through which Ravenna had swum. She cursed her trembling legs, willing her muscles to ready themselves, fighting to still her heart as she calculated her chances of breaking towards it.

'Please!' she gasped, readying her body for action, sucking up all the courage she could muster as she prepared to weave past.

'Natural selection ...' he continued gently, making a stabbing gesture towards her with his flash-light.

The flooding entrance was barely a couple of feet behind her now, the weight of the water - the brooding force of it - almost palpable on her back. 'I'm sorry Eve ...'

The surge of it began to drag at her heels.

Saraceni raised his torch.

'*No!*'

She flung herself sideways, but he was too quick for her, catching her across the shoulders with his torch as she ducked past him, stumbling in a heap beside the flooding entrance. She moaned, gasping breath as she pulled herself from the briny flood, knowing with a horrible certainty that she'd never make the rippling pool.

She ducked as he lunged again, the LED beam arcing blindingly through the frigid space, and then she was yelping as the flashlight clipped her skull; scrabbling back, splashing away in her desperation, knowing he would kill her – knowing he would throw her into the pool where Tarek had died.

'*Stop!*' commanded a firm voice and the torch beam jerked briskly away.

She froze, panting, spitting salt water from her lips as she gazed at the figure silhouetted in his dipping beam.

Deliverance

Ravenna Friere ignored the shivering which racked her body, pushing away the trauma and fatigue of the last twenty minutes as she locked eyes with the man who stood before her.

'I will not fight you,' she said coolly though the voices whispered otherwise. *Just another fool to cut down – just another injustice to be wiped from the face of the earth*. She saw his gaze drop to the short-bladed *falchion* held ready in her trembling right hand.

'Put it down Dr Wilding,' the academic said grimly. He was stood barely a pace from Eve, corralling her by the flooding opening, blocking her escape to the pool. She glanced away as he took a step to his right, blinding her with his torch's bright beam.

'Let her go,' she replied calmly, raising her left to shield her eyes. *Rush him*, the voices said: *you know he is nothing to you – there is already so much blood on your hands!*

She saw Eve shoot her a desperate look, half-pleading, half-resigned. Ravenna glanced almost imperceptibly to meet her gaze, then looked Saraceni firmly in the eye.

'Why did you conceal what you had discovered about me from your colleagues?' she said calmly, '– why didn't you challenge me as soon as I arrived, why did you go along with my story ..?'

'Put the weapon down,' the Italian palaeontologist said grimly, ignoring her attempts to distract him, then paused and laughed to himself, 'just my sense of intrigue,' he said tersely, 'I wished to see how things would play out.'

'Let it go and come with us,' Ravenna returned more gently, 'we can yet live – all of us ...'

Saraceni shook his head. 'Who the hell are you really *Dr Wilding*,' he said derisively, 'and what is this – what is going on?'

Destroy him! the voices seemed to whisper, - *end his life for what he has resolved to do!*

'We must work together!' she called back firmly over the burbling of the flooding chamber, 'let her go - if we help one another we may just ...'

'No,' he said with a shake of his head, the torch held like a cudgel in his hand as he turned towards Eve, '– not until I have answers! This phenomenon – this link to the ancient ocean - it is a discovery which could place the man who found it in the history books, his name in the annals of science amongst Darwin and ...'

She felt the muscles of her hand flex almost beyond her control, mapped the progress of her limbs as her thoughts raced outwards to the movement which would follow, readied her lungs to yell out to her friend as she lunged.

And then the unthinkable happened.

The unexpectedness of it took Eve completely off guard, her terrified mind taking in every vivid detail as the huge animal lunged out of the cave entrance by which she cowered.

A thick tapering snout, like someone had stretched the nose of a killer whale, mottled and grey with huge dagger-like teeth to the fore and serrated shark-like teeth to the rear, wicked sunken eyes, nostrils raised like blowholes high up on its head.

She screamed as its jaws gaped horrifyingly, thrashing wildly towards them for a moment, missing her leg by millimetres, covering her with briny spray before snapping closed like an echoing gun shot: and then it was gone – and Saraceni with it – his horrified scream ending abruptly as the animal vanished in an explosion of broiling spray and deafening echoes.

They looked at one another utterly stunned.

'What the hell was that?' Ravenna exclaimed in a choked whisper.

Dorudon, Eve thought, but her voice seemed not to be working. She began to stumble to her feet, forcing away the image of Saraceni's flailing limbs as Ravenna helped her. She cleared her throat, her mouth gummy, 'a primitive whale - like basilosaurus but smaller.'

They stood in silence for a moment, bathed in the unearthly glow of Saraceni's fallen torch, then scooping it up Ravenna grabbed her arm. 'Come on Dinosaur Girl, we haven't a moment to lose!'

Eve stumbled in a daze, her legs like jelly, her mind now pushed beyond horror to a place of utter numbness. 'We must join Brenna in the cavern beyond – get her to safety.'

Eve nodded, dimly aware of the rising flood, the cave floor now inches deep in water. 'Take a breath Dinosaur Girl.' And then they were swimming, the world a nightmare montage of torch beams and glistening bubbles, the horror of what lay beyond them only registering as she hauled herself into the next cavern, scrabbling desperately up the rocky shore. She coughed and slumped as she caught her breath, dimly aware that the chamber in front of them rose steeply to a shadowy strip of darkness several metres above.

'Where's the Professor?' the American exclaimed desperately as she helped pull her from the churning flood. Eve found herself unable to reply, looking away as Ravenna took her arm.

'I'm sorry,' the Mediterranean girl said softly as she slumped at her side, but the girl just gazed at her, utterly stunned. For a moment Eve thought she was about to yell or else break down, but instead she took a shuddering breath and met the dark haired woman's gaze.

'I've been as far as I can up this cave and it tapers into a tiny gully - I don't think ...'

'There is always a way,' Ravenna cut in firmly and Eve caught her eye. 'Listen to me Brenna - I can make a way where there is no other way.'

Eve felt the breath catch in her throat, hardly able to believe what she was hearing. 'I know that you understand what is happening in this place Brenna – but you must hold this secret within you – if anyone were to learn of it, the consequences would ...'

'What?' the girl exclaimed, 'look – I know Renato had his suspicions – but who the hell *are* you?'

Eve saw the hesitation in the Mediterranean woman's eyes, wondered suddenly what she was about to say. 'I can save us,' Ravenna said firmly, 'but you must swear that you will never tell a soul about this ... believe me, your life depends on it!'

Eve felt welded to the spot, her heart thudding as she gazed at the American palaeontologist.

'I'm sorry,' the girl said determinedly, 'I'm a scientist – I can't just keep quiet and pretend this never happened!'

'But Brenna!' she pleaded, 'please – what Ravenna does …'

'A phenomenon like this,' the girl shot back desperately, 'it's the discovery of the millennium! People have to know – the ocean studied! Can you imagine the understanding we'd gain by examining this eco-system in the flesh?'

But at that moment a deep rumbling gurgle surged through the rock beneath them, sending dust showering down in the motes of their torchlight. They looked at one another – stunned as the sound of rushing water met their ears.

'Oh god!' said Eve in a whisper, turning to the pool they had just exited as the water began to rise – two inches – six inches – ten.

'It's flooding!' Brenna yelled incoherently as they scrabbled up the precipitous incline before them, watching in horror as the water surged forward, rising feet at a time now, pushing them up the slope towards the shadowy ceiling.

'Can't you do your damned thing!' Eve yelled desperately as she pulled herself upwards on all fours, knowing that in moments their heads would crash against the rocky ceiling.

'I need to clear my mind Dinosaur Girl!' the time traveller yelled back angrily over the din of the rising tide, 'and I am not in that *happy place* at present ...'

She broke off, glancing towards the shadowy roof ahead, a thin fissure having revealed itself, a jagged slash of blackness where ceiling met rocky slope.

'*Deo Gratias*,' the time traveller muttered, and then they were straining towards it, Eve grunting with the effort, dimly aware of her shredded finger nails and the blood on her dust-caked hands, knowing the waters were but inches behind. At her side Brenna swore.

'It's too steep!'

They had come to a rocky lip and with a horrifying lurch Eve realised she hadn't the strength to haul herself over it.

'Come on!' yelled Ravenna as she clawed at the rock, pulling herself up and over with the animal grunt of a Wimbledon champion. Eve took a breath, trying to blot out the gurgling roar from her mind, viscerally scared of the darkness which chased them, and in that place of horror found a strength which fuelled her. She gripped the rock, pulling and struggling, feeling her arms strained beyond her ability to endure; and then Ravenna was dragging her, and she was gasping dusty breaths, twisting to offer Brenna her hand.

'Grab on!' she yelled, but the girl was struggling, her fingers slipping through hers as the water rose up to submerge her calves.

'I can't,' she screamed, 'Help me! I can't ...' And then the flood seemed to rise up to take on physical form, Eve's mind struggling to make sense of what she was seeing as the gurgling blackness bulged out in a spray of foam to fill the tapering void.

She felt the world slow down as the girl's eyes shot open in utter horror, the pleading look of shock in her expression etched into her mind as she gasped a horrified breath. She saw Brenna's hands fluttering, droplets exploding around her as a ragged mouth opened wide – dull hide glistening momentarily - and then time seemed to accelerate, wicked teeth visible for a split second as her face vanished beneath the surface.

'Brenna!' she screamed hysterically, but Ravenna was dragging her upwards, pulling her away from the lip and into the narrow squeeze, '... *Brenna!*'

She fought to struggle free, clawing her way past Ravenna, but the time traveller dragged her back. 'Get away Wells, it is too late for her!'

She screamed the girl's name once more, then howled in despair, the horrified look in the girl's eyes burning into her soul as Ravenna dragged her up into the claustrophobic passageway.

'No!' she yelled, 'no – we've got to help her ... got to – like you saved me in the Eocene – saved me from the Ambulocetus!'

Ravenna looked at her fiercely, eyes glistening. 'The creature which grabbed your boot was but a fraction of that animal's size ...'

'No!' she gasped, tears running down her face, 'no - we can't just ...'

'She's gone,' Ravenna whispered, 'and now we must move.'

Breathing Space

Within minutes they were splashing up the tapering fissure, struggling against the rising flow as they climbed the narrowing void.

'It is going upwards, yes?' Ravenna called back to Eve, clearly trying to inject some encouragement into her tone as she led her up the step-like slabs. Eve said nothing. The events of the past hour had been amongst the most horrific of her life – she felt numb – destroyed, unable to shake the memory of the moment Brenna had been taken. 'It is a tight squeeze here,' Ravenna called from ahead of her, 'you must try not to panic, yes?' Almost instantly the torch light seemed to vanish as Ravenna's body blocked the way ahead and she followed in a daze, hands scrabbling desperately at the freezing stone as the waters gurgled close behind. She was gasping, struggling for breath, her right arm jamming for a moment before she was able to wriggle it free.

'Ravenna,' she called breathlessly, 'I don't think …'

'Do not stop!' the time traveller yelled back to her, but she couldn't keep the fear at bay, caught between the knowledge of the rising waters and the uncertainty of what lay ahead. What if the passageway narrowed further? What if they became wedged and … She sobbed with the fear of it, squirming desperately – horrified as for a heart-beat she thought she was trapped – then gasping dropped out into another chamber.

Her heart sank. Just three feet of air space and another brooding saline pool.

Bracing her palms against the rock she wept, her hair brushing the floor.

'Wells, I am sorry,' the time traveller said bleakly at her side, but she hadn't the strength to reply. Behind them the waters were gurgling, sloshing and rushing as they filled the squeeze behind them. Ravenna took a heavy breath. She sounded tired – broken – she rolled on to her side and lay gulping at the stale air.

'We're going to die aren't we?' Eve said softly, turning to glance at the rising darkness, the rippling bubbles almost luminous in the light of their one remaining torch. At her side, Ravenna laughed softly.

'Perhaps … physically at least – this is what I pray for yes … but you?'

Eve pulled herself into a crouch, feeling an odd sense of hope begin to fill her – but whether it came from the primal urge to survive or somewhere else she was not sure. 'There must be something you can do,' she said desperately, grabbing Ravenna's arm to haul her onto all fours. 'Come on, you have to try!'

The time traveller gazed at her for a moment as if considering, then nodded. The water was flowing in around them now, lapping up to their waists, inching towards their shoulders. 'Come on – there must be something you can do!'

Ravenna just blinked at her. 'Perhaps, this is the moment of our end, but …'

'Please,' she returned feeling suddenly beyond her own panic – outside of it somehow – 'I know it's not mine.'

For a moment the diminishing chamber was a maelstrom of echoes and darkness, a place of terror and chaos - then Ravenna nodded her head.

'Leave me Wells and I may have the strength – at the least I must close this rift … make sure this thing can never happen again.'

'Leave you?' Eve yelled over the rush of the water as she gasped the breaths she felt certain would be her last, 'what the hell do you ..?' The water was up to her neck now, fear rising like a scream within her, flooding through her as rapidly as the sea was flooding the cave.

'Go!' Ravenna yelled back almost angrily, 'go and I will close this – end it forever!'

'Go where!' Eve screamed shrilly as the rising flood brought the crown of her head ever closer to the ceiling of the chamber.

'Swim – *downwards* - it is your only hope – I pray you will be guided!'

'What!' she gasped in desperation, the water forcing her up to the roof, barely inches now between the surface and the rocky ceiling. Then her frightened mind made the connection. *Down* –through the sump which already filled the chamber they had entered.

With a terrified glance at her friend she took a desperate gasp, feeling cold water momentarily cover her face. 'I didn't sign on the dotted line to die for this crazy cause of yours!' she spluttered, gasping at the millimetres of air between her and the rocky ceiling, but her friend's eyes were resolute.

'You have no choice now!' Ravenna yelled back over the echoing torrent, 'take a deep breath Eve Wells!' and as she did so felt a hand pushing her under, the flood overwhelming her almost instantly.

She kicked downwards, fighting panic as her mind struggled with all she had just seen, swimming blindly – wildly – hoping she had found another chamber - and then to her horror the current was dragging her – sucking her sideways. Her back collided painfully with the rocky wall – and then she was spiralling, flailing wildly as bubbles clouded her vision, bursting outwards and upwards, dimly aware of a turquoise glow above her as she kicked in a direction she willed to be up.

Her lungs were burning, the need to open her mouth and gasp air almost beyond her ability to control; she felt blackness tugging at her, her chest aching like it would explode, saw silvery flashes begin to dance before her eyes. She was going to die – the surface seemed an infinity away – and even if she did make it which era would she be in?

431

Time seemed to slow and become dream-like, the pain in her head unbearable as her chest burned, limbs slowing as she felt something latch around her leg – a hand, and then there was another at her waist, strong legs kicking, propelling her upwards and then … the world seemed to fade into muted noise and darkness.

End

Eve lay against the rock, gasping breaths like a frightened animal. The moment they had broken the surface was seared into her mind like some memory from her darkest nightmare - the pain and the horror as they had come rushing out of the cave in a tangle of flailing limbs, bursting through another fissure – another era - to be deposited on the canyon's far side.

She closed her eyes.

'They're all dead,' she said softly as if trying to make sense of what had happened, 'everyone …' She barely saw the dry sand of the gorge, hardly heard the last hiss of the waters as they dissipated and drained away - the moment Brenna Wiedermann had been dragged under leaping continually to the forefront of her mind - however hard she fought to forget it. At her side an exhausted figure gasped and coughed.

'I closed the rift,' said Ravenna weakly as the water darkened the sand around them – but Eve barely heard.

'Brenna …'

'The body in the creature's belly,' Ravenna rasped sorrowfully.

Eve felt her shoulders wracked by despair.

'A woman,' she said shakily '… the bones we exhumed were slender: Brenna suspected they were of …' She broke down as the sickening realisation overwhelmed her. Somehow – inexplicably – Brenna Wiedermann was the body in the creature's gut … dragged back into the Eocene depths, crushed by the titanic pressure - *but that was physically impossible.* She closed her eyes, fighting nausea.

Impossible.

'Come Wells,' said the time traveller firmly, laying her hand against the sun baked stone next to hers, 'we have our answer – I will take you home.'

Eve hesitated for a heartbeat, feeling the horror of it all welling up inside her like a red hot wave.

'Answer!' she yelled disbelievingly, 'it was Brenna! And she's *dead* – they're all dead – all of them!'

Ravenna looked at her levelly, yet for once Eve saw a vulnerability in her wide dark eyes.

'I have sealed the rift, Wells,' she said determinedly, 'it can never happen again here.'

Eve broke away, cuffing her eyes. 'I am sorry Eve ...'

She turned away and swore. 'You should have saved her!' she spat without thinking, 'you should never have let her go to the cave in the first place!'

Ravenna just stared at her, clearly stung, eyes wild for a moment before turning to sweep away a strand of the hair which plastered her face.

'Eve, please ..!'

'How ... how the hell can you even do this!' she yelled angrily as emotion overwhelmed her. 'How can you face this kind of thing day after day – and then just ...' She broke off as tears welled, covering her face with her hands. They had almost died – again – experienced the most horrific ordeal of her life – and the words just tumbled out before she could stop them: 'how could you let her die?'

For a split second she saw white-hot anger flash across the Mediterranean girl's face, and then, to her surprise, she hung her head.

'You wish to know how I can do this Eve Wells?' There was a strange look in her eye – passionate yet remorseful, 'because you see this as chaos Dinosaur Girl. You see the horror of what might be. You see endless events and actions and terrifying things which are all far beyond anyone's control. But all I see is order. I know that all the pieces of the puzzle are noted and numbered – every grain of sand, every breath - every hair ...' She broke off and reached out a hand to touch her shoulder. 'I have seen the end from the beginning Eve Wells – I have more than a hope, I have a certainty and I know that come what may I have faith in order – not chaos – I walk into the provision which is made for me sure it will come ...'

Eve pulled free, standing briskly before beginning to fight out of her sodden over-shirt.

'Please child ...'

'I am NEVER coming with you again,' she replied bitterly, laying it across a sun baked boulder to dry, 'however much you need me!'

Ravenna stood, clearly frustrated. 'Do you think I do not hate this too Eve Wells!' - there was a growing anger in her voice– anger and self-recrimination – 'do you think I do not wish that I could ...' She broke off and turned away.

She looked exhausted – older somehow – it was the first time she had ever seen her look truly tired. 'You think I do not wish for this to stop? How often I have longed to crawl out of this body Wells ... this shell – this *thing*! I have known it grow stale and old during the lifetimes I have lived, have prayed for a natural end – but always it is renewed, always I return ...' Eve found herself unable to hold the woman's piercing gaze. 'And always there is another place I am needed.' She turned to gaze out across the darkening desert. 'Always there is one more task.'

Eve took an angry breath, forcing all sympathy from her mind. Brenna was dead and if Ravenna had kept her focus ...

'Look – Eve, you must understand ...'

Eve turned pointedly away. 'Eve Wells, I am sorry ..!'

Eve turned her gaze to the desert, the sun dipping low in an electric blaze of amber and gold. She did not understand – she could not. Brenna and Zalmoud and Renato Saraceni were dead and it need never have happened. She wiped her eyes with the back of her hand, struggling to pull herself together. Would they even have existed at all?

'Just take me home.'

'Wells!' she heard the time traveller say, but she was already walking in the direction of the silent camp, cuffing at the wind-blown sand which stung her tear-stained face.

Part 6

(Envoi) The Other Girl

Rembrandt's Ghost

'Eve ... Dr Wells?'

Eve glanced up from her marking to see one of the junior admin staff craning around the office door. Nearly three months had passed since she had returned from the Valley of Whales, yet still she was jumpy, still she saw movement in every shadow - expected to hear Ravenna's familiar voice. She smiled apologetically, turning her swivel chair to face the girl. She'd been alone in the shared office far too long, and the interruption was more than welcome. 'There's someone here asking for you – think it's one of your friends from the Cranfield in London.'

She felt her heart leap – Polly Nightingale, the only other person who could truly appreciate all she'd been through – the only other girl who had travelled between the boundaries of time. Yet she hadn't said she was going to be in the Midlands?

'Thanks,' she smiled, pushing her misgivings away.

'I'll send her in.'

She abandoned her marking with a heavy sigh. *The boundaries of time.*

Not a day went by when she didn't think about the events in that Egyptian cave, and even in her lightest moments the darkness of that place – and the bitter parting with Ravenna – seemed always to be hanging over her. She took a breath to clear her head. She had drawn a line under that chapter of her life, committed the madness of the past two years to a crazy past she would one day remember with mild wonder – maybe even question whether she had even experienced those insane things at the hands of Ravenna Friere - and yet a part of her longed to talk about them, to unload the darkness and the horror, to seek answers and lay the ghost of Ravenna's intervention in her life to rest.

She felt a flash of hope. Maybe this was providence. Maybe talking to Polly would make all the difference – after all she would understand. She let out a slow breath, emptying her lungs as she realised that a part of her had been avoiding the issue, too scared to phone and open up old wounds: yet now she had no choice. Perhaps fate had thrust this moment upon her, aligned events to bring things to a head ...

A shadow fell across the doorway and sensing footsteps she rose expectantly, unable to suppress a smile – then stopped in her tracks.

'Rav ...' she broke off as her mind processed the fact that neither was it the dark haired girl who had turned her life upside-down. And yet the similarity was enough to make her frown, the inclination of the eyebrows, the set of the jaw - and yet it was not Ravenna. This girl was younger, and there was something almost mocking in her confident smile, an unsettling confidence in the easy twist of her lips.

'Hey,' the young woman began in a disarming North American accent, 'it's a real pleasure to meet you in person Dr Wells.'

Eve stepped forward as the girl removed red leather gloves to shake her hand. 'A real pleasure.'

'I'm sorry,' she frowned after an awkward moment, 'have we met?'

'No,' the young woman continued frankly, 'but we have a mutual friend – two in fact.'

Eve swallowed.

The girl was clearly younger than Ravenna - barely older than her undergrads – yet she possessed a confidence which seemed to outweigh her years by a long way. She broke eye contact, trying not to stare – to speculate - as she resumed her seat.

'I'm sorry if I misled you,' the girl laughed, like it was some kind of private joke they shared. She ignored the chair Eve offered, 'but I kind-of used your friend's name to get up here ...'

Eve felt her blood run unexpectedly cold. 'Polly?' She frowned with a surge of concern. 'Where's Polly?'

The newcomer paused.

'Polly Nightingale won't be able to make it today Eve,' the girl's tone was light, yet deliberate, 'she has her own problems to deal with.'

Eve swallowed, 'Look what on earth ... is she okay?'

The young woman looked at her for a moment, then smiled and began to round her desk. 'She's fine Eve

Wells.' Again it was as if another woman was speaking. She dared to hold the newcomer's gaze.

'Do you know Ravenna?'

For a moment she felt sure she saw amusement flash across the girl's attractive features.

'Yes, we know each other,' the young woman said neutrally, 'Ravenna Friere and I go back a *long* way.' She continued to circle the table, glancing all around her as if assessing her surroundings, as if dragging every scrap of information she could out of the room. It was weird – unsettling – her eyes almost inhuman in the way they darted. She came to a halt, resting her weight against the nearest table.

'You know, Polly really respects you,' the young woman continued obliquely, 'trusts you a lot – that's a rare thing you know, Eve, to find people who you can truly trust – who'll never let you down.'

She thought of Ravenna – all the times she had told her she was safe in her presence – inspired her to be courageous ... told her to trust her judgement. 'Look, who are you?'

'A messenger,' the girl said casually, 'a friend, come to warn you about what's to come if you keep on helping Ravenna Friere.'

Eve felt her eyes narrow. 'I haven't seen Ravenna in months - look, how do you …'

'She's a pirate Eve – an opportunist.' There was a passion in the stranger's eyes, despite her casual speech. 'All her talk about being led – about deeper realms - but she has her own agenda Eve … where do you think she gets the money to live, her food and clothes?'

Eve opened her mouth to reply, yet knew with a rush of realisation that those unanswered questions had dogged her since the very first moment Ravenna had dragged her into the past.

'She threads her way through time at will and creams off whatever she wants,' the young woman continued, 'can you imagine that Eve? Can you imagine what you could do with the kind of knowledge she's amassed?'

There was a look in her eye as if she had glimpsed such knowledge, as if she had been similarly tempted … was she tempting *her*?

'Who are you?' she said softly.

'And you've seen her fight … you know she's taken lives, right?'

Something told her she had to end this conversation right away.

'Look, I don't know who you are …'

'Hear me out,' the girl said raising her hands casually, 'you know you want to … *need to* … haven't you ever wondered how she knows where she's needed – how she finds these anomalies in time?'

Eve found herself suddenly unable to speak, trapped in an almost childlike moment of desperation, hanging on the girl's every word. 'And then there are the *problems* she's dealt with – the people who've gotten in her way.'

'People?' she ventured in a whisper.

The stranger made a casual gesture. 'I mean, that poor girl who disappeared in Cornwall – the girl she abandoned in the past …'

Her thoughts shot to Jess Flynn, the young woman who had triggered their investigation of a big cat loose on the moors. *Abandoned.*

'We never … she wanted to stay behind, she refused to leave!'

'Did she?' the young woman cut in causally, then stepped over to perch on her desk, 'do you really think that she wanted to stay in the Palaeolithic – long-term I mean? Do you really think she was mature enough to know her own mind ..?'

Eve hesitated, almost oblivious to the girl's invasion of her personal space, dangerously aware of how much she wanted to agree with her. Was it really right that the young Cambridge academic had abandoned her modern life and career to live millennia in the past, leaving her family believing she was dead? 'I mean, how hard did Ravenna Friere try to persuade her?'

'Look,' she began, sensing suddenly that she had to object, or else be drawn right along with her, 'we gave Jess every opportunity …'

'But I guess Brenna Wiedermann was different right? I mean, that was just an *accident* that should never have happened...'

Eve felt as if she'd been shot in the chest.

'How do you know all this?' her voice was hoarse when it eventually emerged. The girl just looked at her, her expression impassive.

'Just the wrong place at the wrong time, I suppose.'

Her mind was racing, the terror in the young palaeontologist's eyes flashing vividly before her mind's eye, reliving her white-hot anger at what Ravenna had allowed to happen. She took a breath, aware that she was staring – and when she spoke her words emerged with difficulty.

'Look, I don't know who the hell you are …'

'A friend,' the young woman replied casually, rising from the desk. 'Maybe the best friend you have – though you don't quite realise it yet.' She began to don her gloves, slipping in her fingers with elegant dexterity, and as she did so the similarity to Ravenna Friere was utterly unnerving.

'How … how do you know Ravenna?'

The young woman ignored her. 'Give my regards to Ravenna when you see her – tell her the Mistress' offer still stands.'

Eve pushed back her chair.

'Stop – you can't just walk in here and say this kind of stuff without an explanation! What happened back in …' She found herself unable to say the name, Brenna's terrified scream filling her thoughts, '… it was horrific … and whatever Ravenna had in mind she never intended …'

The dark haired girl looked at her levelly.

'Ignore what I've said,' she continued with a shrug, 'feel free to disbelieve me … but it's all here in black and white.'

Eve hesitated as the girl took a large brown envelope from her shoulder bag and dropped it onto her pile of half-marked essays, 'read it or bin it – it's up to you Eve Wells, but to be honest I'd think twice about trusting your *friend* Ravenna again.'

'Just get out,' she said without thinking. The girl shrugged and turned towards the door, her casualness somehow more chilling than anger.

'Your call Eve,' she said over her shoulder, then paused. 'Hey, did you hear about that European scientist washed up in the English Channel last month?

'What?'

'Trawler pulled out some human remains off the Dutch coast a couple of weeks ago, and by the wonders of modern science the authorities established it was this guy called Rembrandt, a microbiologist who's been missing since the late 90s – hell of a story.'

Eve found herself unable to reply – her mind in another place – trapped in the deserted lab of a university hospital, carried to the place she had felt sure her life was about to end.

'Ravenna Friere doesn't like loose ends Eve ...'

'Stop,' she said desperately, 'what on earth do you mean ?' But the girl was already stepping through the door.

'Take it easy Dr Wells – and watch your back, you need to be careful who your friends are.' And then she was gone.

Eve stood, stunned, her mind running out of control, hand brushing the envelope, fingers pushing back the flap.

'Is everything okay?'

She looked up with a gasp – the girl from the office was looking at her with real concern, 'I heard raised voices ...'

'Fine,' she replied after a moment's hesitation, forcing a smile which wouldn't come easily, then letting out a breath picked up the envelope. It was full of articles – cuttings and print-outs and photos from magazines. *Dozens of them*. Dozens of missing people: *loose ends*.

'Dr Wells?'

'Yeah.' Her voice emerged as a croak, 'fine – I'm just going to take a break,' and swallowing hard stuffed the envelope into her bag.

Acknowledgments

Deeper Realms wouldn't be possible without the help, encouragement, love and support of: Deborah Storer, John Green, Penelope Wallace, Clare Portwood, Simone Greenwood, Jono Renton and everyone else who has given me both the physical and mental space to create the world which Ravenna Friere inhabits.

Ian RobertS

The elusive Ian Roberts is a writer, historian and former tutor of medieval history who has been making-up implausible adventures for as long as he can remember.

Often writing with a strong female lead, he uses the medium of time travel as a way of exploring the past, creating a world where the miraculous is possible - and his brand of quirky historical fiction will be sure to delight lovers of both fantasy adventure and classic science fiction.

38925835R00268

Printed in Poland
by Amazon Fulfillment
Poland Sp. z o.o., Wrocław